CURSE OF THE POPPY

A Penny Green Mystery Book 5

EMILY ORGAN

First published in 2018 by Emily Organ

This edition © Emily Organ 2020

emilyorgan.com

Edited by Joy Tibbs

Emily Organ has asserted her right under the Copyright, Designs and
Patents Act 1988 to be identified as the author of this work.

ISBN 978-1-7200508-0-3

CURSE OF THE POPPY

❧

Emily Organ

❧

Books in the Penny Green Series:
Limelight
The Rookery
The Maid's Secret
The Inventor
Curse of the Poppy
The Bermondsey Poisoner
An Unwelcome Guest
Death at the Workhouse
The Gang of St Bride's
Murder in Ratcliffe

ALSO BY EMILY ORGAN

Penny Green Series:
Limelight
The Rookery
The Maid's Secret
The Inventor
Curse of the Poppy
The Bermondsey Poisoner
An Unwelcome Guest
Death at the Workhouse
The Gang of St Bride's
Murder in Ratcliffe

Churchill & Pemberley Series:
Tragedy at Piddleton Hotel
Murder in Cold Mud
Puzzle in Poppleford Wood
Trouble in the Churchyard
Wheels of Peril
Christmas Calamity at the Vicarage (novella)

CHAPTER 1

The dark spire of All Saints church pierced the summer morning mist as I reached the eastern end of Margaret Street. An inquisitive crowd had gathered outside the townhouse, too busy sharing the news to make way for a carriage which was attempting to pass along the road. The horse shied, parting the mob and frightening the children who were trying to get to their school at the end of the street.

I could see the upper storeys of the narrow, red-brick house. The curtains were drawn across the tall sash windows and the front door was obscured by the crowd.

"Press! Make way!" I called out, hoping this would hasten my progress through the throng. A few people moved, but the majority stayed put. I readied myself with a pencil and notebook in the hope that I might be able to speak to a police officer.

"There 'e is!" came a shout.

"Mr Forster! That's 'im!" someone else cried out.

"Where?" shouted another.

I pushed forward, keen to catch sight of the man who had been tragically widowed after the events of the previous night. Someone shoved me from behind and my spectacles slid halfway down my nose. I pushed them back into place and tried to remain calm.

A row of police constables kept the crowd at a distance from the house. Beyond them I could see an ashen-faced man in a dark suit and top hat standing beside the door. He had copper-coloured whiskers and his eyes darted nervously across the noisy crowd. He was conversing with a police officer, whose uniform bore the insignia of a chief inspector, and a man wearing a blue-checked suit, who I guessed was a detective.

"Keep yer elbows to yerself!" shouted a woman behind me.

"Where was you dug up?" another retorted.

A fourth man, who appeared to be a friend of Mr Forster's, joined the group standing outside the house. He was short and round, smartly dressed and wore a top hat and spectacles. The man rested a hand on Mr Forster's shoulder as a gesture of comfort.

I could hear other reporters in the crowd shouting out questions to the group of men, but nobody responded. It was clear that the police had no wish to speak to the press at that moment.

"Mind yerself, else I'll roll yer in the mud!" shouted the woman who had complained about the elbows.

"Not afore I punch yer face!" replied the other.

With the crowd growing restless and the police ignoring the reporters gathered, I decided to move to a quieter part of the street and find someone who might be of use to interview.

An anxious-looking lady stood in the doorway of the

house next to the church. She wore a dark blue woollen travelling dress and was adjusting her hatpin.

"Excuse me, are you a neighbour of Mr and Mrs Forster?" I asked.

"I am," she replied solemnly.

A maid carrying a heavy portmanteau stepped out from the doorway behind her and pushed past me as she walked toward a waiting brougham carriage.

"I'm leaving town," the lady continued. "I cannot bear to stay here while there are violent burglars about."

"Did you hear anything of the disturbance last night?" I asked.

She glanced at the notebook in my hand. "Are you a reporter?"

"Yes, I'm Miss Penny Green of the *Morning Express*."

She paused for a moment, as if considering whether she wished to speak to me. Thankfully, she continued. "I'm Mrs Yarborough. I didn't hear a thing; that's what worries me. No one had an inkling of what was happening. No doubt poor Olivia cried out for help and no one came because no one heard her! It was well planned, wasn't it? The burglars attacked the staff first so they wouldn't be able to intervene, and then they went for Olivia. I don't suppose they meant for her to die, but she did! And now poor Mr Forster will never get over it. This street will never be the same again. We've lived here happily for almost ten years, but I don't think I could bear to spend another night under this roof. Who wants to live on a street where someone has been so dreadfully murdered?"

I nodded my head in sympathy as I wrote in my notebook.

"And I hear they made such a terrible mess of the house," she added. "Completely vandalised, they say. It was such a beautiful home and now everything is ruined! All Mr Forster's treasures from India... he had so many of them. I should think the valuable ones have all been taken and the less precious ones just smashed to pieces. We had such happy times in their home. Inside it felt as though one had been transported to Bengal with all the beautiful silks draped from ceiling to floor, and a quite delightful fresco of an Indian scene on the wall of the drawing room. Every treasure on display had a story related to it, and Mr Forster did ever so enjoy regaling us with his tales. And we relished hearing them."

"Had the Forsters been back from India long?"

"I seem to recall that they returned at the end of summer last year. They both missed India, which is why Olivia worked so hard to have the home as beautifully furnished as she did."

I felt pleased that Mrs Yarborough was being so talkative.

"Mr Forster worked for a large merchant company there, am I right?"

"Yes, I believe so, based in Calcutta. I forget the name of it now. I heard he made a great fortune out there and brought it back with him, but the thieves have taken full advantage! It's terrible."

The maid carried a bulky leather case out of the house.

"Have there been many burglaries in this street?" I asked.

"No, none. It's been perfectly pleasant living here, and it's so well placed for shopping. I have friends who wouldn't dream of living north of Oxford Street, but Mayfair is so overpriced these days because of all the rich foreigners. They pay such ridiculous sums of money for an *exclusive* address, but that's not our style at all. Fitzrovia suits us much better. Until last night, that is. The level of violence was quite shocking! Why attack people in that brutal manner? Everyone in that household was utterly defenceless!"

"Perhaps if Mr Forster made his fortune in India the burglars knew which house to target," I ventured.

"Possibly, or they may have chosen the house entirely by chance. It could have been any one of us, and that, quite frankly, is what I find so frightening. We've decided to stay at our home in Somerset."

"You have no plans to return?"

"Only to arrange the sale of our house. After the events of yesterday evening, who on earth would want to live here?"

The maid joined us with a small dog under her arm, which bared its teeth at me.

"Do please excuse me, Miss Green, but we must go," said Mrs Yarborough. "I wish to stop thinking about this dreadful unpleasantness, and we have a train to catch at Paddington."

"Thank you for speaking to me, Mrs Yarborough. Have a safe journey."

As Mrs Yarborough was helped into her carriage I noticed the crowd had begun to disperse. Mr Forster, his smart, round friend and the two police officers were walking toward me with a group of reporters in tow.

"When did you last see your wife, Mr Forster?" called out a reporter I recognised as Tom Clifford from *The Holborn Gazette*.

"Leave the man alone," ordered the chief inspector.

"Where were you when your home was being burgled?" another reporter shouted.

Mr Forster ran a hand across his brow.

"My condolences, sir," I said as he passed me.

He gave me a startled glance, as if he hadn't expected to see me standing there. There were dark circles beneath his eyes and his skin looked pallid and clammy. As soon as he caught my eye he quickly looked away again, then muttered something to the detective. To my surprise, the two men began to laugh.

I wanted to ask them what could possibly be amusing on such a misty, dismal morning. Mr Forster's wife had just been bludgeoned to death by a gang of burglars, yet he was able to laugh quite readily.

I simply couldn't comprehend it.

CHAPTER 2

Murder on Margaret Street!

A burglary and brutal murder took place on Tuesday night at a house on Margaret Street, Fitzrovia. The occupier, Mr. Augustus Forster, had left home at seven o'clock for an evening appointment at the East India Club. His wife, Mrs Olivia Forster, had remained in the house and retired to bed at ten o'clock. The housekeeper, Mrs Elizabeth Fereby, was preparing to retire for the evening when she was disturbed by a noise in the kitchen in the basement at just after ten o'clock. Upon investigation, she discovered the kitchen window wide open, and four men armed with cudgels demanding to know the whereabouts of the household's occupiers. Mrs Fereby refused to tell them, whereupon one of the men struck her on the head and rendered her insensible.

The men climbed the stairs to the first storey and threatened a maid they found there, a Miss Harriet Riddiford, who, in a bid to be rid of the gang, told them the details of some valuable vases that were to be found in the drawing room. She was hit about the arms and chest, and ordered to keep quiet if she wished to preserve her life. Two men went into the drawing room and the other two climbed the stairs to the bedchamber where Mrs Forster slept.

While the content of the exchange between these men and Mrs Forster cannot be known, it is clear that she suffered a blow to the head and died from her injury shortly afterward, while the gang decamped with a stash of valuable jewellery and ornaments. The housekeeper recovered sufficiently from the attack to raise the alarm and constables were soon in attendance, alongside Police Surgeon Dr Sweby and Detective Inspector Bowles of Marylebone Lane police station.

Mr. Forster returned home at eleven o'clock to discover the distressing scene. Mrs Fereby and Miss Riddiford continue to receive treatment at the Middlesex Hospital.

Mr. Forster and his wife had recently returned from Calcutta, Bengal Province, India, where Mr. Forster had worked for the merchant Messrs Lewis Sheridan and Co.

"Well done, Miss Green," said my editor, Mr Sherman. "You must have spent quite a bit of time at the scene yesterday to get all this detail. And well done on the interview with Mrs Yarborough, too. You'll notice we've published it in its entirety. None of the other papers managed to get an interview with her."

"It was a bit of luck," I replied. "I saw her step out of her front door just as she was dashing off to Paddington."

"You were in just the right place at the right time," he replied, placing his pipe in his mouth. "That's the skill of a good news reporter." His shirt sleeves were rolled up and he wore a blue serge waistcoat. His black hair was oiled and parted to one side. "You haven't forgotten about the story on the Irish Conference in Boston, though, have you?"

"No, Mr Sherman, I'm working on it now," I replied.

"I need it on my desk by four o'clock."

The editor promptly left the newsroom, leaving the door to slam behind him. The newsroom of the *Morning Express* newspaper was a small, cluttered place with a grimy window looking out over Fleet Street.

"Well done, Miss Green, for being Mr Sherman's favourite today," said my colleague, Edgar Fish. He was a tall, broad man with heavy features and a thin, mousey-brown moustache.

"I'd say that Miss Green has been Sherman's favourite for much of the week," added the corpulent, curly-haired reporter, Frederick Potter.

"Now you come to mention it, Potter, she has, hasn't she?" said Edgar. "That won't do, will it? After all, you and I work a darn sight harder than she does."

"We do indeed," added Frederick.

"What I want to know, Miss Green," said Edgar, "is how you got onto the scene of the Forster murder as quickly as you did. After all, it occurred in Margaret Street and you live in Milton Street, which must be a good three miles away."

"I have my landlady, Mrs Garnett, to thank for that," I replied. "She has a friend who is famed for gossip and always seems to hear of these things before anyone else. I had only just sat down to breakfast at the time."

"Miss Green has an assistant!" said Edgar. "That's how she does it, Potter!"

"She's my *landlady*," I corrected, "and I think she would object to anyone describing her as an assistant."

"But she's a woman," said Frederick, "and we all know the fairer sex has a predilection for nosiness and gossip."

"You've hit the nail on the head there, Potter," said Edgar. "Miss Green and her landlady have a natural advantage over us chaps."

"But aren't your wives inclined to nosiness and gossip?" I asked.

Both men shook their heads.

"That's odd," I replied, "as I'm sure you suggested just a moment ago that these were characteristics all women possessed."

"*Almost* all," replied Edgar. "To tell you the truth, Miss Green, Mrs Fish is really quite distressed about this murder business in Margaret Street. She's fearful that we might be next!"

"But you don't have anything worth stealing in your home, Fish," said Frederick.

"Try telling that to Mrs Fish!" replied Edgar. "She didn't want me to leave for work this morning, and I've been instructed to be home by six o'clock at the very latest."

"That's a shame," said Frederick. "It means you won't be able to have your customary tipple down at Ye Olde Cheshire Cheese."

"I know. Customary tipples are quite out of the question at the moment, Potter. I'm afraid they won't be permitted until Mrs Fish has found a way to calm herself."

"Tell Georgina not to worry," I said. "I'm quite sure the burglars won't be paying you a visit any time soon."

"But you can't be sure of that, Miss Green," said Edgar. "Your interview with Mrs Yarborough just goes to prove that many people are fearful. No one can bear the thought that it might happen to them. You just don't know where these villains are likely to strike next."

"I don't think this was an opportunistic attack," I said.

"Is that what the police are saying?" asked Edgar.

"No, not yet. It's just what I think. It sounds as if the burglary was carefully planned. And I don't really believe that the motive was burglary at all."

Edgar groaned. "Oh no, Miss Green, you're theorising again. Leave all that to the police."

"I can't help it, Edgar! I saw Augustus Forster yesterday morning, and there was something about him which didn't quite ring true."

"Are you suggesting the chap burgled his own house?"

"No, but I happen to think it rather convenient that he wasn't there at the time."

"But surely the fellow should be allowed to enjoy an evening at his usual club without being accused of committing a shocking crime! Perhaps the burglars knew he would be out and simply seized their chance."

"Perhaps so, but if they were merely after some valuable items, why not wait until the middle of the night when everyone in the house was fast asleep? They'd have had a better chance of pulling it off undisturbed."

Edgar pondered this. "That's an interesting thought. Then you really think they wished to attack Mrs Forster and her servants?"

"I believe so. Otherwise, why would such violence have been employed? There was no need to attack everyone in that forceful manner; I'm sure threatening them would have had the desired effect."

"Perhaps they were set upon by the staff."

"No, I think the burglars must have chosen to harm them from the off in order to approach Mrs Forster unchallenged."

"Then Mrs Forster was the intended target?"

"Yes, I believe she was intentionally murdered. The burglars struck when her husband was out of the house. They ensured that the servants were incapacitated and were devastatingly brutal once they reached the poor, unsuspecting woman. The theft of valuable items was nothing but a half-hearted attempt to disguise the true motive of this crime."

"Only you're saying it wasn't; that it was, in fact, murder?"

"I can't say for sure, Edgar, but it's the most plausible theory I have at the moment."

"Well, it's not a bad one. Have you discussed it with your detective friend, Inspector James Blakely of the Yard?"

"No, not yet."

The mere mention of James' name made my stomach flip. I hadn't seen him since we had shared a forbidden kiss in my sister's hallway the previous week. It was an incident which I both felt ashamed of and treasured. James was supposed to be marrying his fiancée in just six weeks' time.

I also had a terrible suspicion that the kiss had been witnessed by my friend Mr Edwards, a man who had once held what I believed to be a deep affection for me.

"Are you all right, Miss Green?" asked Edgar. "Has your mind wandered elsewhere?"

CHAPTER 3

"Your theory is an interesting one, Miss Green," said Detective Inspector Bowles as we stood outside Mr Forster's home. A constable guarded the door and several onlookers lingered in the midday sun. Bowles was a thick-set man with a thin moustache, and a left eye which appeared to be looking over my shoulder while his right eye was firmly fixed on me. "However, we are continuing to treat the incident as a burglary at the present time."

"But Inspector —"

He raised his hand to prevent me from talking any further. "That's enough, Miss Green. I have an important job to be getting on with and I can't stand around being detained by news reporters any longer."

Inspector Bowles was the detective I had seen with Mr Forster the morning after the murder. I wanted to ask him what he and Mr Forster had been laughing about, but instead I sighed and tucked my notebook and pencil back inside my carpet bag.

"You think there's something more to this, do you,

madam?" I turned to see a man with bushy brown whiskers. He wore a top hat and a long, dark coat. His eyes were grey and watery.

"Were you listening in to our conversation?" I asked.

"Apologies, madam. Miss Green, isn't it? That's what I heard the inspector call you. I'm Mr Charles Mawson, a friend of the Forster family."

"I offer you my deepest condolences, Mr Mawson. This must be a most difficult time for you."

"It is, rather. I came here looking for Forster, but I don't know where the chap has gone. I don't suppose he'll want to set foot in his home again after the terrible tragedy that has taken place within its walls. I'm interested in this idea I over-heard you mention to Inspector Bowles. Do you really think the incident could be something other than a straightforward burglary?"

"I have no idea, Mr Mawson. I suppose it's in my nature to speculate on these matters. You should ignore most of what I say; I'm nothing more than a nosy news reporter!"

"Ah, I see. For a moment you seemed rather earnest about your thoughts on the matter. Do you know how the burglars got inside the house?"

"Through a kitchen window at the rear of the house."

"Oh dear. So they set upon the staff at first?"

"Apparently so."

"Bludgeoned with cudgels, weren't they?"

"Yes."

"And then they went upstairs and attacked poor Olivia." He shook his head. "Dreadful business. How many of them were present, do you know?"

"Four, I believe."

"They would have covered their faces, I imagine, so it will be quite impossible for the police to catch them unless the stolen goods appear for sale at some market stall in the near future, which might arouse suspicion. Though they could sell the valuables in another city altogether, couldn't they? That would cover their tracks rather well. You can see how solving these crimes becomes a battle of wits between the criminals and the police, can't you?"

"You can indeed."

"I wonder what evidence the police have uncovered so far. I should like to find out."

"Have you known the Forster family for long, Mr Mawson?"

"Yes, for some years, in actual fact. I spent some time in India and became acquainted with Mr Forster there."

"He worked for a large merchant company, did he not?"

"Yes, Sheridan and Company."

"What sort of merchant is it?"

"It trades in a number of items; principally cotton and opium. It's one of the largest firms in Calcutta and employs a number of people here in London too."

"Did you work for the same company while you were there?"

"No, I worked for the Indian government. I first met the Forsters while dining at a club in Calcutta, and subsequent to that we often enjoyed riding, shooting and picnicking together; that sort of thing. I returned a year ago." He sighed. "I do miss those days, and now everything has changed. I don't suppose you know where Mr Forster has gone, do you?"

I was surprised that Mr Mawson didn't know the answer to this question himself.

"I'm afraid I don't. He was here yesterday morning, but I suppose he must wish to stay away from the house for the time being. Do the Forsters have any children?"

"A son and a daughter. The son is at Oxford and the

daughter is married to a chap in Bristol. He works in shipping. Dear me, I struggle to believe that we have lost poor Olivia in this frightful way. I do hope Forster's all right. I wish I knew where he was."

"The police might have an idea as to his whereabouts."

"They might, mightn't they? I say, Inspector!"

Inspector Bowles turned to acknowledge him.

"Do you know where Forster is at the moment? I'm Mr Mawson, a friend of the family."

"I'm not at liberty to say where he is," Bowles replied, suddenly distracted by a man who was swiftly approaching. "Good afternoon, Inspector Blakely."

I caught my breath before slowly turning to face James.

"Penny!"

He grinned at me and I felt my face redden. He wore his customary bowler hat along with a smart grey suit and waistcoat. He held my gaze with his sparkling blue eyes.

"Hello, James."

"It's terribly sad, isn't it?" His face grew solemn as he glanced up at the Forsters' house.

Mr Mawson wandered off to speak to a police constable, presumably hoping to find out where his friend might be.

"Immensely sad," I said. "I was here yesterday morning and spoke with the neighbour, Mrs Yarborough. She's headed off to Somerset now."

"I read your interview with her in the *Morning Express* and I'm not surprised she has decided to leave. This whole business is rather unpleasant."

"Miss Green has been trying to persuade me that this was more than just a violent burglary, Inspector Blakely," Inspector Bowles interjected.

"What makes you think that, Penny?" asked James.

"A few things —"

"No, don't you be getting into all that again," said Bowles, "there's important work to be done. Come on, Blakely, I'll show you the crime scene."

"I'll be with you in two minutes, Inspector Bowles," replied James. "Do you mind if I have a quick word with Miss Green?"

The inspector shrugged in reply and James glanced around, looking for a quiet place for us to talk privately.

"Let's nip over to the church, shall we? There's a little courtyard there."

We walked the short distance to All Saints church with its red and black patterned brickwork. The courtyard could be accessed via a brick archway. Once we were beneath the tall, arched windows and looming spire, James stopped. I felt nervous about what he was about to tell me. Surely it would relate to that stolen kiss.

James cleared his throat, looking every bit as uncomfortable as I felt.

"I must apologise to you, Penny, for my despicable behaviour the other evening."

"No, you mustn't apologise, there's no need. Besides, it wasn't despicable at all —"

"Mr Edwards," said James, interrupting me. "I think he saw us."

"Yes, I think he must have done. He avoided my gaze for the remainder of the evening."

"I'm so sorry, Penny. I fear that I may have ruined any chance there might have been of a courtship between you and Mr Edwards."

"There was never any chance of that," I replied.

"Are you sure? Because I felt certain that you were beginning to hold him in a higher regard than you had previously."

"I was, and still do, but I don't lament the loss of a potential husband."

"Have you seen him since the incident?"

"No, I haven't." I had deliberately avoided the reading room of the British Library, where Mr Edwards worked as a clerk. At the present time I felt too embarrassed to face him. *Would he mention the kiss or remain silent on the matter?* I couldn't bear the thought of finding out.

"Penny, I will be married next month."

I sighed, and my heart felt heavy. "You don't need to remind me of that."

"I wonder if I should perhaps speak to Mr Edwards and explain the mistake I made that evening."

My heart gave a lurch. "You consider it a *mistake*?"

"Yes, Penny, it had to be."

I stared at him, saddened by his words. "And that will be your explanation to Mr Edwards? That it was simply a mistake?"

"Yes, a mistake which I take full responsibility for. He might be more understanding of the situation if I were to explain it that way."

"I doubt it very much."

"But he cares for you a great deal, Penny, and I'm sure that you would feel the loss of his acquaintance acutely. Perhaps more than you realise."

"You seem rather keen for me to remain good friends with Mr Edwards," I said.

"I am, Penny."

I paused to consider this.

"Perhaps it makes you feel better that I have Mr Edwards at my side," I said. "Maybe it makes you feel less distressed about your own impending marriage, which you seem intent on continuing with despite everything."

"I have to, Penny."

"As you've explained to me in the past."

"I'm sorry if my actions have in any way given you hope

that the marriage might be called off. That's why I wished to apologise to you in private."

I felt tears pricking the backs of my eyes as I looked up at the tall church windows. I had harboured a vague hope that the kiss might have prompted James to cancel his nuptials, but I finally realised that it would go ahead regardless and there was nothing I could do about it.

I clenched my teeth in anger.

"Well, I suppose you could explain matters to Mr Edwards," I replied, intrigued as to how James would approach the conversation. Perhaps a vengeful part of me wanted him to be placed in such a difficult situation. "I'm not sure what he'd make of it at all. I can't imagine him being particularly polite about the matter."

"Then I shall do so, Penny. I shall explain to him that the kiss was no one's fault but my own, and that you were entirely blameless."

"That would make me seem very virtuous indeed."

"It's the truth, and it's important that he knows it."

"Then that settles it, James. Shall I tell you my theory about Olivia Forster's murder?"

"It's settled? You're happy to simply change the subject to something completely different?"

"No, I'm not, but there's nothing I can say that will change the situation, is there? If you must know, I enjoyed our kiss and I was not at all blameless in the matter. You don't have anything to apologise for, but your impending marriage has no doubt left you feeling remorseful about the incident, so if you wish to apologise and explain matters to Mr Edwards I shall leave you to do just that."

"I see."

An uncomfortable pause ensued.

I had the urge to plead with James to call off his wedding.

I wanted to tell him he wasn't being truthful to his fiancée, Charlotte. Most of all, I wanted to tell him that he was making a mistake. But if I revealed the strength of my feelings for him I knew there was a possibility I would drive him away. Instead of explaining how I truly felt, I told James what had made me suspicious about the burglary and Olivia Forster's death.

"I'll have a good look around inside the house and see what I can deduce from it," he said once I had finished. "I shall also speak to the staff when they're sufficiently recovered."

"But do you agree that my theory holds weight?"

"It cannot be ruled out, Penny."

"Good. Do you know who I think is behind this? The husband."

"Mr Forster?"

"Yes, he was conveniently absent at the time, and when I saw him here the morning after the murder there was something rather odd about his manner. Do you know, I actually heard him laugh?"

"Really?"

"Yes, as if he and Inspector Bowles were sharing a private joke. Something's not quite right, and I have heard of so-called burglaries being used to cover up an alternative motive before."

"So have I, Penny, and I can see how there might be some truth to your speculation. I'll find out what Inspector Bowles has discovered so far and carry out my own investigations into the matter. I'll also try to ascertain what they were laughing about."

"Thank you, James. You will let me know how you get on, won't you?"

"Of course I will. I know how keen you are to know every detail of each case you report on." He smiled.

"Perhaps we can meet at the Museum Tavern again to discuss it," I suggested. "Oh, I've just remembered that we're not supposed to meet there any more. Charlotte wouldn't like it. Forget that I ever mentioned it. I shall see you again soon, no doubt."

CHAPTER 4

"What a delightful pair of vases, Mrs Billington-Grieg."

"Oh, thank you. I'm so pleased you like them, Mrs Lennox," my sister Eliza replied.

About a dozen of us were sitting in her drawing room in Bayswater, gathered together for a meeting of the West London Women's Society.

"The vases are Cantonese," continued Eliza, "and although I would like to say they were gifted to me, they were in fact gifted to my husband, George. A show of gratitude from a wealthy client of his. I forget his name, but he trades in Chinese wares, and thankfully for me George is quite happy to have these vases displayed by our fireplace so that visitors such as yourselves can enjoy them."

"I've been collecting Chinese porcelain plates for some years now," said Mrs Lennox, "and on my birthday I ask the housekeeper to serve dinner on them. For the remainder of the year they remain solely on display!"

This anecdote was met with genteel laughter. I leafed

through my notebook waiting for the polite conversation to end so that Eliza could begin chairing the meeting.

"My sister, Miss Penelope Green, has joined us at last!" she announced to the group. "Welcome, Penelope. I'm aware that as a working woman you struggle to find the time to attend our meetings regularly. I'm extremely pleased you could join us today."

I smiled and wished all the faces would turn away from me. I was only there because I felt guilty for not having turned up to any of the meetings for several months.

Eliza stood between the Cantonese vases and updated us on the progress, or lack of it, in women's suffrage over the past few weeks. Like me, she was fair-haired and brown-eyed. She wore a divided blue skirt made of soft cotton with a matching jacket. Over the past year she had begun to adopt rational dress: comfortable, functional clothing which allowed her to ride her bicycle with ease. Glancing around the room I could see that some of the other ladies were wearing similar attire, though a number still conformed to the traditional corseted style with a tight bodice and full skirts. I felt too accustomed to my corset to abandon it altogether, but it was loosely laced and my blouse and skirt were of a practical, rather than decorative, design.

"I think the Bishop of Carlisle's letter is extremely encouraging," commented a lady with a beak-like nose and silver hair. "Never before has such a high-ranking member of the Church conceded that women should have the vote."

"*Unmarried* women," corrected a younger woman with dark hair so curly it was fighting back against its pins. "The bishop maintains that married women should not have the vote because husband and wife must be as one on the matter. If the husband has the vote there is no need for the wife to have it as well."

"Such a ridiculous notion!" said Eliza. "George and I never agree on anything!"

"Ah, but in the eyes of God you are *as one*," said the curly-haired woman with a smile.

"If only we were," replied Eliza. "George is still concerned about the case of Mrs Cynthia Leonard, an American lady he read about in the newspaper."

"Who is she?" asked Mrs Lennox.

"It's reported that she went to a women's suffrage confer-ence in New York and then refused to return to her husband. Apparently, she wishes to be 'untrammelled in her life's work'."

"Hurrah for Mrs Leonard!" I piped up, instantly wishing I hadn't as all the faces immediately turned toward me again.

Eliza scowled in response to the interruption. "A judge in New York has now granted her the divorce," she added.

"While I cannot deny that women's suffrage is a noble cause, it seems a step too far to be divorcing one's husband over the matter," said the silver-haired lady.

"It does indeed, Mrs Knatchbull," said Eliza, "and I now find myself having to reassure George that I'm not about to do the same thing! Poor chap."

"I always refer prophets of doom to the queen," said Mrs Lennox. "When they complain about women's suffrage I ask them whether they're aware that a woman has governed the destinies of this country for forty-seven years! And I might add that she has done so with more diplomatic skill and grace than any man could ever have achieved."

This statement was met with many nods of approval.

"Agreed," said a red-haired lady in a tightly laced dress. "Our great queen is often overlooked in this debate."

. . .

"I do so enjoy it when the West London Women are here," said Eliza as she plumped up a cushion once the ladies had left. "Did you enjoy the debate?"

"Indeed I did, Ellie." In all honesty the time had seemed to drag. Some interesting points had been made, but there had been a good deal of superfluous chatter, which always bored me.

"This is the first opportunity I've had to ask you, Penelope," said Eliza, "but did something irregular pass between you and Mr Edwards at the dinner party we had for Mr Fox-Stirling last week? I couldn't help but notice that the man was rather sullen following Inspector Blakely's brief visit."

"Not that I'm aware of, Ellie." I willed my face not to redden as I told the lie.

"James called in to update you on the case you had been working on together, and then, to my knowledge, you spoke for a while in the hallway. I asked Mr Edwards to fetch you for pudding, but when the pair of you returned I swear that not a single word passed between you for the remainder of the evening."

"Really? That's not how I remember it."

"Were any cross words exchanged between Mr Edwards and Inspector Blakely? I suppose there must be a little resentment on both sides."

"Resentment? What nonsense!" My voice sounded less than convincing. "If Mr Edwards became sullen I cannot imagine why. Perhaps he was tired, or maybe he's prone to changeable moods."

"It was certainly changeable that evening," said Eliza. "Which is a shame, as he had been enjoying Mr Fox-Stirling's tales of adventure, hadn't he?"

"He had. And I was pleased that Mr Fox-Stirling agreed over dinner that he would start the search for Father in Colombia again."

Our father had vanished in Amazonia nine years previously while undertaking one of his famous plant-hunting expeditions.

"Yes, isn't that wonderful news? And it's encouraging that he has agreed to take a Spanish interpreter along with him this time. I'm still in a state of wonderment that Mr Edwards should have donated such a large sum to aid the search effort. It's incredibly generous of him, and certainly demonstrates the size of the torch he holds for you, Penelope. Don't ever upset him, will you?"

I smiled meekly.

"Now we have only the remainder of the money to raise," continued Eliza. "I shall organise some fundraisers, but I shall need your help with those."

"Of course."

She watched my face for longer than felt comfortable.

"I still think there's something you're not telling me, Penelope."

"Regarding what?"

"Oh, never mind. I can see that you're not in the mood to admit anything to me at the present time, but the truth will out sooner or later."

CHAPTER 5

I had begun to make progress on the book I was writing about my father's life. By committing time to it each evening I had managed to write between five hundred and a thousand words each day. Some comprised transcriptions of his letters and diaries, so I had found it quite difficult to add my own narrative. However, with perseverance and much crossing out, I was finally beginning to achieve something.

The ending of the book would depend on the result of Mr Fox-Stirling's search for my father, which had been planned for the following year.

I worked at my writing desk in my garret room in front of a little window which looked out over the rooftops. My cat Tiger was usually close by as I worked, either sitting out on the roof watching the birds on the chimneys or resting on my desk. Sometimes she was determined to sit on the piece of paper upon which I was trying to write.

It was usually when I was most absorbed in my work that my landlady would come knocking at my door with a message.

"There's a gentleman here to see you, Miss Green!"

Could it be James? I wondered. My heart skipped hopefully, but then I reminded myself of our conversation beside All Saints church. His wedding was going ahead and I would have to do my very best to suppress any affection I held for him.

I smoothed down my cotton skirts and adjusted the pins in my hair.

"Miss Green!" my landlady called impatiently.

I opened the door. "Yes, Mrs Garnett?"

Her steel-grey curls sprung out from beneath her bonnet. A widow of about fifty, she had come to London from British West Africa as a child. The whites of her eyes contrasted with her dark skin as she gave me an excitable look. She lowered her voice to a whisper.

"It's that lovesick gentleman from the library!"

It was Mr Edwards.

"I see. Thank you, Mrs Garnett."

"Well come on, then. Don't keep him waiting!"

I reluctantly descended the narrow wooden stairs behind my landlady. *Why was Mr Edwards here? What had he come to say to me? And what could I say to him in return?*

I could feel the heat rising in my face as I thought about the kiss with James, which Mr Edwards had undoubtedly witnessed.

I followed Mrs Garnett down the wide, carpeted staircase which led to the hallway as a prickly ball of shame rolled in my stomach. I wished I could be anywhere but here.

Mr Edwards stood by the hallway table holding his bowler hat in one hand. He wore a pale grey summer suit and the fringe of his sandy hair partly obscured his spectacles.

"Mr Edwards," I said as cheerfully as possible. "What a pleasant surprise!"

"Miss Green."

His greeting was polite but solemn, and I steeled myself

for a difficult conversation. Having once agreed we'd refer to each other by first name, we appeared to be on surname terms again. Mrs Garnett remained in the hallway with us, looking from one to the other as if waiting to see who would speak next.

"Mrs Garnett, I hope it isn't untoward of me to request this, but please may I speak to Miss Green alone for a few minutes?"

My landlady sucked her lip disapprovingly.

"What about a chaperone?" she asked.

Mr Edwards nodded. "I understand your concern, Mrs Garnett, but please rest assured that I only wish to have a quick conversation with Miss Green. My intentions are entirely honourable, and I can assure you that I would never take advantage of a lady." He spoke these last few words with emphasis, as if referring to my kiss with James.

"I should hope not!" retorted Mrs Garnett. "However, it would not be appropriate for me to allow the two of you to use my parlour. I have known all matter of mishaps occur in parlours."

"I'm sure it will be quite suitable for us to speak here in the hallway," I suggested.

Mrs Garnett nodded but showed no sign of moving.

"The evening air is quite pleasant," said Mr Edwards. "Shall we talk outside on the steps?"

"What an excellent idea, Mr Edwards," I replied.

We stood on the third step down from the front door in the hope that Mrs Garnett wouldn't be able to overhear our conversation. As Mr Edwards fidgeted with the brim of his hat my mouth suddenly felt dry. The street was quiet at this time of day, with only a few carriages passing by. Streaks of cloud above the rooftops began to glow orange.

"I had a conversation with Inspector Blakely yesterday evening," said Mr Edwards, staring at the houses opposite us.

"Oh?" My voice croaked.

"It was at quite a pleasant establishment, actually: The Marquis of Cornwallis in Bloomsbury. Have you ever been there?"

"I haven't."

"It was Inspector Blakely's idea. He was waiting for me when I finished work at the library. He gave me a thorough explanation with regard to recent... events."

"Oh?" I said again, unsure as to what else I could say.

"Yes, and I must say I respect the man's ability to express such contriteness. First and foremost, he has been extremely concerned about the effect the incident may have had on you."

"Is that so?"

"Yes. He explained that it was nothing more than a moment of weakness on his part. He was tired and had spent a long, busy day on that Borthwick case. He stated that he has no idea how the emotion overcame him, but overcame him it did. I cannot recall ever seeing a man so filled with regret."

"I see."

"He was most regretful about the fact that he has ruined your honour."

"I think that he is overstating it, rather. It was a simple mistake, and I feel sure that my honour remains intact."

"He would be pleased to hear you say that, I'm sure. I believe he has already apologised to you."

"He has."

"He apologised profusely to me and I should say that, after some consideration, I have accepted his apology."

"That's very obliging of you, Mr Edwards."

"I can't say that I initially felt obliging, but having spent some time in the chap's company I can say that I respect him and his work, and I consider him to be of generally good character given that he appears willing to recognise and apologise for his mistakes."

I smiled to myself as I realised that Mr Edwards considered me entirely blameless in this matter. The idea that I might have wanted James to kiss me did not seem to have entered his head.

"So there's no need for me to say any more on the matter," Mr Edwards said, turning to face me. "I haven't seen you in the reading room recently, Miss Green."

"Oh, I've been rather busy reporting on this Forster murder case. And the book about Father's life is coming along rather better now. I've been devoting more time to it."

"Good." He smiled. "Well, I hope to see you there again soon. If there's anything you would like me to research on your behalf you know where I am."

"Thank you, Mr Edwards, and I appreciate the time you've taken to come and speak to me about the other matter this evening. I do apologise —"

"I won't hear an apology from you, Miss Green. You were a victim of the man's passions. Detectives such as Inspector Blakely must endure much stress and strain in their work, and lapses will naturally occur. Others lapse into drink, of course. You were merely in the wrong place at the wrong time. It could have been any woman who happened to find herself standing in front of Inspector Blakely that evening."

I felt my heart sink at the thought that James would have kissed any woman he might have encountered that night, but it was clearly a thought which afforded Mr Edwards some comfort, so I remained silent.

CHAPTER 6

"Stay back!" came the shout.

People knocked into each other as they tried to lift their feet from the rivulets of water running off the pavement and into the gutter.

Another pail of water was emptied onto the paving slabs with a loud slosh, and brushes scrubbed the decks with great fervour.

"Move away!"

A group of constables were doing their best to keep the crowd away from the London Library in the corner of St James's Square. Tom Clifford from *The Holborn Gazette* elbowed me as he tried to get closer. I stood on my tiptoes, hoping to see an inspector who might be in charge of the scene, but everything appeared rather chaotic.

More water trickled past my feet and my stomach churned when I saw that it was streaked with red. Additional staff emerged from the stone portico of the East India Club, each equipped with a pail of water and a broom.

"What's 'appened?" asked a woman in a brown dress and tattered shawl who had appeared at my side.

"I'm not exactly sure yet," I replied. "All I've heard is that there's been a murder."

"That's what I 'eard an' all. What they washin' the path for?"

I chose not to answer as she pushed past me to get closer to the action.

There was an early morning chill in the air. Mrs Garnett had woken me shortly after dawn with the news, her knowledgeable friend having called at the house to give her the scoop.

I decided it was time to break through the crowd and find out what had happened.

"Press!" I shouted as I began to push my way to the corner of the square. "Press! Let me through!"

I was knocked and jostled as I battled my way through the throng. My toes were stepped on and I almost lost my notebook in the melee.

"Move back! Move back!" cried the police constables.

Behind the line they were maintaining, the paving was still being scrubbed by the staff of the East India Club. The crowd surged forward and my face was pressed up against the chest of a black-whiskered reporter from the *News of the World*. We avoided each other's gaze, equally embarrassed by our close proximity.

"Who was the victim?" I asked his jacket.

"Augustus Forster."

"*Mr Forster?*" I looked up at the dark whiskers. "The man whose wife was murdered during that burglary a few days ago?"

"Same one."

"He's also been murdered? But how? Why?"

The reporter tried to shrug but could barely move his arms. "It's baffling," he replied as he was lurched into me. "Oops, I am sorry."

The man I had suspected of murdering his wife was dead himself.

As I struggled to comprehend this, a wiry inspector with a wispy moustache skipped over the wet pavement and called out to us. "Gentlemen! Can I have some calm, please? If you're from the press, follow me. No one else has any business being here. Get back to whatever it is you ought to be doing."

He strode off in the direction of the East India Club and everyone in the crowd turned to follow. I was able to extricate myself from the reporter's chest, but the next moment I received a shoulder blow to my chin.

"Miss Green?"

"Edgar?"

"I thought I'd got here before you this time."

"I'm afraid not." I smiled. "Did you hear the inspector's announcement? We're to follow him into the East India Club."

"Righty-ho," said Edgar, shuffling into an about-turn.

The police constables tried to disperse the crowd while the rest of us made our way toward the club.

"Why here?" I asked Edgar.

"The chap was staying here, apparently," he replied.

"Have you heard that it was Augustus Forster? The man whose wife, Olivia, was murdered in the recent burglary?"

"It's *him*?" said Edgar. "Well I never!"

We reached the cream portico of the East India Club and began to climb the stone steps. I overheard the inspector ahead of us telling a reporter he had been permitted to use the smoking room for his briefing.

"I'm rather impatient to find out what has happened," I said.

"It must have been a stabbing," replied Edgar. "Did you see all the blood?"

"I tried not to look at it."

"My apologies, madam, but ladies are not permitted inside the East India," said a young man in a dark suit with gold buttons. He rested his hand on my forearm to gently reinforce his words.

"Oh, it's quite all right. I have no wish to become a member; I'm simply a reporter attending the police briefing."

Edgar walked on into the club without me.

"Indeed, madam, but I'm afraid you're not permitted inside."

"I'm a reporter for the *Morning Express* newspaper! Here, let me find you my card." I pulled my arm away from his hand and rummaged around in my carpet bag for it.

"That may be so, madam, but the rules of the club state that membership is for gentlemen only."

"But I have no wish to become a member!" I hissed.

All the reporters except me were inside the building by this point.

"Madam?" He held my forearm again and glanced toward the door.

"Presumably you don't usually allow a crowd of reporters inside your club," I said, "so on this unusual and tragic day perhaps you could make allowances for a single woman."

"I'm afraid not, madam. Please do accept my apologies and thank you for agreeing to my request without creating an embarrassing scene."

I glared at him, knowing that any further protest would be useless. I turned and made my way back down the steps.

CHAPTER 7

"Where did you vanish to, Miss Green?" asked Edgar when he returned to the newsroom that afternoon.

"I wasn't allowed inside the East India Club."

"Well, I can't say I'm not surprised. It only takes a single glance to realise you're trouble." He laughed.

"I didn't find it funny at the time."

"You truly weren't allowed inside? I thought you were joking."

"The East India is a *gentleman's* club, Edgar," said Frederick Potter. "Miss Green is a member of the fairer sex."

"Yes, I realise she's a lady. Thank you, Potter," said Edgar. "But I didn't realise the club would stop you going in altogether, Miss Green. That's a bit out of sorts, isn't it?"

"Do you ever see ladies at your club, Edgar?" asked Frederick.

"No, it's not a place for ladies."

"And that's precisely why Miss Green wasn't allowed in."

"But surely an exception should have been made!"

protested Edgar. "She's a news reporter and works just as hard as you and I do."

"Thank you, Edgar," I said. "Perhaps you could have helped me explain that to the man on the door."

"I hadn't even realised he'd stopped you, Miss Green. I do apologise."

"He wouldn't have allowed her in even if you had explained it," said Frederick. "Rules are rules."

"Let's forget about all that now," I said. "Did you write down everything the police had to say, Edgar?"

"I certainly did."

"What happened to Mr Forster?"

"The unfortunate chap was staying at the club after all that terrible business with the burglary and the murder of his wife. Yesterday evening he decided to step out into St James's Square for some air, and that's when the attacker struck. A knife in the back, it was."

I winced. "Were there any witnesses to the murder?"

"Not that the police are aware of. It's believed that Mr Forster was lying there for a while before he was discovered by a constable doing his rounds."

"At what time was that?"

"About two o'clock this morning. The constable had previously walked the perimeter of the square shortly before midnight and all had been quiet at that point. And then at some time between midnight and two o'clock, the poor fellow was done in. The chap on the reception desk at the club said he thought Forster had left for his walk shortly after midnight. He'd had a few drinks at one of the lounges beforehand and had presumably decided to take some air before retiring for the night."

"Has there been any sign of the murder weapon?" I asked.

"Not yet."

"But why? Why would someone wish to murder him?"

"That's the question everyone asks, isn't it? I can't see why there should ever be a reason to murder anyone."

"Oh, I can think of a few good reasons," said Frederick.

"Perhaps someone knew that he'd had his wife murdered and then killed him in a quest for revenge," I suggested. "Or perhaps he somehow found out the identity of the men who had killed his wife and was murdered to prevent him from telling anyone."

Edgar nodded. "Either theory is possible."

"Or," I continued, "the people who killed his wife had also intended to kill him that same evening but were unable to because he was absent, so they finally caught up with him."

"Anything's possible, Miss Green," said Edgar, "but it's not for us to conjecture. We must leave the detective work to Inspector Paget of C Division."

"I've just thought of another scenario!" I exclaimed. "Perhaps his death has nothing to do with his wife's, and instead he had an argument with someone at the club. That person may have followed him out and stabbed him in the back."

"Maybe, maybe not," said Edgar. "Why are you hurling all these theories at me? Do I look like a detective?"

"I'm just trying to make sense of it all," I replied.

"There are many things I wish to make sense of, Miss Green, but striving to consider every possible explanation isn't a sensible use of my time."

"We need to find out more," I said.

"And we will, in good time."

"Thank you for writing everything down, Edgar. If you could pass me your notes I'll get the article written up."

He scowled at me. "I shall be the one writing the article, Miss Green."

"But I was there before you!"

"Were you?"

"Yes!"

"At what time?" asked Edgar.

"I left my home at half-past five. How about you?"

"I left at six, but I live nearer to St James's Square than you, so I was there first."

"You were not! I managed to get further into the crowd than you, which confirms that I was there earlier."

"That doesn't mean anything."

"Edgar, I have to write this article because I wrote the one about Mrs Forster's murder."

"Ah, but it's not the same story."

"It is! It involves the same family."

"But it's a separate incident."

"I saw Mr Forster the morning after his wife's murder. I'm closer to this story than you."

"It's an entirely different story, Miss Green."

"If I'd been allowed inside the East India Club this story would have been mine!" I fumed.

"Maybe, but then again maybe not," said Frederick. "You'd both still be bickering about it whether you had been allowed into the club or not, Miss Green."

"Thank you, Potter," said Edgar. "I'm pleased you agree that the story is mine."

"I said nothing of the kind," replied Frederick.

"Whose story should it be, then?"

"Miss Green's, given that she wrote the story about the wife."

Mr Sherman marched into the newsroom. "Good Lord!" he declared. "What's all this noise about?"

"Miss Green and I have been arguing about who should write the story on Mr Forster's murder," said Edgar. "I say it should be me as I was on the scene first and was able to listen to Inspector Paget's briefing at the East India Club. Miss Green wasn't permitted entry because she's a woman."

"I see, well get on with your article then, Fish," replied the editor. "Less talk and more writing, please."

"Edgar gets the story?" I said. "But I covered Mrs Forster's murder. It's only fitting that I write this piece!"

"I cannot abide discord, Miss Green," replied Mr Sherman. "I want four hundred words from you about the funeral of Bishop Claughton, and you'll need to typewrite it quickly as the deadline is fast approaching."

CHAPTER 8

I left the newsroom that evening feeling angry that Edgar had been given the story. It made no sense to me that the two murders should be treated as separate incidents. *Surely Mr Forster's death was related to the murder of his wife?*

With Edgar working on the article it would be difficult for me to find out how the investigation was progressing. I was desperate to discuss the murders with someone, and James was the only person I could think of. We usually met at the Museum Tavern by the British Museum to discuss our work, but James' fiancée Charlotte had begun to express her disapproval of our meetings. I felt I could no longer send him a telegram and ask to meet at our usual place. He had probably left Scotland Yard for the day, so the only alternative was to visit his home.

I had never called on James at home before and I wasn't sure how he would receive me. Besides discussing the Forster murders I also wished to hear more about his conversation with Mr Edwards.

. . .

James lived at Henstridge Place in St John's Wood. One side of the street was lined with large stucco buildings and James lived in one of the smart terraced houses on the opposite side. An unseasonably chill wind blew along the street as I approached number twenty-five. My heart pounded heavily as I knocked at the door and waited.

I knew James would be surprised to see me, and I also knew that it wasn't entirely ladylike for me to be here.

As I had hoped, James answered the door. His shirt sleeves were rolled up and he had unbuttoned his waistcoat.

"Penny! Is everything all right?"

"Yes, everything's fine, nothing to worry about. I just found myself passing by and thought I'd call in on you for a moment."

"Passing by?"

"Yes." I grinned.

I had expected him to invite me inside, but instead he stepped out onto the top step with an uneasy expression on his face.

"You've heard about poor Mr Forster, I presume?" I asked. "I was down in St James's Square this morning, but Edgar has been given the story."

"Yes, I heard. It's quite shocking. I expect Inspector Paget of C Division has the matter in hand, but no doubt he'll call on the Yard if he requires our assistance."

"Have you discovered anything more about the gang that broke into Forster's home?"

"I've spoken to the housekeeper and the maid, who have both given me their accounts. There's a boy who worked there, too, and he managed to escape unharmed. I have a description of the men, but they disguised themselves quite well with hats and scarves over their faces. I made sure the descriptions were sent out to all the police divisions as it's possible some of them may have encountered the gang before."

"Could the same men have murdered Mr Forster, do you think?"

"It may be the same men behind both attacks. It's terribly tragic, and it begs the question *why*."

"Do you think Inspector Paget and Inspector Bowles are capable of finding that out?"

"I don't doubt their competency, but there are two separate divisions working on this now: St James and Marylebone. I'll have to see what I can do to coordinate the effort."

"I don't suppose you spoke to Mr Charles Mawson, who was hanging about the Forsters' home when I saw you there?"

"The chap with the bushy whiskers? No, I didn't. Did he have anything interesting to say for himself?"

"Only that he had known the Forsters in India. He seemed rather keen to find out where Mr Forster was. I had assumed he was asking out of concern for his friend, but now I'm beginning to wonder whether he had another motive."

"He might have wanted to find him so he could stick a knife in his back, you mean?"

"It's possible, isn't it?"

"One of many possibilities at this stage, I should think."

"The man was asking a lot of questions about the burglary. He seemed keen to find out what the police knew."

"But that doesn't make him a murderer."

"I realise that, but he may know something. I wish I could find him again."

"Why don't you try?" James asked.

"It would be like looking for a needle in a haystack! That's why I hoped you had spoken to him. I wondered if there was an easy way to track him down."

"Why don't you ask Inspector Bowles?"

"Yes, I will. I know he spoke to the man, at least briefly.

Perhaps he's also suspicious of him. Thank you, James. I won't detain you any longer."

I felt disappointed that we had conducted our entire conversation on the doorstep. It appeared that James considered it ungentlemanly to invite me inside.

"Hopefully we shall see one another again soon," I continued. "Perhaps when you have made some progress with Mrs Forster's murder you could let me know."

"Inspector Bowles would be better placed than I, Penny."

"I suppose he would be, yes, I'll ask him to update me. I shall be on my way then, James. Oh, I had a visit from Mr Edwards yesterday evening."

"Is that so?" James' brow furrowed.

"He told me about your conversation. You seem to have taken full responsibility for what happened at Eliza's home, and he respects you for doing so."

"Does he?" James lowered his voice. "Well, I do take responsibility for it, Penny, and I hope that the friendship between yourself and Mr Edwards is unaltered."

"Yes, thankfully no great damage appears to have been done, which is quite miraculous given the circumstances."

"He seems to be quite forgiving where you are concerned."

"Thank you for speaking to him. Matters would no doubt have remained quite awkward between Mr Edwards and myself otherwise."

"I wanted to do what I could to right the situation."

"Well, things are righted now, thank you. Mr Edwards considers me a lady of virtue once more."

I laughed and James smiled. We held each other's gaze for a moment until I was startled by a woman's voice from beyond the door.

"Who are you speaking to, darling?"

James gave a brief look of alarm before swiftly regaining

his composure. The door opened wider to reveal Charlotte, whom I had met once before. She had a wide, apple-cheeked face framed by fair curls. I blinked and forced a smile onto my face.

"Miss Green!" she said. "What a surprise." Her mouth smiled, but her blue eyes did not match it.

"Who is it?" came another voice. Behind Charlotte was an older woman with the same face, though decorated with age lines. It was Charlotte's mother.

"How lovely to see you again, Miss Jenkins," I said, trying my hardest to sound sincere.

"What is it you want?" Charlotte asked abruptly. Her tone was not as polite as it had been when I had met her last.

"I was passing by and needed to tell James something about a case I'm reporting on. That was all, Miss Jenkins. I'm just about to leave."

"Charlotte and her mother are here to discuss wedding arrangements," said James as cheerily as possible.

"How lovely," I said. "It's not long to go now, is it? Just six weeks, I believe. I shan't detain you any longer; you must have a great deal to discuss."

CHAPTER 9

"Thank you for your information regarding Mr Mawson, Miss Green. I shall bear him in mind."

Inspector Bowles closed his notebook and tucked it into his jacket pocket. We stood in the wood-panelled waiting room at Marylebone Lane police station.

"I had hoped you would know where to find him," I said.

"No, I'm afraid not. I don't know anything about the man."

"Don't you think he seems rather suspicious?"

"It sounds as though he was simply enquiring about the whereabouts of his friend when you spoke to him."

"He wished to find his friend, and then his friend was murdered. What if he only wanted to locate Mr Forster so that he could carry out the deed?"

"That seems rather unlikely to me," Inspector Bowles replied.

"But it's a possibility. Who else do you suspect may have been behind Mr Forster's murder?"

"C Division is investigating *Mr* Forster's murder; I am investigating *Mrs* Forster's murder."

"Aren't you communicating with one another about the two cases?"

"Absolutely. We know how to do our job, Miss Green."

"Do you think the same person might be behind both murders?"

"That's for myself and Inspector Paget to decide. Please allow me to proceed with my work now," Inspector Bowles replied, "You're fortunate I'm speaking to you at all. Many police officers have no time for news reporters, you know."

"I'm aware of that, Inspector. There's something else which has been troubling me since I saw Mr Forster the morning after his wife was murdered. I recall that you and he walked past me discussing something, and then he laughed."

"Did he?"

"Yes, and I thought it rather an odd thing to do considering that his wife had just died. Do you not recall it?"

"I can't say that I do. It's not as if we can ask the chap now, given that he's dead."

"You don't remember him laughing?"

"No, I don't."

"I see. Well, thank you for your time, Inspector Bowles. I realise this has become quite a complicated case, but I'm sure Scotland Yard could be of some assistance."

"I've already had Blakely from the Yard sniffing about and that will do for the time being. D Division is quite capable of handling this case. Thank you, Miss Green. You've taken an extremely keen interest in matters but please concentrate on your job and allow me to do mine."

As the omnibus carried me along Oxford Street I reflected on the frosty reception I had received from Charlotte Jenkins the previous evening. Although I resented the manner in which she had spoken I knew that she had every right to be suspicious of me. Having asked James to stop meeting me at the Museum Tavern she must have been deeply annoyed to find me standing on his doorstep.

I wondered if she had discussed me with him after I left. I pictured an awkward conversation between James, Charlotte and her mother. After that they had probably forgotten all about me and discussed their plans for the wedding: which guests should be seated together, which should be kept apart and what they should all dine on.

How I envied Charlotte and wished I were the one discussing wedding plans with James. An advert for Pears Soap situated above the passenger opposite me caught my eye. Beaming out from the picture was a woman who looked just like Charlotte, all apple-cheeked and happy.

I closed my eyes and tried to think of other matters. My father. The book I was writing about my father. My cat. Charlotte may have been betrothed to James, but she didn't have a cat as adorable as Tiger. Though it was but a small consolation, it offered momentary relief.

❧

"You seem perplexed, Miss Green," whispered Mr Edwards as I sat at my desk in the reading room. "A penny for your thoughts."

"I wouldn't waste your penny, Mr Edwards." I smiled. "I'm not perplexed; I'm just wondering how I might find out more about a person I met only briefly. He was a friend of Mr and Mrs Forster, and I think he may have been in possession of some useful information."

"The Forster family who fell victim to that dreadful burglary and murder business?"

"Yes."

"It's horrifying, isn't it? I cannot understand why they should have been harmed in such a manner."

"Me neither. And the police haven't made much progress with the case as yet. I think they should be speaking to the people who knew the Forsters."

"I'm sure they already are."

"But not all of them. I spoke to a chap who Inspector Bowles thought was of no consequence at all. I'm not convinced he's interested in speaking to the man, though I think he may have some valuable information."

"Is this the man you wish to discover more about?"

"Yes. His name is Charles Mawson, and he told me he was living near the Forsters while he was working for the Indian government. There's a periodical which summarises news and appointments in India, isn't there? I'm trying to remember the name of it."

"*The Homeward Mail?*"

"Yes! That's the one, Mr Edwards, thank you. Presumably there are copies held here?"

"There are indeed. Do you intend to search for a mention of this Mawson chap?"

"Yes. There might also be something in there about the Forsters."

"I believe it's a weekly publication, Miss Green, which means there would be quite a lot of information to search through. It could take you a long while."

"Mr Mawson told me he returned about a year ago. Hopefully there are passenger lists in *The Homeward Mail*."

"I seem to recall that just about everything is listed in that publication. What is it exactly that you wish to find out?"

"Whatever I can. I should like to find Mawson and ask him what else he knows."

"I'll show you where it's stored, and hopefully something will leap out from its pages for you."

I followed Mr Edwards, feeling relieved that he had returned to his usual self after witnessing the events of that unforgettable dinner party. After a short walk we reached the newspaper storage area of the British Library, where shelves from floor to ceiling held tall, leather-bound volumes.

"Here we are. *The Homeward Mail*, July to September 1883," he said, pointing at a heavy-looking volume. "Do you think this might include a reference to your chap Mr Mawson?"

"He told me he had returned a year ago, so he must be in the passenger lists if nothing else."

"Let me lift this off the shelf and carry it into the newspaper reading room for you, Miss Green. It's rather cumbersome."

We walked to the newspaper reading room where Mr Edwards rested the volume on a rack over one of the desks.

"There you are," he said with a smile. "I hope you find what you're looking for. It seems rather a daunting task."

"Thank you, Mr Edwards."

"And do let me know when you need to look through the other volumes, won't you? They're rather heavy to be carrying about by yourself."

"I'll manage. Thank you, Mr Edwards."

"I mean it, Miss Green. I wouldn't wish for you to injure yourself."

I spent much of the morning leafing through copies of *The Homeward Mail* hoping to find any mention I could of the Forsters or Mr Mawson.

I skimmed through various articles on the Indian budget, schools, military intelligence, stocks and shares, the cotton trade, shipping intelligence, births, marriages and deaths. I found no mention whatsoever of Mr Mawson in the passenger lists.

I eventually ran out of time. The volume was heavy, as Mr Edwards had warned me, but I managed to return it to the shelves. The time had come to write my article about the prime minister's recent speech on fruit farming.

CHAPTER 10

"It fills me with fear that a woman could be murdered in her own home," said Eliza. "Whenever I think of poor Mrs Forster I shake like a leaf!"

"And now the husband's dead too," added her husband George. "It's a terrible state of affairs."

I was dining with Eliza and George at their large home in Bayswater. My brother-in-law was a lawyer: a tall man with wavy brown hair swept to one side. He had thick mutton-chop whiskers and the buttons on his waistcoat strained around his generous girth.

"Please don't worry, Ellie," I said. "I don't think Mrs Forster's death was a case of a burglary gone wrong. I think it's more likely that she was the intended target."

"That's even worse!"

"I know it's dreadful, but it should be of some reassurance. I'm quite sure nobody wishes to murder you."

"But how do you know that? Presumably poor Mrs Forster had no idea that someone wished to murder her, yet they did exactly that!"

"And don't forget about the husband," said George, sawing

away at his lamb cutlet with a blunt knife. "Stabbed to death outside the East India. That's only a few streets away from my club! It could just as easily have been me stabbed in the back."

"There's no denying that it's horrific," I said, "but someone must have had a reason to attack Mr Forster. It wasn't just a man lying in wait for any old gentleman to step outside his club of an evening. Someone had a reason for wanting the Forsters dead."

"But what could that reason have been?" asked my sister.

"That's what the police need to find out," I replied.

"It wouldn't surprise me one bit if you were trying to find out as well, Penelope," she said.

"I'm taking an interest in the case. I spoke briefly to a friend of the Forsters, who I'm sure must have some clue about who might wish to murder them. Perhaps it was the chap himself! The trouble is, I don't know how to find him again."

"There's a surprise," said George. "If he's the man behind it I expect he's scarpered. He's probably escaped to the continent by now. Switzerland. That's a good place to escape to; nobody bothers a chap in Switzerland."

"Adjust your serviette, George, or you'll end up with gravy on your shirt," scolded Eliza.

Her husband did as he was told.

"But I still don't understand the motive behind the two murders," she continued. "What could they ever have done to harm someone to such an extent? They were a respectable married couple living in a respectable home without bothering anyone."

"And rather wealthy, too," added George.

"But why murder them?" asked Eliza.

"We don't know enough of the detail about their lives as

yet," I said. "Perhaps they did harm someone and we don't know about it."

"Nonsense, how could they?" said Eliza. "Wealthy people who live in respectable homes don't go around harming people, do they George?"

"They most certainly do not."

"They led a whole life in India which we know nothing about," I said.

"That makes them even more respectable!" said George. "What did Forster do? Indian government? Military?"

"He worked for a merchant in Calcutta."

"Eminently respectable," said George, taking a sip of wine. "We look after the legal affairs of several Indian merchants. You don't find anyone more respectable than them."

"I have learned very little about Mr Forster so far," I said, "but I did hear that he once worked for a merchant who dealt primarily in cotton and opium."

"The opium trade?" asked Eliza. "Oh dear. How I detest the opium trade. I don't understand why the government won't abolish it."

"Because it makes too much blessed money, that's why," said George. "Not as much as it used to, but still a fair amount."

"But it's immoral, darling!" protested Eliza. "Have you seen what opium does to people? It turns them into empty, vapid husks of their former selves. Opium addicts become selfish and neglect their families, and eventually they neglect themselves as well. It's nothing short of a tragedy."

"But if John Chinaman wishes to smoke opium it's not our duty to stop him," replied George.

"But it's bad for him! It's bad for China! I feel sorry for all those poor little Chinese babies whose parents show far more interest in their opium pipes than their charges."

"The Chinaman has smoked opium for hundreds of years," said George. "And if the British didn't sell it to them they'd only grow it themselves. In fact they do, and I hear it's rather poor quality when compared with the opium of Malwa or Bengal. Better that they smoke ours, and that we make some money from it in the meantime. The Chinese government also makes money on it from the import duty! It's not as if we're smuggling it any more; it's all perfectly above board these days."

"It may be above board, George, but it's still immoral," said Eliza.

George laughed. "Trust a woman to consider morality above revenue! Do you know how much the opium trade is predicted to make for us this year? In excess of eight-and-a-half million. Abolish the trade and where on earth could we raise eight million pounds from instead? Do you think the British taxpayer would be willing to cover the deficit? I should think not. And we're not just talking about money here; we're also talking about trade. How else would we get our hands on fine silk and porcelain? You're rather fond of the Canton vases, Eliza. In order to display such fine Chinese porcelain in our homes we must trade something in return. The British have nothing that is of interest to the Chinese save for opium, so opium it is."

"If that's how we came by the Canton vases I think they should be sent back," said Eliza sulkily.

George laughed again. "All the way back to Canton? I knew it would be hopeless trying to explain such matters to a woman! It's easy to throw one's hands up in the air at the plight of poor little Chinese babies, but far more difficult to understand the economics of the modern globe. This is how empire operates, Eliza, and it's what my clients have to continually explain to the empty-headed chaps at the Society for the Abolition of the Opium Trade."

"I think that sounds like a very worthwhile society," said Eliza. "I should like to join it."

"I think you belong to quite enough societies for the time being," said George. "And many of these so-called societies are founded on passions of the heart rather than on anything factual, or indeed any knowledge of how the world really works."

"I'm not sure I always agree with the way the world works," I said.

"Neither do I, Penelope," said George, "but this is what we are up against."

"But isn't it admirable to demand change?" I asked.

"Yes, when it makes sense to do so," he replied.

"But perhaps it doesn't always appear to make sense at the time," I said. "When it was first suggested that women should have the vote many people said it made little sense."

"And many still say it," said Eliza.

George groaned. "Oh, not that topic again. If you think I'm about to ruin my dinner discussing women's suffrage with the pair of you, you're sorely mistaken. I happen to have a lot of work to do for a client who is just about to land a lucrative contract with the India Office. Do excuse me while I get on with that." He stood and dropped his serviette onto his plate. "I shall take pudding in my study," he said to the butler on his way out.

"I do apologise on behalf of my husband, Penelope," said Eliza once he had left the room. "He's so terribly stubborn and old-fashioned."

She was trying to smile, but I noticed that her eyes were damp.

"There's no need to apologise. I've known George long enough to recognise his views on most things."

"But don't you find it all rather frustrating?" she asked. "You and I can see the things that are wrong, and we want to do something about them. We want to *change* them. But as long as men like George remain in charge we have no hope, do we?"

"There is always hope, Ellie. We just have to keep speaking up and making ourselves unpopular."

Eliza laughed. "It seems to be the only way. Do you know who I should like to see again, Penelope? Mr Edwards. He's a good conversationalist. How is he?"

"He's well. In fact, he has been assisting me in my research today."

"Oh good. I think an excursion with him is long overdue, don't you? And besides, we need to speak to him about Mr Fox-Stirling's search for Father. As a generous benefactor Mr Edwards needs to be closely involved, don't you think? Some time spent with him will take your mind off that troublesome inspector's forthcoming wedding."

CHAPTER 11

"Here you are, Miss Green," whispered Mr Edwards, placing some papers on my desk. "I spent a bit of time perusing *The Homeward Mail* and made some notes for you."

"There was no need to do that!" I whispered in surprise. "It must have taken you ages."

"It didn't take that long, and I had some spare time anyway," he replied. "I began at January 1882 and worked through to December 1883. I found a few mentions of the Forsters and Mr Mawson in the listings."

"That's extremely helpful of you, Mr Edwards, thank you. You must have put an enormous amount of your time into this. I really don't deserve it."

"You don't deserve it, Miss Green? What nonsense!"

James had done such a convincing job of persuading Mr Edwards of my virtue that he seemed content to spend as much time helping me as he had done before, but I felt rather guilty about the whole affair. I knew I had been partly to blame for the kiss, yet Mr Edwards considered me entirely innocent.

"Thank you again, but there really is no need to go to such great lengths on my behalf."

"But why ever not, Miss Green? I've helped you with your research in the past and I'm simply continuing in the same vein. Has anything changed?"

"No, I suppose not."

He softened his whisper further. "That business with Inspector Blakely is all forgotten about. There is no need to feel ashamed about the matter."

"Thank you, Mr Edwards. I would prefer not to be reminded of it."

"I shan't mention it again, Miss Green. Perhaps we could enjoy another walk out together in one of the parks again soon. You could invite your delightful sister to accompany us."

"Perhaps we could."

"I should very much like to discuss the search Mr Fox-Stirling is to conduct into your father's whereabouts."

"Oddly enough, Eliza said the same thing at dinner time yesterday. You have made an extremely generous donation to the search, and it is only right that you should have some say in how it is undertaken."

"Oh, I don't wish to have any say, Miss Green! I merely wish to take a keen interest. Mr Fox-Stirling will be in charge of it all."

"Yes, I daresay he will."

"Perhaps you could ask your sister when might be a convenient time for her."

"I will do, Mr Edwards."

"Good." He smiled. "I shall leave you alone with your work now. I know how busy you are."

"How is Inspector Paget getting on with the investigation into Mr Forster's death?" I asked Edgar in the newsroom that afternoon.

"I've visited him several times at Vine Street police station, but he's rather fed up with me questioning him," replied Edgar.

"Inspector Bowles is the same with me," I said. "Between us we're duplicating quite a bit of the effort, aren't we? It makes sense for just one of us to be working on the story."

"Yes, but there's little we can do about that now. It was the editor's decision."

"What was the editor's decision?" asked Mr Sherman as he marched into the newsroom, leaving the door to slam behind him in his customary manner.

"The decision to have me working on Mrs Forster's murder and Edgar working on Mr Forster's," I said. "It means that we're both putting a lot of time into what might have been treated as one story."

"Ah, I see." Mr Sherman puffed on his pipe as he gave this some thought. "I suppose we could consider it one story given that they were husband and wife."

"Exactly," I said. "I think it would be better for one of us to work on the murders, Mr Sherman, as they must surely be linked."

"They might well be," he replied. "The chances of both Mr and Mrs Forster being killed in unrelated attacks within a matter of days must be fairly slim." He paused a moment longer. "Fish!"

"Yes, sir?"

"You will take both the Forster stories."

"But sir!" I protested. "I've already done a lot of work on the Forsters!"

"Work I asked you to do? Or work which you have undertaken because you fancy yourself the detective, Miss Green?"

"Work I felt necessary in order to understand the case," I replied, feeling aggrieved.

"Well, no need to worry about it any longer as Fish has the story now. I want you at Limehouse Mortuary tomorrow afternoon to report on the inquest into the death of a chap who was pulled out of the river. They think he was the chief engineer on the steamship *Gaia*, which collided with the SS *Hoxton*. I believe they have recovered all the bodies, but an update from you would clarify that nicely. In the meantime, you have Mr Gladstone's fruit farming speech to be getting on with."

"Mr Sherman, I beseech you to let me work on the Forster case."

"You will work on the stories I give you, Miss Green. Now get on with it, and no more of your perpetual detective work."

CHAPTER 12

I sat at a table with several other reporters in the dreary, high-ceilinged courtroom of Limehouse Mortuary. Opposite me was Tom Clifford of *The Holborn Gazette*. He grinned at me, his slack jaw chewing on a piece of tobacco. On raised benches behind him sat the jury, and behind me was the witness stand. Members of the public occupied the benches to my right.

"Didn't I see yer in St James's Square?" Tom Clifford asked me.

"Probably," I replied brusquely.

Tom and I had experienced a number of disagreements in the past.

"That Forster bloke, weren't it? Stabbed in the back, I 'ear."

"Nasty business," said Tom's immediate neighbour, a reporter with a sandy moustache.

"Wife bludgeoned an' all," continued Tom. "Unlucky, ain't it?"

We stood to our feet as the coroner entered the room, placed his top hat on the windowsill behind him and sat on the raised stand at the end of the reporters' table. He had a bald head, thick grey whiskers and gold spectacles.

I made notes as the inquest into the death of twenty-six-year-old Alfred Holland was officially opened. Moments later the jury filed out of the room to view the body.

Tom folded his arms and gave a quiet whistle. "I wouldn't want ter be looking at a bloke who's been shot in the 'ead."

"I thought he drowned," I said.

"Drowned?" Tom said with a laugh. "How could he 'ave drowned? He was shot in the 'ead!"

"By whom?"

"No one knows as yet."

"The chief engineer on the steamship was truly shot in the head?" I asked incredulously. "The accident was not the result of a collision, then?"

Tom laughed louder. "Do you even know what inquest you're attendin', Miss Green?"

"Is it for someone else?"

Tom nodded with great mirth and I felt my teeth clench.

"Alfred Holland was shot dead inside an opium den," explained the reporter with the sandy moustache. "I believe the inquest into the chief engineer's death will be held after this."

"Thank you for the explanation," I replied. "This afternoon's inquests are not in the order I had expected."

"That's the *Morning Express* for yer," replied Tom. "You don't know yer 'ead from yer tail!"

I wondered why I hadn't heard about Mr Holland's death before now. I decided to remain where I was and find out anything I could about what had happened.

Once the jury had returned from viewing the body, the coroner summoned his first witness and asked him to introduce himself. I had to turn around in my seat to look at him in the witness stand. A man of about thirty, he had lank, black hair and a bulbous nose.

"John Spratling. Mr 'Olland was lodgin' in my 'ouse at twenny-four George Street."

"How long did he lodge at your house?" asked the coroner.

"Since last autumn."

"And when did you first become concerned with regard to his welfare?"

"He never come 'ome that evening."

"Had you been expecting him home at a certain time?"

"No, sir. He come 'ome whenever 'e wanted, it's just that I never 'eard 'is boots on the stairs that night, and I always 'eard 'is boots on the stairs when 'e come 'ome. Always woke me an' the missus up, it did."

"And what did you do when you realised he hadn't returned to your home?"

"I thought nuffink much of it. But then I 'eard a commotion outside and folks was sayin' there'd been a murder."

"At what time was that?"

"About eleven o'clock. I stepped out the front to see where the murder'd 'appened, and some bloke told me it were in one o' the opium dens, so when I went down there I saw a big crowd o' folk."

"And you ventured inside the opium den?"

"Yeah, I went in 'cause I 'adn't seen Mr 'Olland and I wondered if it were 'im what 'ad been murdered."

"You were aware that Mr Holland was a regular opium smoker, were you not?" the coroner asked.

"Yeah."

"And that he frequented the opium dens in the Limehouse area?"

"Course. So I went in and I told 'em 'e were missin' and

could I just see who 'e was, and they showed me." Mr Spratling's voice grew tremulous.

"You were in the same room as the deceased?"

"I were, but not fer long."

"Long enough for you to recognise the deceased gentleman as your tenant?"

"Aye. It were the clothes what looked familiar. I didn't see much of his 'ead. Well, I couldn't... There wasn't..."

His face grew pale and the coroner thanked him for his deposition.

The coroner summoned his next witness; a dishevelled-looking Chinese man called Ming Tan, who was the owner of the opium den. His hair was greased back from his face and he wore a scruffy, collarless shirt. He shifted uneasily from one foot to the other.

"At what time did Mr Holland visit you on the evening of his death?" asked the coroner.

"He visit about eight thirty."

"And he was a regular visitor?"

"Regular. Yes, sir."

"How regular? Weekly? Daily?"

"Normal daily."

"And during his visits did he impart much information about himself?"

"Not much information."

"He wasn't particularly talkative?"

"Not talkative, sir."

"So he visited your establishment purely to smoke an opium pipe?"

"Yes, sir."

"In the weeks leading up to Mr Holland's death, was there

any indication either from what he said or did that suggested someone might wish to attack him?"

"No, sir."

"So the attack came as a complete surprise to you?"

"Complete surprise. Yes, sir."

"At what time did the man with the gun appear?"

"I don't know exact time. I think must be ten o'clock or after."

"So by that time Mr Holland had been with you for about an hour and a half?"

"Hour and a half. Yes, sir."

"And, considering the effect of opium upon the mind, in what state of alertness was Mr Holland when the man with the gun visited?"

"He could be asleep. He did look asleep."

"This is a common state for a man who has recently smoked opium, am I right?"

"Common. Yes, sir."

"Can you describe the man with the gun?"

"Dark suit. Dark hat."

"Anything else?"

"No, sir."

"The colour of his hair?"

"Look dark."

"Had you smoked opium yourself before the gunman entered, Mr Tan?"

"Yes, sir."

"So it's possible that your recollection of the assailant may be a little hazy?"

Mr Tan shrugged.

"Should I take that as a yes?"

"Hazy. Yes, sir."

"How many other gentlemen were in the room when the attack took place?"

"Three."

"So there were three gentlemen in addition to Mr Holland and yourself in the room when the gunman arrived?"

"Yes, sir. Three."

"Do you believe the gunman deliberately targeted Mr Holland?"

"Yes, sir."

"So he took a good look at everyone in the room before firing the weapon?"

"Yes, but I did not know he have a gun. He walk in and look at us, then he look at Mr Holland and shoot with the gun."

"He kept the gun concealed until he identified the man he wished to shoot. Is that what you believe?"

"I believe it. Yes, sir."

"And what happened once the gunman had fired his shot?"

"We all panic. We don't know what is happening. We try to wake him up."

"Mr Holland, that is?"

"Yes, but I see..." Mr Tan pointed at his head. "I see he will not wake up."

"And the gunman?"

"He's gone."

"As soon as he shot Mr Holland?"

"Yes, sir. Gone."

The three other customers from the opium den were summoned as witnesses: two Indian sailors who spoke little English and a Norwegian sailor with a wide grin. Their recollection of the murder and the potential culprit was hazier than Mr Tan's.

Following this, a quite different witness came to the stand: a young woman in a black bonnet and mourning dress.

She had soft features, but her lips were pushed into a harsh, thin line.

"I'm Miss Emma Holland, the sister of Alfred Holland," she said in response to the coroner's request to introduce herself. "I live at number seven Drummond Street, Euston."

"When was the last time you saw your brother?" asked the coroner.

"Christmas time."

"And whereabouts?"

"At my parents' house in Hillingdon."

"Did your brother have regular employment when you saw him last?"

She shook her head sadly. "No."

"Had he ever had regular employment?"

"Yes, he worked for the Indian government in Ghazipur."

The mention of India aroused my interest.

"What did he do there?"

"He was an opium agent."

"And when did he return to England?"

"It was in the summer of last year."

"And he found no regular employment on his return?"

"That's correct."

"Do you know why that was?"

"It's because he was unreliable. He took up a few jobs, but no employment after that first one lasted for long."

"Was the cause of this unreliability his regular opium habit?"

"I fear that it was, yes."

"How long was your brother in India?"

"Five years."

"And what did he do before he found work there?"

"He studied at Cambridge."

"He was an intelligent and capable young gentleman, no doubt," commented the coroner, slowly shaking his head as if saddened by the disappointing demise of someone who had shown such early promise.

"He was," said Miss Holland. "He was clever and kind, and I adored him. I wish that my brother had never encountered opium. It was the ruin of him."

"Have you any idea who might wish to harm your brother?" asked the coroner.

"No, none." Miss Holland dabbed at her eyes with a handkerchief.

"Did he mention that he had been in any trouble with anyone? Perhaps there had been an argument. Or perhaps he owed someone money."

"If he did I never knew of it," she said sadly.

Inspector Henry Reeves of K Division described the bloody scene as he had found it, and then the police surgeon described Mr Holland's injuries in detail. Miss Holland stepped out of the room during his deposition.

The inquest eventually reached its conclusion. The coroner stated that Mr Holland had been barbarously murdered in cold blood and the jury returned a verdict of wilful murder against some person or persons unknown.

CHAPTER 13

After the inquest I found Inspector Reeves outside the mortuary smoking a pipe. He was a slight man with wide-set green eyes and a black moustache. He acknowledged me with a nod as I introduced myself.

"You have a puzzling murder case to solve," I said. "How is the investigation progressing?"

He removed the pipe from his mouth. "There's no doubt the killing was the result of some feud. Mr Holland was deliberately set upon, as we heard in there."

"But your witnesses are not very reliable."

"They're not; however, we do have a few witnesses who saw the gunman before and after the attack, so we've put together a reasonably good description of the man."

"Which is what?"

"A young man in dark clothing with no obvious distinguishing features. Made no attempt to speak to anyone either before or after the event. Remarkably calm and unflustered. I'd say he was a hired assassin."

"That could make him rather difficult to track down."

"We have our methods." Inspector Reeves gave a conspiratorial smile and popped his pipe back in his mouth.

"Tom Clifford, *Holborn Gazette*!" came a voice from behind me. I sighed. "You caught the killer yet, Reeves?"

Inspector Reeves gave Tom a sidelong glance. "What do you think?"

"I'm guessing no, or you'd 'ave said otherwise at the inquest."

"Your guess is correct."

"Any suspects?"

"Not yet."

"Any idea why they went after Mr Holland?"

"None so far, though as I've just explained to your colleague here we believe the gunman was a hired assassin."

"Oh, she ain't my colleague."

"That's not a particularly polite way to speak about the young lady."

"I'm used to it, Inspector Reeves," I said.

"That makes it even worse! No lady should have to become accustomed to rudeness. You must apologise, Mr Clifford."

Tom stared at the inspector and then at me.

"But she's used to it," he said.

"If you desire my co-operation, Mr Clifford, you will apologise," said the inspector.

I felt a smile appear on my face.

"Apologies, Miss Green," said Tom, "it's just that we've 'ad our differences over the years."

"Of course you have," replied the inspector. "That's what happens when you work for rival newspapers. Now, how about I give you both a story your editors will thank you for?"

Tom nodded eagerly.

The inspector lowered his voice. "How would you like to visit an opium den? Every reporter worth his or her salt visits an opium den in the course of their career. Charles Dickens did just that."

"Isn't it dangerous?" I asked.

The inspector gave a hollow laugh. "Not with me it isn't. You'll be in safe hands, and they know me well down there. I have to do the rounds every so often, and now and again I take a few reporters with me. If you're interested there would be a moderate fee to cover my time and expenses."

"How much?" asked Tom.

"Three shillings."

"All right. When then?"

"How about Thursday?"

"I'll come too," I said. I couldn't bear the thought of *The Holborn Gazette* carrying a story about an opium den and the *Morning Express* missing out.

"Good," replied Inspector Reeves. "Both of you it is, then. I shall meet you by the Chinese laundry just a little further up the road on Thursday at nine o'clock." He pointed to his right.

"What's the name of this road?" asked Tom.

"Commercial Road. The laundry's opposite the soda factory, you can't miss it. Bring payment with you."

Inspector Reeves bid us a good day and walked away.

"Do you think he's a bit shifty?" I asked Tom.

"Enterprising's what I'd call 'im."

There seemed little use in reading through the notes Mr Edwards had made for me about the Forsters and Mr Mawson. With Edgar working on the story there was no need for me to devote any attention to them, but as Mr Edwards had spent so much time on the research I felt obliged to read what he had written. And having initially worked on the piece I still had a keen interest in the case.

I sat at my writing desk that evening and read through Mr Edwards' notes. Tiger spent a few minutes on my lap before jumping out of the window to stalk a pigeon on the rooftops. The sun began to set and a train hooted as it pulled out of nearby Moorgate station.

Mr Edwards was always thorough in his work and had been able to find the Forsters and Mr Mawson on the departing passenger lists. He had also written down every mention of Sheridan and Company, the merchant Mr Forster had worked for.

A record for Mr Mawson in late August 1883 caught my eye:

INDIA OFFICE. ARRIVALS REPORTED IN LONDON: Mr C. G. D. Mawson.

I smiled as I read this. *Surely the India Office was where I would find the mysterious Mr Mawson.*

CHAPTER 14

The India Office formed part of the imposing government buildings in Charles Street, Whitehall, and was only one street away from the prime minister's residence in Downing Street.

I walked through an archway beneath the grand stone facade and entered a quadrangle bordered by arched windows and columns. I turned left and made my way across the gravelled courtyard until I reached the door marked 'India Office'. I had worn my smartest jacket, skirt and hat, adopting an air of self-importance as I entered the building.

"I have an appointment with Mr Charles Mawson," I announced to the uniformed man in the hallway. I pretended to be unmoved by the splendour of my surroundings: the marble columns, the elaborately carved stone, the intricately tiled floor and the shimmering highlights of gold wherever my eyes cared to rest.

I gave the man my card as I introduced myself. It was swiftly handed to another man in livery, who placed it on a salver and carried it away.

Then I waited and prayed that Mr Mawson would play along with my ruse.

It seemed that he had, as a few minutes later the liveried man returned with Mr Mawson in tow. He was as I remembered, with bushy brown whiskers and watery grey eyes. A smile spread across his face as he approached me.

"Miss Green, the reporter! What brings you here?"

"We arranged an appointment, did we not?"

"Did we?"

"Yes," I replied through a clenched grin.

"Oh yes, I remember now," he replied unconvincingly. I felt relieved that he appeared happy to keep up the pretence.

"Is there a convenient place we could talk?" I asked.

"Absolutely," he replied. "Just follow me."

We left the entrance hall and stepped into a long corridor with oak wainscoting and ornate arches at regular intervals for as far as the eye could see.

"How did you find me here?" he asked.

"Through a listing in *The Homeward Mail*."

"Clever," he replied with a smile. "I don't think a lady has ever gone to so much trouble to seek me out before."

"After our conversation outside the Forsters' home I wished to find you and express my condolences for the sad death of your friend, Mr Forster," I said.

He stopped and looked at me. "That's terribly kind and thoughtful of you, Miss Green. It's been a huge blow, it really has. I cannot make head nor tail of it."

"When we last spoke you were trying to find him. Did you succeed before his tragic death?"

"I did. I found out that he was residing at the East India, which I should have guessed, anyhow. We spent a pleasant evening together the night before he died."

"*Pleasant*? Even though his wife had just been murdered?"

"I chose my words unwisely, Miss Green, I do apologise.

The chap had been through the most appalling time and it was the first opportunity he had found to enjoy some whisky and a chat with a friend. I shan't pretend that it was easy, but it was convivial. The fellow was in need of some light conversation; a brief respite from the darkness into which he had been plunged. I don't understand why such a pleasant, friendly couple should have had their lives taken from them in such a dreadful way. Mrs Forster was a delightful lady, the daughter of a tailor. Her family were Somerset folk and she never lost the slight burr in her accent no matter how hard she tried to conceal it."

We reached an ornate door.

"Have you ever seen the inner courtyard before, Miss Green?"

"No, this is the first time I have ever been here."

Mr Mawson pushed it open and we stepped out onto a flight of steps that led down to an expansive marble floor. A glass roof stretched high above our heads, and surrounding us were three storeys of elegant arches, columns and balustrades.

"The Sultan of Turkey was received here in 1867," said Mr Mawson. "Impressive, isn't it?"

"It certainly is."

"Mrs Forster was instrumental in organising the walks and picnics in India, and colossal picnics they were too!" continued Mawson. "She would have her servants working for an entire day to prepare the food, and then they would have to carry it all, of course. Mr Forster and I dined at the club each Wednesday evening, and we'd go out shooting partridge on a Saturday afternoon. He was an accomplished whist player and a good dancer. There was at least one dance a week in those days."

"It seems you and the Forsters were kept quite busy out there."

"Oh, we were, and the lawn tennis tournaments were also

enjoyable. I don't consider myself much of a player, but I did manage third place once."

Mr Mawson seemed keen to impress upon me the lifestyle he had enjoyed in India, but he had told me little about himself. I wondered whether his achievements were, like his tennis ability, rather mediocre.

We walked across the highly polished floor toward a flight of steps at the far end of the courtyard.

"What did you do in Bengal, Mr Mawson?" I asked.

"I worked for the Indian government in various capacities; most of them administrative and extremely dull, I'm afraid. I spent time at a few locations in Bengal and some in Calcutta itself. The work didn't hold much interest for me, but the social life, as you have heard, more than made up for it."

He paused to look up at the roof. "This courtyard takes my breath away every time I walk through it. Does it have the same effect on you, Miss Green?"

"There's no doubt that it's an extremely impressive sight, Mr Mawson."

I thought of the wealth that must have been required to build such a beautiful place, and the eight million pounds of opium revenue came to mind. I was astonished that the British government made so much money from the trade. Then my thoughts shifted to the death of Alfred Holland at a miserable opium den in Limehouse.

Somehow it all seemed to be part of the same intricate web.

"Have you ever come across a man named Alfred Holland?" I asked Mr Mawson as we ascended the steps.

"No, I can't say that I have."

"I attended the inquest into his death yesterday. He was shot dead at an opium den in Limehouse."

"Oh goodness, how unfortunate." He opened the door in front of us and we stepped into another elaborate corridor.

"You may have come across him," I continued, "because he also worked for the Indian government. He was an opium agent in Ghazipur."

"Was he indeed? There are many chaps employed up there, you know. It's the largest opium factory in the world."

"You haven't heard any mention of him? Or of his murder?"

"Not until you mentioned it just now."

"I realise the topic of murder is rather a gloomy one, but I hope you don't mind me asking whether you have any idea who might have wished to murder Mr and Mrs Forster?"

"None at all, Miss Green. Forster had no idea who had attacked his wife, but he believed the motive to be burglary. And as for who attacked him, I simply don't know. I wasn't aware of any grievance he had with anyone."

"Do you think they were murdered for the same reason?"

"Who can say? But it has to be more than just a coincidence. Someone clearly wanted them both dead, but I can't for the life of me think why."

"Have the police interviewed you?"

"No, why should they?"

"Because you knew the couple. Perhaps you unwittingly know something about them which could help the police investigation."

Mr Mawson laughed. "I think you're overestimating me, Miss Green. I merely socialised with them. I had no knowledge of their intimate affairs."

"I'm wondering whether there's a connection between their deaths and Mr Holland's."

"Why should there be?"

"Both men worked in India and were involved in the opium trade."

"I wish you every success in finding a connection, Miss Green, but I cannot think of one."

"I wonder where I might find someone who worked with Mr Holland. Would you be able to find out for me, Mr Mawson?"

"Such as who?"

"Someone who worked with him in Ghazipur, perhaps. Preferably someone who is back on home soil now."

Mr Mawson grimaced. "I could try, but I don't know how successful I'd be. A lot of chaps have worked there, I suppose, but the chances of finding someone who knew this Holland chap seem rather slim."

CHAPTER 15

A s arranged, I met Inspector Reeves by the Chinese laundry in Commercial Road. Tom Clifford was already there when I arrived.

"Oh, you turned up, Miss Green," he said disappointedly as he chewed on his tobacco.

"Of course I did. I wouldn't let *The Holborn Gazette* be the only newspaper to carry a story about an opium den."

The inspector removed the pipe from his mouth and held out his hand for payment. Once we had each handed over three shillings we were on our way.

The sun was setting as we left the busy thoroughfare of Commercial Road, turning into a side street which led us beneath the railway.

"You'll need a strong stomach for where we're going," said Inspector Reeves. "Have you reported on many murder cases before?"

"Yes," I replied.

"Which ones?"

"Lizzie Dixie, the St Giles' murders, Sophia Glenville, Richard Geller —"

"I've done that lot an' all," interrupted Tom Clifford. "And I've done more 'an that. The man who's been found in the canal and that other one where he got pushed under a train."

"The same man?" I asked with a smile.

"No, they was different murders. You can't get pushed into a canal *and* under a train."

"Not unless you're extremely unlucky," said Inspector Reeves.

"Miss Green's very friendly with an inspector down the Yard," continued Tom Clifford.

"Which one?"

"Inspector Blakely. Turns out 'er and the inspector's quite the double act when it comes to murders."

"Is that so?" asked Reeves.

"Not really," I replied curtly.

"The rest of us reporters don't get no chance when it comes to the Yard. Miss Green's the favourite."

We found ourselves in a narrow street of cramped dwellings with several people watching us from dark doorways.

"Evenin', Inspector," called a man from outside a ship chandler's store.

"Evening, Juggins," replied Inspector Reeves.

The man stared at me and I suddenly felt out of place.

Outside a noisy pub, a group of dark-skinned sailors sang in a language I didn't recognise. A woman in a brightly coloured dress and headscarf quickly ducked out of sight.

"Mr Holland was an opium agent in India. Is it possible that his habitual use of the drug began there?" I asked Inspector Reeves.

"It's a possibility. After all, he was surrounded by the stuff in Ghazipur, wasn't he? But not all men come back from there addicted to opium. Perhaps he had a weaker character than most."

"I'm surprised that a man who had shown such promise should have his life ended in such a sad manner."

"It happens, Miss Green," replied Inspector Reeves. "Education and wealth aren't always enough. A man must rely on the strength of his character."

"True enough," added Tom Clifford.

"Do you think Mr Holland's sister would be happy to speak to me?" I asked.

"I don't know, but you could try calling on her. You'll have her address from the inquest, no doubt, but be aware that she's grief-stricken, so don't go upsetting her."

"Has she been able to tell you anything useful about what may have led to his murder?"

"No, she knows very little of what he'd been getting up to," replied the inspector. "He kept his opium-soaked life to himself."

We crossed the road and walked briskly through a dingy alleyway which ran between two enormous warehouses. The alleyway opened out into Regent's Canal Dock, where tall sail ships were moored beside rows of coal barges. Heavily loaded carts lumbered past us, seagulls wheeled above our heads and an unpleasant, dank smell rose up from the water, which lapped at the slimy stone walls.

Inspector Reeves strode along the quay beside me with Tom Clifford following closely behind. Beyond the dock stretched the River Thames, its shore lined with warehouses, chimneys and cranes, which were silhouetted against the darkening sky.

Without warning, the inspector turned sharply to his right and into a passageway I would otherwise have walked past without noticing it was there. A putrid odour hit my nose and I felt forced to hold my breath as we walked along the cobblestones. Tom Clifford mumbled a string of curse words relating to the stench.

Inspector Reeves paused beside a door with flaked paint on it. I placed a hand over my nose and mouth in a vain attempt to keep the smell away.

"Mr Tan has permitted us to visit his establishment," announced Inspector Reeves.

"We're goin' to see the gaff where Mr Holland was shot?" asked Tom Clifford.

"We certainly are," replied the inspector proudly.

Tom eagerly pulled out his notebook and pencil, while I clasped my carpet bag and shivered. The alleyway was so wretched and miserable I wasn't sure how prepared I was for what lay beyond the door. It reminded me of the misery I had encountered in St Giles' Rookery during a previous murder investigation.

Inspector Reeves knocked at the door and eventually it opened slightly. He and the occupant exchanged a few words, and then the door opened just wide enough to permit us entry.

"Ladies first," Tom said with a grin.

"I'll follow you," I replied, feeling rather hesitant.

The dingy corridor smelled almost as bad as the alleyway had. I could hardly see where I was going.

"Mind the steps, there are a few missing," said Inspector Reeves as we clambered up a narrow, greasy staircase.

The hazy figures of Inspector Reeves and Tom Clifford turned right at the top of the stairs. I followed and knocked into the back of Tom, unaware that he had stopped.

"You remember Mr Tan from the inquest, don't you?" said the inspector.

I couldn't quite see the man from the doorway that led into a dimly lit room.

"Yes. Evenin', Mr Tan," said Tom as he entered breezily.

I remained where I was and simply peered in. My eyes

slowly adjusted to the gloom, and I saw that Mr Tan nodded a brief acknowledgement when he saw me.

A thick layer of smoke floated above a dim paraffin lamp. A person lay on a mattress on the floor and two other forms lay prostrate on a bed. A fourth person was sprawled over a mattress lying upon some tea chests. In the gloom I could see that this person was reclining with a long pipe in his hand, the end of which was held over a small flame. A sweet, rich, floral smell mingled with the odour of unwashed bodies.

I had worried at first about what the men in this place would think of a woman visiting, but I realised they were too insensible even to notice my presence. I considered the romantic idea of the opium den portrayed in theatre and art with its colourful wall hangings, silk cushions and paper lanterns. The room I saw now was a truly pitiful place. *How dreadful had Mr Holland's life become that he had needed to seek solace here?*

"Show the reporters where the bullet holes are, Mr Tan," instructed Inspector Reeves.

Mr Tan nodded and walked toward the dishevelled man lying on the tea chests. The man gazed at Mr Tan nonchalantly as the proprietor pointed beyond his shoulder at some marks on the wall.

"Bullet hole," he said.

I shivered as I pictured Alfred Holland lying in that place and receiving the fatal gunshot to his head. I imagined how loud it would have sounded in this small room. Mr Tan seemed remarkably calm for a man who had been through such an ordeal. I reasoned that the opium had most likely dulled his senses.

"Thank you, Inspector Reeves and Mr Tan," I said. I was beginning to feel nauseous and craved clean air. "I think I've seen enough now."

"How does the opium pipe work?" asked Tom.

Mr Tan picked up a thick bamboo pipe, which was about the length of his arm. It was etched decoratively and a small silver bowl was attached to one end. Mr Tan proceeded to explain how the opium was placed in the bowl and then heated over the flame.

"I can't 'ave come all this way up 'ere not to give it a go!" said Tom cheerily.

"But a man died in here," I said. "Don't you wish to leave immediately?"

"I should imagine that a good few men have died in here," said Inspector Reeves.

"I'm going back outside now, Inspector," I replied, "Thank you for your time."

My stomach turned as I stumbled down the staircase, and I held my breath until I was safely back at the quayside of Regent's Canal Dock.

CHAPTER 16

A light drizzle fell the following morning as I arrived at Drummond Street. The Euston Hotel and a row of terraced houses lined one side, while on the other was Euston station with its enormous, sandstone arch, which wouldn't have looked out of place in ancient Greece. The word 'Euston' was etched into its architrave in gold lettering.

I found number seven: a modest, three-storey terrace. I took a deep breath to calm my nerves and hoped Alfred Holland's sister Emma would be willing to speak to me.

A maid with a black armband answered the door and asked me to wait in the hallway while she took my card to her mistress. I felt relieved when she returned and informed me that Miss Holland was prepared to see me.

I was led into a parlour at the front of the house. The curtains were drawn, the mirror above the fireplace was covered with black crepe and the room was lit by two gas lamps. Miss Holland stood by the fireplace, her face and hands white against the black of her mourning dress. I guessed she was about twenty-three years of age.

"Thank you for agreeing to see me, Miss Holland," I said.

"Please accept my condolences for your brother's untimely death."

She nodded warily and waited for me to continue.

"I realise this must be a difficult time for you," I said, "and I hope not to detain you for long. I attended the inquest and I should like to find out more about your brother. It seems he led rather an interesting life."

"Why do you want to discover more about him?" Her eyes were a hard, sharp green.

"To understand why someone might have wished to harm him."

"But isn't that the job of the police?"

"It is, yes, and I know that Inspector Reeves is working hard to find your brother's murderer. But I am interested to find out whether Alfred's murder might be connected to the death of a couple from Fitzrovia; a Mr and Mrs Forster. They also worked in India. Bengal, to be precise."

"I read about them in the newspaper, but I don't think Alfred would have known them. They once lived in Calcutta, didn't they?"

"Yes, they did."

"Alfred was in Ghazipur, which is more than four hundred miles from Calcutta."

"Yes, I can see how their paths may not have crossed, though Mr Forster worked for a merchant which traded in opium, and Alfred was an opium agent."

"But a great many people work within the opium trade. I don't see any reason why the two should have necessarily known each other."

I sighed. "No, I suppose the chances are rather slim."

As her eyes remained on me I wondered exactly what I had hoped to achieve. My conviction that Alfred Holland and the Forsters had somehow known one another seemed rather weak, but I couldn't think of anything else to suggest.

"Would you like some tea, Miss Green?" she asked, her expression softening a little.

"Only if it's not too much trouble, Miss Holland. Thank you."

She called for the maid and gestured for me to take a seat on the settee. Once she had asked for some tea to be brought in she seated herself in an easy chair next to the fireplace.

"I haven't spoken to many people about Alfred," she said. "He had lost many of his friends, and our parents had disowned him."

"Because of his opium habit?"

She nodded. "It turned him into a selfish person. He was my brother and I loved him dearly, but I didn't like the man he became. The past year has been especially difficult. Since his death I have received few condolences, and as for my parents..." she paused as her eyes grew damp "...I can't tell whether they're sad or relieved. He brought great shame on them after his return from India."

"And before he went there?"

Her face brightened. "They were extremely proud of him. He was clever and good-natured. He had lots of friends and enjoyed life. He studied at Cambridge, and when he began working for the Indian government my parents anticipated great things for him. We all did."

"And he was in India for five years?"

"Yes, how do you know that?"

"You said so at the inquest."

"Oh, yes."

"Did he come home at all during those five years?"

"Once or twice, and he seemed a little more serious than when he had first departed for India, but I suppose that was to be expected. He travelled over as a boy and became a man out there. I suppose it's only natural for someone to lose their spontaneity and sense of fun in those circumstances."

"Do you put the change solely down to age, or do you think there was another reason for this new display of maturity?"

"No, just age. And I suppose living and working in a foreign country would change a man, wouldn't it? Nobody stays the same forever."

"Was he happy in Ghazipur?"

"Yes, he seemed to be. Mother and Father went out to stay with him for a while, but I didn't go."

"So you saw little of him during that time."

"Yes, and when he returned for good he was quite different."

The maid brought in the tea.

"When did you find out about the opium?" I asked.

"It was after he'd lost his second job. He worked as a clerk for a tobacco merchant on his return, and then he ran errands for the Metropolitan Board of Works. It wasn't the usual sort of profession you'd expect a Cambridge graduate to be pursuing. Neither job lasted long and he confessed to me that the only enjoyment he found in life came in the form of opium. He had first tried it in India and subsequently began to make regular use of it. He told me that if he went for any length of time without it he was overcome by sickness. The only way to stop the sickness was to take it again."

"Presumably he had no idea that he would become so dependent on it."

"He told me he had first taken it for toothache, and that it had given him a sensation so pleasurable he never found anything else that could compare. Not even love, it seems."

"Was there ever a chance of marriage for him?"

"He told me there had been a girl in India at one time, but she had brought their courtship to an end. Whether it was her choice or her family's I cannot tell, but I think he was more upset about that than he was willing to admit."

"You last saw him at Christmas, is that right?"

"Yes, and it was so dreadful I vowed never to see him again. It transpired that I kept that vow."

Her eyes grew damp and her hand trembled as she lifted a cup of tea to her lips.

"What happened at Christmas?" I asked.

"He had terrible rows with Mother and Father; with all of us, including my cousin and her husband, with whom I share this home. We all found him detestable."

"What was the nature of his work in Ghazipur?"

"He weighed the pots of opium when they arrived at the factory. It doesn't sound like much, but he told me it was quite an important job because opium is as precious a commodity as silver. Forms had to be filled in and certificates signed, and everything was done under lock and key. Apparently, there was tight security to prevent any of the opium falling into the wrong hands."

"There's nothing in what you have told me to explain why someone might have wished to kill your brother," I said.

"No, I cannot understand it. All I can think is that he had a disagreement with someone. Perhaps he owed money to the wrong people. He somehow managed to pay for his opium, though he didn't have a job."

"Was there any money from the family?"

"A little from Mother and Father. I can only hope that the police find out who did this to him and why. I realise he probably got himself into some dangerous situations, but I need to understand why this happened, no matter how unpalatable the truth may be."

CHAPTER 17

I stepped out of the *Morning Express* offices and into the rain that evening. I began searching among the traffic on Fleet Street for an omnibus to take me home.

"Penny!"

I turned to see James standing beneath his umbrella outside a stationer's shop and I felt a flip of excitement in my chest.

"James! What are you doing here?" I hadn't seen him since the day I had called at his home and accidentally encountered Charlotte and her mother. I had been trying my hardest not to think about him, knowing how close his wedding was, but I felt pleased that he had sought me out.

"Were you waiting here for me?"

"I was just passing your offices and thought you'd probably be finishing for the day about now. I read your article about the opium den." He gestured for me to join him under his umbrella.

"Oh, did you?"

"What on earth were you doing in an opium den? It's not a safe place for a lady to be at all."

"Or for anyone, in fact, especially not after the murder of Alfred Holland."

"Indeed. Have you the time to take a walk?"

"Of course."

We walked west in the direction of the Strand.

"I don't like the thought of you wandering about Limehouse visiting opium dens," said James.

"Oh, it wasn't quite like that. Inspector Reeves of K Division took us."

"Us?"

"Myself and Tom Clifford from *The Holborn Gazette*."

James groaned. "Oh, no! I remember that man from the St Giles investigation."

"Have you come across Inspector Reeves before?"

"Once or twice. He's a slippery character. I can't imagine he took you on a tour of the opium den out of pure goodwill. Did he ask you for money?"

"Yes, three shillings."

James shook his head.

"We visited the opium den where Alfred Holland was shot."

"So your article said."

"I met with Alfred's sister this morning, and she has no idea who might have wanted to murder him."

"I can't imagine Inspector Reeves having much of an idea either," said James.

"Alfred Holland came from a good family," I said. "His death seems to have marked the end of a tragic descent into destitution. He worked in India, did you know that?"

"I didn't. I'm afraid I'm not terribly familiar with the case."

"I've been trying to find out whether he met the Forsters while he was out there."

"The odds of that are fairly slim, aren't they?"

"I realise that, but both Mr Forster and Mr Holland worked within the opium industry."

"Along with a good many other people."

I sighed. "I don't think I'll ever convince anyone to consider the possibility that the murders could be connected."

We paused beside the lofty arches of the law courts.

"Let's cross here," said James.

We darted between the carts and carriages, and turned into Essex Street.

"If the murders are connected we need to find the evidence that links them," said James. "I'm assisting D Division with Mrs Forster's case and working on Inspector Paget of C Division to allow me to help with Mr Forster's case. As for Mr Holland, that's K Division and I must say that I don't trust Inspector Reeves one bit. I sometimes wonder who he's actually working for."

"What makes you say that?"

"Just rumour. But you understand what I'm saying, don't you? It's rather difficult to pull all these separate incidents together and try to connect them."

We passed the Essex Head Tavern and made our way toward a handsome archway at the end of the street.

"But you work for Scotland Yard," I said. "You're well placed to work on all these cases and discover the connection."

"I can't just march in and demand that I take over these cases, Penny. I'm not senior enough to seize control."

"But you know there's little possibility that Inspector Bowles or Paget will consider that a murder in Limehouse could be linked to the murder of the Forsters in Fitzrovia and Mayfair. They're very different parts of London. What this situation needs is a detective like you to consider the cases side by side."

James sighed and we paused beside the arch. A flight of worn steps ran beneath it to the street on a lower level.

"It's not as simple as you make it sound, Penny. Scotland Yard can't spend all its time trying to establish whether a crime carried out in one part of the metropolis has anything to do with a crime committed in another part."

"You managed it with the St Giles murders."

"Because we were quite certain from early on that there was only one culprit."

"Do you think the three murders might have been committed by the same person?"

"I wouldn't completely rule it out, but there's no evidence to suggest it."

"What about the opium connection?"

"There could be something in it, or it may simply be coincidence."

"But you would consider it if I could find some evidence to support the theory?"

"Of course, Penny, but you're a news reporter and it's not really your job to go about trying to establish such things."

"But if I don't do it who will?"

"If there's a connection between the Forsters and Alfred Holland I'm sure something will come to light sooner or later."

"You're content to just wait for something to *come to light*, are you? And what if it doesn't?"

"Then perhaps there is no connection after all."

"What an extremely lackadaisical manner of doing things!" I fumed, marching down the stone steps before James could respond.

CHAPTER 18

"Penny, you'll get soaked without an umbrella!" James called, following me down the steps. "The Yard only has so many men. Chief Inspector Cullen won't allow me to get involved in any case I pick and choose. And I feel sure that the divisions will make the Yard aware as soon as they need our help."

"But they don't even know when they need help," I retorted. "I'm surprised at your reaction to this, James. I thought you would want to be involved in these cases."

"It's not that I don't want to, Penny, but my hands are tied. At least I've been involved in Mrs Forster's case. Perhaps there's something I can do from my work on that."

"What progress has there been so far?" I asked.

We stood under James' umbrella beside a row of trees which bordered Temple Gardens. Beyond them was the Victoria Embankment and the River Thames.

"The staff at the Forsters' home say the gang was well organised and its members seemed to know what they were doing. They used their cudgels to incapacitate the staff but inflicted wounds on Mrs Forster which were deliberately intended to end her life. They kept asking the servants where Mr and Mrs Forster were."

"As if they were after them rather than the valuables?"

"Exactly. They remained calm for most of the time, using intimidation and violence only where necessary. The house-keeper told me she felt sure the men were comfortable with what they were doing, as if they were well-practised at it. It's interesting that they completely spared the errand boy."

"Because he's a child, perhaps."

"Possibly, but there might be another explanation. It's intriguing that the gang knew exactly how to break in. I think they had been given information about the layout of the house before the break-in."

"Do you think the boy might have told them?"

"It's possible. The gang may have bribed him with some-thing. He might not have considered that he was doing anything wrong at the time. I have tried asking him whether that's what happened, but he has given me little information so far."

"If someone bribed him and he tells you who it is that could lead you straight to the men who carried out the act."

"Absolutely, so I'm hoping that if he has something to tell us he will do so very soon."

"Do you believe the gang also intended to attack Mr Forster that evening?"

"Yes, they were probably disappointed to find him out of the house."

"Which explains why he was tracked down just a few days later and stabbed in St James's Square."

"Yes."

"So Inspector Paget of C Division should allow you to be involved in Mr Forster's case considering that the murders were almost certainly carried out by the same people."

"I'm trying to convince him of that at the present time."

"The Forsters may have been murdered by people who were paid to kill them," I said, "and Inspector Reeves has the same theory regarding Mr Holland's murder. He believes the culprit was a paid assassin."

"That may be the very connection we're looking for. We just need more evidence."

"Inspector Reeves has a few witness statements from people who saw the gunman before and after he shot Mr Holland. Maybe the description bears some resemblance to one of the men described by Mr and Mrs Forster's staff."

"Perhaps I should speak to Inspector Reeves about the case, then. That's what you want me to do, isn't it?" James said with a smile.

"Yes." I smiled in return.

The rain was starting to ease. We crossed Victoria Embankment and stood overlooking Temple Pier, where numerous passengers were embarking a pleasure steamer for an outing downriver. I told James about my meeting with Mr Mawson at the India Office.

"He seems innocent of any wrongdoing," I said, "but I can't help recalling how keen he was to find out Mr Forster's location after the murder of Mrs Forster. Perhaps he passed the information on to someone."

"Have you told Inspector Paget about him?"

"No, I haven't met with Inspector Paget and I'm not supposed to be working on the story at all. Edgar Fish has it."

"Oh dear, really?"

"Yes, it's all rather frustrating. I suppose I could ask Edgar to mention Mr Mawson to Inspector Paget, but he doesn't like doing any more work than he absolutely has to. You should visit Mr Mawson at the India Office; it's only a stone's throw from Scotland Yard. Mr Mawson was with Mr Forster the evening before he died, so he might be able to tell you something useful."

"I'll see what I can do, but neither you nor I can officially take control of the work. We must leave it to the other detectives and reporters."

"The other incompetents."

James laughed. "It seems you have a high opinion of our colleagues."

A break in the cloud allowed the setting sun to cast its golden light across the river, bathing the ships and barges moored by the wharves on the south bank.

"I miss our meetings at the Museum Tavern," I said. The words had left my mouth before I had time to consider them.

James gave a small sigh. "They're not over yet. We'll have more of them."

I turned to look at him. "Are you sure? I thought the future Mrs Blakely was rather disapproving of our conversations at that establishment."

"I put it down to her pre-wedding nerves."

"Do you have pre-wedding nerves?"

James thought for a moment before replying. "No."

"Why not? It's a life-changing event."

"I don't like to think of it changing anything so very much."

"Of course it will! If Charlotte won't allow you to meet with me at the Museum Tavern now she's even less likely to after the wedding."

"Nonsense, she'll be fine."

"Are you sure? I don't think she will be."

"You don't know her as well as I do, Penny. Once the wedding is over and done with she will become her usual calm self again."

I quietly disagreed but chose not to argue with him. "I do apologise for interrupting your evening with Charlotte and her mother the other day."

"It was a welcome interruption."

"It wasn't really, was it? You weren't able to invite me in and Charlotte didn't seem particularly pleased to see me."

"Pre-wedding nerves, as I say."

"I don't think she likes me."

"Of course she likes you, Penny!"

"I wouldn't like me if I were her."

"You're beginning to confuse me with statements like that. How's Mr Edwards?"

"His usual self. Sometimes I feel you only bring him up to make yourself feel better about your impending wedding."

James gave me an incredulous look.

"What does that mean?"

"Perhaps you feel less guilty about your choice knowing there is a potential husband for me waiting in the wings."

"You think I should like to see you married to Mr Edwards?"

"Yes, I think you would. It would reassure you that you're making the right decision. It would mean there was no longer any alternative. It would suggest that fate rather than your free will had determined events."

James scowled. "I have no idea what you're talking about, Penny. It doesn't make any sense."

"It's why you tried so hard to ensure that Mr Edwards and I remained on friendly terms, isn't it? You were even willing to paint yourself as the villain in order that he would forgive me. He doesn't for a moment consider that I was willing to kiss you that evening; he believes me to be an innocent victim. In fact, he probably feels sorry for me, which is deplorable."

"I apologise if my attempts to repair your reputation were somewhat clumsy."

"I didn't need you to repair my reputation, James!"

"No?" He fixed me with his bright blue eyes. "And what would Mr Edwards have thought had he known you were a willing participant in that kiss? What would he have told people about you, Penny? The thought of you becoming a topic of gossip was too much to bear. What if your sister had found out? You're an intelligent, respectable woman, and you don't deserve to be the topic of tittle-tattle across West London's drawing rooms."

"I'm sure it wouldn't have come to that."

"I believe it would have done, but if Mr Edwards considers you blameless your reputation is saved. And as for all this nonsense about me wanting you to marry him, nothing could be further from the truth. Do you think I can bear the thought of you hanging on to another man's arm?"

"It would make you feel better about your own nuptials."

"It would do nothing of the sort! If you were to ask me honestly what I think about Mr Edwards I would say that I wish the man had never taken up employment in the reading room and found you there. I wish the man didn't even exist!"

"Now you know how I feel about Charlotte."

There was a long silence.

James stared at me and I boldly looked him in the eye, not regretting for one moment what I had just said.

CHAPTER 19

"Did you actually have to go inside the opium den, Miss Green?" whispered Mr Edwards in the reading room. "Would a description of it not have satisfied you?"

"That wouldn't have been proper news reporting, Mr Edwards," I replied softly. "It's important to be able to report on such information first hand."

I had been carrying out some tiresome research on the Franchise Bill when Mr Edwards approached me.

"I think it terribly irresponsible for a police officer to allow a lady into such a place!" he said with a frown.

"I don't think Inspector Reeves minds who comes along on his opium den tours so long as he gets his three shillings," I replied.

"That's even worse! The man has no scruples."

"I can't say I enjoyed my visit, but it meant I could write authentically for others to read. If just a handful of people who read my article are dissuaded from frequenting these places my work has surely served a purpose."

"I suppose so, but I don't see why you should put yourself at risk, Miss Green."

"I have put myself at risk in this job before, Mr Edwards, and I shall probably do so again. My work often leads me to unpleasant people and places."

He sighed and handed me some papers. "I've gone through *The Homeward Mail*'s 1881 editions, and here are some references I found. I don't know how useful they might be. Did you find my last set of notes helpful?"

"I certainly did. They led me to Mr Mawson and I was able to speak with him."

Mr Edwards' face brightened. "That's good news indeed! Did he have anything interesting to tell you?"

"A little more about the Forsters, and I asked whether he knew anything about Alfred Holland."

"Ah yes, that Holland chap is the reason you visited the opium den, isn't he?"

I nodded.

"I'm relieved you got out of there alive," he said.

I stifled a laugh. "Of course I did. There was no danger there."

"We're talking about opium addicts, Miss Green!"

"Opium sends them into a stupor, Mr Edwards. They weren't even aware that I was present."

Mr Edwards shook his head disapprovingly. "Have you thought of a suitable date for a walk in the park with your sister and myself?"

"Oh, I think so," I said, having forgotten all about it.

"When would suit?"

"This Saturday, perhaps? I'll need to make sure Eliza is available."

"Good. I shall await confirmation from you. I'll leave you to your work now, Miss Green." He smiled and gave me a little bow.

. . .

I tried to concentrate on my article about the Franchise Bill but it was proving difficult. The conversation with James by the river kept running through my mind. I felt surprised at myself for stating that I wished Charlotte didn't exist, but I still could not bring myself to regret the words I had spoken.

Although it had been extremely useful to discuss my work with James I had found our past few meetings rather uncomfortable. With his wedding just weeks away our conversations felt fraught with tension. There was no escaping the event that was about to change everything. James had said that it wouldn't, but I knew he was pretending even to himself. Once he became a married man our relationship would inevitably change. People would disapprove of any time we spent together, even if it was arranged merely to discuss work. His wife would have a legitimate hold over everything he did.

❧

"Ah, Miss Green! The close friend of Tom Clifford's," said Edgar as I entered the newsroom just in time to meet my deadline that afternoon.

"Nothing could be further from the truth," I replied curtly.

"But Tom is telling everyone down at Ye Olde Cheshire Cheese how much he enjoyed your company in Limehouse."

"He's using sarcasm, Edgar," I replied.

"Actually, I don't think he is. He was rather flattered by your company, I believe."

I gave an empty laugh.

"And if I may say so, Miss Green, your article about the opium den was far better written than his," added Edgar.

"I doubt that would be much of an achievement," I said.

Edgar lowered his voice. "So, did you try it?"

"Try what?"

"The opium! John Chinaman selects the very best of it, doesn't he? Opium can be found all over London, but if you want the best quality a Chinese opium den in Limehouse would be just the place to find it, don't you think?"

"I don't know, Edgar."

"Tom tried it," he said. "He told us all about it at the Cheshire Cheese. He confessed that it's most gloriously perfumed, and induced in him a soothing, floating, dreamlike state."

"He said he felt as though he were a spoonful of gently warmed syrup," added Frederick.

"I'm pleased to hear that he enjoyed it," I said.

"You weren't tempted?"

"Not for a moment. It was one of the most miserable places I have ever set foot in, besides the fact that a man was shot there!"

"That's not particularly pleasant," said Edgar. "I think that would have put me off trying it as well."

"I would have gone to a different opium den," said Frederick.

"Exactly, Potter. I don't think I could feel at ease in a room where I knew a man had been shot to death," said Edgar.

"While we're on the topic of murder," I said, "have Inspector Bowles or Inspector Paget made any progress?"

"Paget's done a bit of work. It seems Mr Forster had complicated legal affairs," said Edgar. "He bought a trading company in Calcutta about ten years ago but it ran into financial difficulties. For a few years he maintained the belief that its fortunes would rise again, so he funded the company with loans. When he came close to defaulting on them he decided to use his property in London as a source of income."

"The house in Margaret Street?"

"Yes. The Forster family has owned it for many years and it was occupied by a tenant while they were in India. When he arranged a mortgage to fund his company in India there were problems with the bill of sale."

"Such as what?"

"It became clear to the individual who was advancing the mortgage that Forster was, in fact, trying to submit a fraudulent bill of sale."

"Why should he do that?"

"Forster needed to provide a bill of sale for his home and furniture in order to be granted the mortgage advance, but he didn't want to provide a legally binding document. The reason for his deception was that the house wasn't strictly his to mortgage. It was part of his father's estate, which was being held in trust."

"I see, though I think I may have lost the thread now."

"I did as well. It takes a few iterations to get your mind around this situation."

"But I don't understand. I thought Mr and Mrs Forster were wealthy?"

"They probably were once upon a time. And then these financial difficulties arose, and Forster clearly did a good job of pretending he still had money."

"Like many a good man," Frederick chipped in.

"So, to continue," said Edgar, "Forster managed to find another individual who wasn't so eagle-eyed with the bill of sale, and that person advanced him a sum of ten thousand pounds, which Forster put into his failing company in India."

I briefly mulled this over. "Are you saying that he fraudulently obtained the money as he didn't own his house?"

"Exactly, Miss Green. And despite his best efforts the company in India failed for good, leaving a number of creditors in its wake. Over the past few months his chickens came home to roost. The chap who had given him the ten thousand began pursuing him through the courts to recover his funds, and his father's estate took legal action against him for mortgaging a house he didn't own."

"So the long and short of this sorry tale is that he owed money?"

Edgar nodded. "Vast amounts of it. Tens of thousands of pounds. He owed it to various people, both in India and in Britain, and a number were getting rather impatient with him about it. Only a few days before his death he had been in court requesting more time to settle his debts."

"It would have taken more than just time by the sounds of things. What a desperate situation to be in. Does Inspector Paget think a creditor had him murdered?"

"That's one line of investigation."

"And a very complicated one, it would seem. But why should someone he owed money to decide to have him killed? Surely they would want to keep him alive so they had a chance of seeing their money again one day."

"I agree with you, Miss Green. Having gone to great lengths to understand the ins and outs of this case my conclusion is the same as yours. I don't know why he should have been killed for owing money."

"Was it some sort of punishment?"

"Perhaps, but when you're dead you're not really being punished any more, are you?" said Edgar.

"Unless you're in hell," Frederick piped up. "Perhaps Forster's killer intended for him to suffer in purgatory."

"Despite Forster's debts, he may be of greater financial worth now that he's dead than he was when he was alive," I said. "Perhaps there is a life insurance policy the creditors can claim against, or something else in his estate which could be accessed."

"That's an interesting theory," said Edgar, "and it could

explain why the wife was also murdered. It meant she couldn't inherit his estate."

"But the Forsters have children," I said, beginning to feel alarmed. "What if this mess passes down to them?"

"It will do, won't it?" said Edgar.

"Has anyone warned them?"

"I have no idea."

"Do you know who began the legal proceedings against him?"

Edgar flicked through his notebook, then read aloud from the relevant page. "One is a law firm representing his father's estate, Sadler and Campbell, and the other is a chap named Mr Chakravarty."

"Do you know anything about either of them?"

"Nothing at all."

CHAPTER 20

"Penelope, I do believe this is the most foolish thing you have ever done," said Eliza as she sat on my bed at my lodgings. "An opium den! It's just about the worst place you could have visited in the entire world!"

"I'm sure there are worse places, Ellie," I replied, "and its abjection was the very reason I went there. I wanted to convey how simply dreadful these places are, and what an unpleasant drug opium is. It ruined the mind of Alfred Holland; a man who was born into comfort and wealth. Just think what it must do to the lives of so many people we never hear about."

"Oh, I know what it does. That's why we argued with George over dinner recently, wasn't it? But surely you don't need to visit these places in person, Penny. You're putting yourself in terrible danger."

"I like to think that by doing so I have helped educate a few more minds about the effects of opium."

"You could do the same thing without going inside these dens."

"Not at all. A first-hand account is what people most

enjoy reading. They don't wish to be lectured on the dangers of opium; instead, they desire to somehow experience its effects from the safety of their own homes."

"While you put yourself in danger!"

"I wasn't in danger, Ellie. I was accompanied by a police inspector and another news reporter, and I'm rather tired of being scolded for the decision I made. Three of you now – yourself, James and Mr Edwards – have berated me for doing what I consider to be an important part of my job."

"It's only because we care about you, Penelope!"

"Anyone who really cared would understand my need to do it."

"Oh, I see. We care but we don't care the way you would like. Is that what you're saying?"

"No, it's not. All I ask is for a little more acceptance."

Eliza snorted in reply.

"You should welcome articles such as mine," I continued. "Didn't you mention that you wished to join the Society for the Abolition of the Opium Trade?"

"Actually, I have spoken to a very nice gentleman there."

"Did you show him my article?"

"No, I hadn't read it by that point. But having spoken to the chap I've decided to propose that we add the abolition of the opium trade to our list of causes at the next meeting of the West London Women's Society."

"That's excellent news, Ellie."

"And the nice gentleman is to be our guest speaker."

"Even better! What does George think about the idea?"

"Oh, I haven't told him yet, but we both know what his reaction will be, don't we? You can't talk any sense into the man. I feel sure that he likes to think we're still living in 1850. Please tell me you're not planning a return visit to that opium den."

"Of course not, it was a horrible place."

"Good. Perhaps you can come to our next meeting and describe your experiences there."

"I'd be very happy to, Eliza."

"Splendid, I look forward to it! Now tell me, when are we next meeting Mr Edwards to discuss the search for Father?"

"Would this Saturday be convenient?"

"That would be absolutely fine with me. Oh, I have such a fondness for Mr Edwards. Isn't he a delightful chap? What it must be like to have a brain as clever as his. I do hope he hurries up with his proposal. I can't help but wonder why he's dragging his heels."

"Perhaps he has no intention of proposing."

"Oh, of course he does, but he must hurry up! You're thirty-five now, Penelope. Do you know what I think will spur him on a little? The marriage of Inspector Blakely. I think poor Mr Edwards must be aware that you and the inspector hold some sort of affection for one another."

"We don't."

"Oh, Penelope, look at your face. It's gone quite red! You're a hopeless liar. Now mark my words, as soon as Inspector Blakely is married Mr Edwards will surely propose."

My heart sank. I wasn't looking forward to either event.

CHAPTER 21

I found James at his desk in the drab, smoky offices of Scotland Yard.

"Penny!" James stood to his feet as soon as he saw me. He wore a dark blue suit and there was a gold pin in his silk tie.

At a desk nearby sat Chief Inspector Cullen, a police officer who cared little for me. He was about fifty-five with a thick grey moustache and silver-rimmed spectacles. Having experienced a number of disagreements with me in the past he acknowledged me with only a slight nod and continued reading the papers on his desk.

"I was just passing," I said to James, realising as I spoke that these words were becoming a common excuse between us.

"Of course." He smiled.

"Edgar Fish explained Mr Forster's complicated financial affairs to me."

"Did he? That's impressive, as they are extremely complicated."

"And presumably the reason he and his wife were murdered."

"Possibly. It cannot be denied that the man got himself into quite a bit of trouble. I've learnt a fair amount about the case from Bowles and Paget of C Division is happily co-operating with me now too."

"Both a law firm and a banker were pursuing him in the courts, were they not?"

"Yes, that's right."

"Do you know much about them?"

"Sadler and Campbell specialise in family law. I believe they were acting on behalf of his father's estate. I've spoken to a clerk there but have not yet found the opportunity to meet with either Mr Sadler or Mr Campbell. Mr Chakravarty owns a deposit bank in Change Alley in the City of London."

"Mr Chakravarty is the man who advanced Mr Forster the mortgage loan, I believe."

"On the house Mr Forster didn't own, yes, that's right. I've spoken briefly to Mr Chakravarty, but he claimed he had no time to speak to me. I need to go back and have a more structured conversation with him. I don't think he particularly likes speaking to the police. He strikes me as a man who has something to hide."

"Such as what?"

"Unscrupulous money-lending tactics, probably," Chief Inspector Cullen piped up. "I've come across his sort before."

"Unscrupulous enough to have a man murdered?" I asked.

"Perhaps so." Chief Inspector Cullen stroked his moustache and maintained an impassive expression, as if he knew more than he was prepared to say.

"Oh dear," I said. "It seems Mr Forster chose the wrong man to borrow money from by deception."

"Forster was a fool," retorted Chief Inspector Cullen.

"He didn't deserve to be murdered, though, did he?" I said.

"If a man plays with fire, sooner or later he will be burned," he replied.

"But what about his poor wife? And their servants who were also attacked?" I said. "Surely you must have some sympathy for the family?"

"It's not our job to be sympathetic, Miss Green, it's our job to catch people who break the law," stated the chief inspector.

"Do you know much about the murder of Alfred Holland in Limehouse, sir?" I asked.

"I've heard of it."

"I think his death may be connected to the murders of Mr and Mrs Forster."

Chief Inspector Cullen gave a hollow laugh. "You're doing a spot of detective work again, are you? If and when the Metropolitan Police decides to admit the fairer sex to its ranks we shall have to consider you, though you'll be required to lose some of those weak feminine traits, such as sympathy."

I took a deep breath and tried to quell the anger brewing in my chest.

"The good news is that C and D Division are co-operating well with each other and with me," said James, "and we're certain now that the errand boy who worked for the Forsters was bribed by the gang, as five shillings were found in his possession, though he says he found the coins in the street. The officers at D Division are doing what they can to get him to talk."

"Doing what exactly?" I said. "He's only a boy. Presumably he's frightened?"

Chief Inspector Cullen emitted another sarcastic laugh and I glared at him.

"I'll check with Inspector Bowles," said James. "You're right, Penny, the boy is only young and probably has little understanding of the position he has found himself in."

"Have you had an opportunity to speak to Inspector Reeves yet?" I asked.

"Good grief, Miss Green!" exclaimed Cullen. "Fancy yourself as the Commissioner of the Yard now, do you? No, Blakely has not spoken to Reeves in Limehouse, nor is there any need for him to do so. Now stop bothering the man and let him get on with his job!"

"Sir, I don't think there's any need —" James began.

"No defending her, Blakely! I've had enough of the woman's interference. She's an ink-slinger with ideas above her station, and I'm not having her distract you from your work any longer." He pointed a fat finger at me. "If you don't stop this, Miss Green, I shall have a word with your editor at the *Morning Express*."

"Sir, it's most impolite of you to speak to Miss Green in this manner," said James.

"I'm not a polite man; you know that, Blakely. Now this woman has charmed you for long enough. Ask her to leave immediately."

"There is no need to ask me. I'm already on my way out."

"Penny, I..." James' eyes were full of concern, but I knew that I couldn't stay here for a moment longer.

"You have your work to get on with, James. Thank you for taking the time to listen."

I turned and left, angered by the hot tears pricking the backs of my eyes.

CHAPTER 22

As I sat at my writing desk that evening I wondered whether there was any truth to what Chief Inspector Cullen had said. *Perhaps I was interfering in the police investigations too much. It had been wrong of me to call on James at his home and his place of work.* I realised that my actions were borne out of frustration, and that I wanted to see James even more than I wanted to secure justice for the Forsters and Mr Holland.

Perhaps it's time to accept that my hands are tied, I mused. *I can't keep telling James that I just happened to be 'passing by'.* Time and time again I had tried to accept that he was marrying someone else, but I simply couldn't. His betrothal to Charlotte should have quelled my affection for him, but it never had. If anything, it had made it stronger.

Not only did I enjoy James' company, but working with him had proved invaluable on many occasions. We had solved a number of cases together and I had never met anyone else I could work with so effectively.

I tried to remind myself that I was just a news reporter: that my job was to report on events and tell people what was happening. It wasn't my job to influence an investigation; that had to be left to the police. It was frustrating, however, when the police failed to ask the right questions and missed important witnesses or evidence.

I looked around my small lodgings with the bed at one end and the little stove at the other. I didn't have a large house like my sister, or a husband and children to distract me. My job consumed all my waking hours because there was little else occupying my life. It was no wonder I became so involved in each story I worked on, or that I had invested so much in James.

I realised Chief Inspector Cullen had been right to accuse me of being overly sympathetic, and that I sometimes allowed my emotions to take precedence over logic. *Was it because I was a woman? Could I persuade myself to care less?*

A knock at the door startled me, but before I could answer it swung open. Mrs Garnett marched in with my cat under her arm and a scowl on her face.

"There she is!" I said with a smile. "I was wondering where Tiger had got to."

"I found her asleep by my stove again," said Mrs Garnett, dropping Tiger onto the floor. "I've told you many times before that I won't have her in my rooms. When you took her in you assured me she would be a roof cat."

Tiger remained where she was with her fur ruffled and wearing a scowl that almost matched Mrs Garnett's.

"She is! I don't even know how she gets into your rooms. I am sorry, Mrs Garnett."

"Through the window is how she does it. I fling water at her but she doesn't care!"

"Naughty Tiger," I scolded unconvincingly.

"You'll have to get rid of her if she keeps doing it."

"Oh, no! She only likes to sleep by your stove, Mrs Garnett. Surely that's not so very terrible?"

"She's scratched my chair and she jumps up onto my shelves."

"I'm sorry."

"And she gives me sneezing fits."

"I hadn't realised that."

"I'll be sneezing all night now. I shan't get any sleep."

"I'm sure that's not true, Mrs Garnett."

"It *is* true! The only thing that stops it is scrubbing my floors with carbolic soap. I can't say I want to be doing that at ten o'clock at night. Do you want to come and scrub my floors?"

"No, I don't."

"Then keep your cat out of my rooms!"

"I'll try, Mrs Garnett, I'm sorry, I..."

A sob threatened to interrupt my words. The scolding from my landlady on top of the rebuke from Chief Inspector Cullen was proving a little too much.

"Oh, there's no need for tears, Miss Green," said Mrs Garnett, passing me her handkerchief.

I lifted up my spectacles and wiped my eyes. "I know there isn't, I'm sorry. I've had quite a busy day and I've been thinking about things too much."

"What sort of things?"

"Work things."

Mrs Garnett sucked her lip. "You should do a different sort of job, Miss Green. I've said it before and I'll say it again."

"But I like my work."

Mrs Garnett gave a soft laugh. "So it seems."

"I just need to learn to forget about it at the end of each day." I dabbed my eyes again with the handkerchief.

"You absolutely do. That's what my husband Hercules did, you know. Once he was at home you couldn't move him from his chair. He would sit there like a giant boulder not worrying about a thing. Meanwhile, I was the one fetching and carrying all over the place. The only thing that would get him to move was a tap on the knees with the carpet beater."

I laughed. "Knowing you, Mrs Garnett, it was more than a tap." Tiger jumped up onto my lap. As I stroked between her ears she gave a little murmur and began to purr. "I think the best solution is to treat my profession as an office clerk would treat his. I just need to work the usual hours, go home at a regular time and not let each story consume me."

"If you say so, Miss Green. That all sounds sensible to me."

"It's what my colleagues Mr Fish and Mr Potter do."

"I'm sure they do. Men don't seem to bear the weight of the world on their shoulders like us women. Hercules wasn't often the type I could learn from, but he did know how to sit down and not worry about anything."

"Except you and the carpet beater."

"Exactly. That was all he had to be concerned about."

Tiger remained on my lap long after Mrs Garnett had left. I thought about James and decided I would have to start avoiding him. The less I saw of him the less I would miss him.

But how could I get by without him?

I thought of the contentment I felt whenever I was with him. No one else had ever made me feel like that. And I knew the feeling was mutual, hence why he had kissed me at Eliza's house. Had I known that he cared nothing for me it would have been easier to persuade myself that I should never see him again.

Perhaps I was still harbouring a small hope that he would change his mind about the wedding. Was that what I was waiting for? It was a vain hope, but perhaps Charlotte would call it off, or maybe her mother would. It felt selfish to feel this way, but I couldn't help myself.

I thought of my father and how he would have felt if he could see me now. I hoped he would be proud. He had always known that I wanted to be a writer, but I wondered whether he would be proud of the manner in which I had conducted myself over the past few days. I couldn't be sure. I knew I had inherited his relentlessly curious spirit, but I wondered whether I had gone too far.

Taking a step back and striving not to care went against my very nature, but I knew that I would need to balance my impetuosity with what was expected of me or I would be in danger of making enemies.

CHAPTER 23

"Oh, do paddle carefully, Francis. I heard somebody drowned here last week," said Eliza.

I perched with my sister and Mr Edwards in a small rowing boat on the Serpentine lake in Hyde Park.

"Don't worry, Mrs Billington-Grieg. I was on the rowing team at university."

"Were you indeed? It seems there's no end to your talents. Do please call me Eliza."

"What lovely weather we're having," I commented, unable to think of anything interesting to say.

The sunshine had brought an unprecedented number of people to Hyde Park. Bathers splashed in the water around us while others promenaded along the edge of the lake and rode down Rotten Row.

"Oh, watch out! We're going to collide!" shrieked Eliza.

A boat containing four young men drew close and we were purposefully splashed with water from their oars while they cackled at us.

"Scoundrels!" shouted Eliza as they rowed away again.

"Just high jinks," said Mr Edwards, pulling on the oars and

propelling us smoothly across the surface of the water. He had removed his jacket and rolled up his sleeves, which was uncharacteristically informal. He wore a light grey waistcoat and trousers with a straw boater hat.

"There's a bather just behind you to your left, Francis," said Eliza. "Oh dear, I do worry that these people swimming about will be hit by a boat. And there are so many swans. I can't say that I really care for swans. They can be rather aggressive, can't they?"

"Only if you trouble them," replied Mr Edwards.

"I should say that it would be quite easy to trouble them on a busy day like today," said Eliza. "There's hardly any room left for them, and I can imagine them becoming rather angry about it."

Mr Edwards paused for a moment and mopped his brow with a white handkerchief. The strains of a military band rose from a nearby bandstand.

"Have a rest now, Francis, you look quite exhausted," said Eliza. "We can float about here for a bit. Are you enjoying yourself, Penelope? You seem a little quiet."

"I'm enjoying myself immensely, Ellie," I replied. I was struggling to shrug off the despondency which had settled over me since the previous evening. And despite the bright sunshine, music and happy chatter of people around me I kept recalling the dismal opium den where Alfred Holland had met his tragic end.

"I took the liberty of drawing a map," said Mr Edwards. He picked up his jacket, which was neatly folded on the seat next to him, and reached into one of the pockets.

"Oh dear, it's a little damp from when those oafs splashed us."

He carefully opened out the folded piece of paper to reveal an immaculately drawn map of the northern and central part of Colombia. He had drawn maps for me before and I had always been impressed by his drafting skills.

"That's a terrible shame! Some of the ink is spreading," said Eliza.

"We can still read it, though, can't we?" He held up the map so we could all see it. "I drew out Mr Fox-Stirling's proposed route to find your father. He'll be disembarking at Savanilla up on the northern coastline here, then he'll take a steamboat south along the Magdalena River for five hundred miles or so until he reaches Honda."

"Which is where the steamboat has to stop," I said.

"You're right, Miss Green. Steamboats are unable to navigate the Magdalena beyond Honda. What he must then do is travel by mule for about two hundred miles in a south-easterly direction to Bogotá."

"So that's seven hundred miles in total," said Eliza.

"Ah, but that's not all," said Mr Edwards. "It's another day's ride from Bogotá in the southwest to El Charquito on the banks of the Funza River."

"And the Falls of Tequendama," I said.

"Precisely. That's where the falls are, and the little village of El Charquito is where Mr Fox-Stirling found the hut your father had been staying in."

"And this time he'll have a Spanish translator with him," said Eliza, "so he'll be able to have a proper conversation with the natives rather than relying on his own poor understanding of the language."

"Yes, that was a serious oversight last time," I said. "He persuaded us that his Spanish was better than it actually was."

"Have you found a translator for him?" asked Mr Edwards.

"He's found one himself; an explorer friend recommended a man he has used before, apparently."

"Good news indeed," said Mr Edwards.

I felt happy that he was to help us plan this new search for Father. Although Mr Fox-Stirling was a seasoned traveller he also struck me as the sort of man who was rather set in his own ways of doing things. Mr Edwards offered an intelligence and pragmatism which had undoubtedly been missing when the last search was carried out. I felt that he had donated his money to the search not only out of affection for me but also because he had a genuine interest in Father's work and travels.

"The crossing of the Atlantic will take about eleven days, and there's usually a stop-off at Haiti or Jamaica, or sometimes both," said Mr Edwards. "It will probably take him two weeks to reach the shores of Colombia, and then the journey inland will take between four and six weeks."

"So it will be between six and eight weeks before Mr Fox-Stirling arrives in El Charquito," I said.

"That's if all goes well," replied Mr Edwards.

"And he won't be going until next year as he has his Himalayan expedition to do first." I sighed. "It feels like rather a long time to wait."

"We've only recently decided to carry out another search, Penelope!" said Eliza. "These things cannot just happen immediately, you know."

"I know. I'm afraid I'm not a terribly patient person. Once a decision has been made I like to get on with it."

"Life doesn't always fit in with our wants, Penelope, and there's still a little more money to raise. Instead of grumbling about having to wait perhaps you could help with the fundraising efforts."

"Yes, I should be happy to."

"Thank you for drawing such a detailed map, Francis," my sister said. "For the first time I've been able to properly imagine what this next search will entail. I think I was rather too grief-stricken last time to consider it in great detail. It has made me realise what a long journey Mr Fox-Stirling has ahead of him. I can't say that I should like to ride for two hundred miles on a mule. Or travel for five hundred miles along a foreign river in a steamboat after two weeks on a steam ship!"

"That's why some people are explorers and others aren't," I said.

"Mr Fox-Stirling is clearly the sort of chap who enjoys it," said Mr Edwards.

"And talks about it a lot," I added. "I prefer him being out and about on his adventures rather than boring people at home with unnecessary details."

"Unlike Francis here, who always has something meaningful to say, doesn't he, Penny?" said Eliza.

"Absolutely," I said.

He gave me a bashful smile.

Was Eliza correct in her assumption that he would propose to me as soon as James married? I wondered. I had always been reluctant to consider it, but perhaps I simply didn't know what was best for me. Having realised that I needed to be less involved with James and my work, perhaps I needed to consider the possibility that the potential for a marriage was staring me in the face.

"Thank you, Miss Green."

"Please call me Penny."

"I'd be delighted to." He grinned. "*Penny.*"

CHAPTER 24

"**M**iss Green! Thank goodness you've arrived! How do I use this darned thing?" asked Edgar. He was seated at the typewriter, closely examining its keys.

"You'll need to put some paper in it to start with."

"And how do I do that?"

I placed my carpet bag on my desk, walked over to the typewriter and showed him how it was done.

"Did you see that, Potter? It's rolled onto a cylinder!" said Edgar. "Now, where do I find the letter 'A'? Why aren't these keys in alphabetical order?"

"We've discussed this before, Edgar," I said. "There's the 'A' on the far left."

"Actually, I don't require an 'A'. I require an 'M' for the name Mr Godfrey White."

"'M' is on the bottom row, over on the right."

Edgar pressed it. "And that has put something on the paper, has it?"

"Yes, you can just about see it behind the ink ribbon."

"I can typewrite, Potter!" said Edgar cheerily. "Now where's 'R'?"

I pointed it out to him.

"And now I press this long rectangular key for a space, don't I? And now for 'G'... Don't tell me, Miss Green, I want to find it for myself. There it is! How's it looking?" He peered closely at the paper. "Oh, darn it. It's all in lower case!"

"Sorry, Edgar, I forgot to explain about the shift key."

"What, this one here?"

"Yes. For an uppercase letter you need to hold the shift key down at the same time."

Edgar sat back in the chair looking deflated. "Now I've lost all my enthusiasm for the project."

"It's quite easy, Edgar. Just put in another piece of paper and start again."

"No, no, I haven't the time for that sort of fussing about. I'll find out if Miss Welton is in an amenable enough temper to typewrite it for me. Thank you for your help, Miss Green."

I sat back at my desk and leafed through the morning's edition. I was reading about a new elephant at the Zoological Society's Gardens when an announcement caught my eye:

Sir Archibald Duffield will preside over a dinner for gentlemen interested in Indian affairs at the Burlington Hotel on Thursday the 21st of August. The guest of honour will be the merchant Mr. Lewis Sheridan, whose Calcutta company has contributed greatly to the commercial and material interests of India. Among those present will be Lord Wallace, Sir Edmund Nicholl, Sir Thomas Horsman, Colonel Worthing, Mr. Cornelius Redington and Mr. Rajah Rogay.

I showed the announcement to Edgar.

"Do you think you might be able to secure yourself an invitation?" I asked.

"I doubt it. Besides, it would be exceedingly dull."

"But you know who Lewis Sheridan is, don't you?"

"No, who is he?"

"Oh, Edgar, I thought you were covering the story of the Forsters' murders!"

"I am! What of it?"

"Then you must know who Lewis Sheridan is."

"Oh, wait a minute." Edgar clicked his thumb and forefinger together as he thought it over. "Yes... it sounds familiar. Yes! It's that merchant Forster worked for in Bombay, isn't it?"

"Calcutta."

"That's it, Calcutta."

"It would be interesting to speak to him, don't you think?"

"Why?"

"To find out what he makes of his former employee's death."

"I suppose so. I can't imagine he'd have much to say other than to express his sympathies."

"Can you attempt to get an invitation to the dinner? Your father has plenty of good connections, doesn't he?"

"He does, but I don't see what use there could be in me attending. Mr Sheridan will hardly want to discuss Forster's death with me, will he? It's rather a gloomy topic."

"It needn't be an in-depth discussion; it could merely be a few words to express your condolences and ask for his thoughts on the tragedy."

"To what end?"

"He might have some useful information about who may be behind it."

"If so he's probably already told the police."

"Not necessarily. People don't always think to tell the

police seemingly trivial pieces of information. Often they think what they know is rather small and of no importance, but when it's pieced together as part of a bigger puzzle it can be extremely significant. And it's difficult to find out these pieces of information without asking people. Conversation is often the best way; especially accompanied by a glass of something to loosen the tongue."

"I see what you're getting at, but I don't think I have any chance of securing a place at that dinner. Why not attend yourself if you're so interested?"

"You're forgetting something, Edgar. I'm a woman."

"Oh yes, so you are."

"I wasn't allowed into the East India Club for Inspector Paget's briefing, so it's unlikely that I would be invited to this dinner. And it's not really my story, is it? It's yours. I've already been scolded by Chief Inspector Cullen at Scotland Yard for getting too involved in it all."

"Oh dear. I suppose I'll have to go instead if I can."

"You'll enjoy it. You like dinners, don't you?"

"I do like a good dinner, but it's much more fun when I'm not there for work purposes."

"So you intend to request an invitation?"

"I'll try, but I don't know what good it will do."

"Edgar, I have just explained it all!" I began to feel exasperated by his lack of interest. "Can't you see how useful it would be to find out Mr Sheridan's opinion on the matter?"

"I can't say that I do. Forster wasn't even working for him when he was killed. He left the company last year, did he not?"

"Yes, he did, but I'm surprised by your laxity, Edgar. You're a news reporter. Surely you feel compelled to get to that dinner and speak to Mr Sheridan?"

"It's simply not in my nature, Miss Green. I can't say that I care too much for investigative work. That time I went undercover in St Giles' Rookery represented the worst few weeks of my life. I like the stories to come to me."

"But they don't always do so. Most often you have to go looking for the information."

"Only I let the police do that. They have detectives for that sort of thing."

"But the police aren't always looking in the right places."

"You're not criticising your friend Blakely with that comment, are you?"

"No, not at all. But Inspector James Blakely's work is constrained by what his superior tells him to do. And having recently spoken with Chief Inspector Cullen about this case I can see that he has no imaginative ideas on how to approach it."

"My work is constrained by what my editor, Mr Sherman, tells me to do," replied Edgar. "There's really no point in creating extra work for myself."

I sighed. "I see that you prefer to take the path of least resistance."

"Of course I do. Doesn't everyone? Everyone apart from you, that is."

We were interrupted by the editor's secretary, Miss Welton, entering the room. She wore a woollen dress, which was buttoned up to her throat, and a pair of pince-nez. She was accompanied by a young woman in mourning dress, whom I recognised as Emma Holland.

"You have a visitor, Miss Green," said Miss Welton.

"Miss Holland!" I rose to my feet. "This is a surprise indeed."

"I'm sorry to disturb you at your place of work," she said, glancing around the room nervously. "I hope you don't mind me visiting you here."

"Not at all. Would you like to take a seat? I'm afraid there isn't a lot of space." I pushed all my papers into a pile and removed another stack from a chair so that she could sit down.

"Take the young lady to a refreshment room, Miss Green," said Edgar. "This inky den is no place for women's conversation."

"That's quite a good idea, Edgar. Shall we do that, Miss Holland?"

She nodded.

CHAPTER 25

Emma Holland and I sat at a table in the oak-panelled tea room of Anderton's Hotel on Fleet Street. The gas lamps were lit, as the only natural light came from a window overlooking a dingy courtyard. The darkness of the room made Miss Holland's face seem even paler, and I tried to imagine what she must have looked like before grief had held her in its grip.

"I read your article about the opium den, Miss Green," she said. "I didn't realise you had visited the place. What was it like?"

"Much as I described it, I'm afraid. Extremely dismal."

"Oh dear. Why ever did Alfred choose to spend time in such an awful place?"

"I don't think it was a free choice he made; he was dependent on the drug, Miss Holland."

"Please call me Emma."

"And you may call me Penny." I smiled. "He wasn't of sound mind when he went to that place, I feel sure of it. Opium has that effect on people."

"It's horrible." She shuddered. "I hope you don't mind me

131

distracting you from your work, it's just that I feel rather help-less in terms of what I can do about my brother's death. He wasn't a well man at the end of his life and he may have got himself into trouble, but that doesn't explain why someone should wish to go into that opium den and shoot him dead."

"I wish I had some idea why," I replied. "Have you spoken with Inspector Reeves about his progress on the case?"

"I've tried, but he hasn't been a great deal of help. And then he told me that for a payment of three shillings he would take me on a tour of the places where Alfred spent most of his time."

I felt angered by this. "What an irresponsible way to behave toward the sister of a murder victim. You declined, I presume."

"Of course. I'm not convinced Inspector Reeves is partic-ularly committed to finding Alfred's murderer."

"I'm sure he is." I secretly agreed with her, but felt I should try to offer some reassurance. "It's his job to find the culprit."

"But how long will it take him?"

"Hopefully not too long."

"I feel rather lost. I've never encountered a situation like this before."

"Few people have, Emma. It's natural that you should feel lost."

"But you have experience with this type of thing, haven't you? When I spoke to Inspector Reeves he told me about the other cases you have reported on."

"There have been a few."

"How were the culprits found?"

"Each case has been different. The only similarity was the compunction to keep going, no matter how impossible it seemed at the time."

"That's how I feel at the moment. It seems impossible to me that Alfred's killer will ever be caught."

"And that's why we must never give up."

"But it's rather difficult when you're reliant on the police to solve it. I wish there was something I could do myself. That's why I've come to see you, Penny. I feel sure that you can do something about Alfred's murder."

I felt a pang of alarm. "I'm not a police officer, Emma. I have no legal powers at all. I would wish to see every murder I report on solved, but my involvement is no guarantee of that." I felt worried that her faith in my abilities was somewhat misplaced.

"I realise that, but you have significantly more influence than I do. Who would listen to me? I can't even convince my parents to take an interest in the case. They washed their hands of my brother a long time ago."

"So you want me to help you," I said, taking a sip of tea.

"Yes please, Penny."

"I may have worked on other cases, but it isn't always as easy as it sounds. In fact, just a few days ago I resolved not to get too involved in either this case or that of the Forsters. I received a ticking off at Scotland Yard for supposedly interfering."

"That sounds rather unjust."

"I'm not certain that it was. I am only a news reporter, Emma, and although I have a good friend who is a detective at Scotland Yard there are many other police officers who have little time for me."

"Inspector Reeves spoke highly of you."

"That is most probably because I paid him three shillings for his opium tour!"

"So what's your answer to my request? Are you telling me you cannot help?"

"I want to, Emma, and I shall, but please don't rest all your hopes on me as I may be unable to do anything at all."

"But you might be able to do something. You have experience of working on some terrible murder cases."

"I do, and the experience is useful, but it doesn't make me an expert. You may be able to do more yourself than you realise."

"But I have no idea where to begin."

"Do you know if your brother left any diaries or correspondence behind?"

"There are some papers among his belongings which I collected from his landlord."

"Have you looked through them?"

"I've tried to, but I find it too upsetting."

"I understand, however it's important that you read them as we need to find out who your brother was consorting with during the last few months of his life. Please try to read through everything you have and write down the names of any people he has mentioned. It would be particularly interesting to find out whether there was someone he had a disagreement with or anyone he owed money to. We discussed that when we last met, if I recall."

"I can do that," Emma said with a nod. "It won't be easy, but I think I can manage it."

"Good. It won't be easy, as you say, and you'll need to do it quickly as Inspector Reeves will soon ask you for your brother's diaries and correspondence if he's doing his job properly so that he can do the same. Once he is in possession of them it may be a while before they're returned to you. If I were you I would go home right away and make a start."

Emma nodded. "And when I've done it, shall I come and show you what I've found out?"

"Yes, please do. You mentioned that you picked up his

belongings from the landlord. Did the landlord have anything useful to say for himself?"

"No, not really."

"It might be worth your while returning to him and asking about your brother's acquaintances. Perhaps you could take the list of names with you and ask if he has met any of them."

"That's another good idea, Penny, thank you." Emma smiled. "It's a relief to feel that there's something I can do after all."

"Of course there is. And if you discover anything else among the papers or from the people you speak to, just write it down. As I discussed with my colleague Edgar earlier, the smallest piece of information can sometimes be surprisingly useful."

Emma's face looked a lot brighter and I realised that, despite my warnings, she was placing all her trust in me. I returned her smile, but it dawned on me that I was now firmly committed to finding out what had happened to Alfred Holland.

CHAPTER 26

As I left the *Morning Express* offices that evening I found James waiting outside the stationer's shop again.

"Were you just passing?" I asked with a smile.

"No, I confess that I am purposefully here to see you, Penny." He grinned.

The sun felt warm on my face as we walked toward the Strand.

"I must apologise for Cullen's rude behaviour when you visited the Yard," he said.

"Oh you mustn't apologise for him. I know what he's like."

"But he was unnecessarily obnoxious, and I didn't like the idea of you being upset by it."

"I have come to expect it of him."

"But you shouldn't expect it! Even though I respect the man I consider his behaviour toward you utterly unreasonable."

"He was angered by my interference."

"You weren't interfering, Penny."

"I'm inclined to think I was a little. I had a think about it afterwards and decided that I need to be far less involved in the stories I am reporting on. I should leave the investigating work to you and the other detectives."

"Do you really think so?"

"Yes, although I came to the decision with some reluctance."

"But you don't really believe that, do you? I hope not, as you're an extremely useful asset to the police force."

I laughed. "You must be the only police officer in London who thinks so!"

"I'm sure Cullen feels the same. He just has a gruff manner."

"He certainly does. I don't know how you put up with him."

"He's good at his job, and extremely experienced. Anyway, I came here to ask you a favour."

"What is it?"

"I'm struggling to speak to this Chakravarty gentleman."

"The one who was defrauded by Forster?"

"That's right. He won't give me any of his time. As I mentioned before, I suspect he's engaged in some other sort of business which he doesn't wish to be uncovered. I could become heavy-handed about the whole affair and march him down to the nearest police station but he's not an official suspect and I would prefer not to do that just yet."

"But if he's not keen on speaking to a detective why should he wish to speak to a news reporter?"

"I don't think he would speak to a news reporter, either. However, he would most likely speak to a lady who shows an interest in borrowing some money from him."

"And you would like me to be that lady, would you?"

James' expression was apologetic. "Would you consider it, Penny?"

"His suspicions will be raised when I begin asking him questions about Forster, won't they?"

"You're right, they will. The information would need to be coaxed out of him in the course of general conversation. And to hold his interest you'll need to present yourself as a woman of significant means."

"In which case, why would I need to borrow money from him?"

"Wealthy people are always borrowing money, Penny. What's important is that he can see that you'll be able to pay back the sum with interest."

"I see. Sadly, I don't have any clothing that would fit the bill."

"What about your sister's clothes?"

"She possesses a number of expensive dresses she no longer wears because she can't ride her bicycle in them."

"There you go."

"I'd have to scrub the ink off my hands," I said, glancing down at them. "They seem to be permanently stained. It's impossible to find a pen which doesn't leak."

"Couldn't you wear a pair of gloves?"

"Yes, I suppose so."

"So you'll do it?"

"What do you know about the man?"

"His grandfather came to Britain from India at the end of the last century and worked for a nabob. His son, Chakravarty's father, owned some vapour baths in Knightsbridge. Mr Chakravarty has worked in the banking sector for many years and keeps a tight circle, but in the right company men like him have been known to brag, so you may get something useful from him."

"If he wants to impress me, you mean?"

"Exactly. He has no interest in impressing me; however, I should think he would quite like to charm you, Penny, and have you borrow as much money as you can possibly stretch to."

"I don't know if I could be convincing enough."

"Hopefully he'll do most of the talking."

"Even if he does I'm not sure I can pass for a lady of great wealth. It would be easier if I was pretending to be a maid, as I have done before."

There was a pause as James considered this.

"Perhaps it's a foolish idea after all," he said. "Forget that I mentioned it. It puts you under duress and I have no wish to ask you to do something you feel unsure about."

"I'll do it, James."

"No, no, I'll think of another way to find out what Chakravarty knows."

"I said I'd do it! I wasn't sure when you initially suggested the idea, but I should like to meet Mr Chakravarty. He might even become a suspect, mightn't he?"

"He might. Are you sure you're happy to meet with him?"

"I'm certain. Now what of the legal firm that was pursuing Forster? Would you like me to meet with them as well?"

"There's no need; they've been much more co-operative. I've spoken to both Mr Sadler and Mr Campbell and they answered my questions comprehensively. I can find no evidence to suggest that they have behaved dishonourably."

"But they're lawyers."

"Indeed. Lawyers often consider themselves to be above the law, but at this stage I have come across nothing to suggest that they would wish to harm Mr Forster or his wife. They were extremely saddened to hear of the attacks."

"Largely because they've lost out on the legal fees now the case has come to an end, wouldn't you say?"

"Oh, Penny! Not every lawyer is so very mercenary!"

We both laughed.

"Inspector Bowles has been rounding up ne'er-do-wells

who he suspects were members of the gang which burgled the Forsters' home," continued James. "There's no doubt the poor errand boy was paid to ensure that a window was left unlocked that night. There's a good deal of anger about that, of course, and I'm keeping a close eye on the lad. D Division wish to prosecute him."

"But presumably he was too young to understand the implications of what he was doing."

"Bowles says if the boy is old enough to work he's old enough to understand the responsibilities that accompany his employment. The lad has been extremely helpful in providing us with a description of the man who approached him a few days before the murder and that's helped him in making an arrest. Needless to say the chap is already known to the police. I've spoken with Inspector Reeves, and interestingly the descriptions of the gunman seen shortly before and after the murder of Alfred Holland are not too dissimilar to the boy's description of the ringleader."

"So there's a possibility that the same man could have been the ringleader of the attack on both the Forsters' home and Alfred Holland?"

"Indeed."

"And could he be the same man who attacked Mr Forster in St James's Square?"

"Possibly, but Inspector Paget has been unable to find any reliable witnesses to that incident."

"The same man has to be behind all three deaths."

"I don't know, Penny. Three different murder weapons were used: a cudgel, a knife and a gun. That suggests to me that we have three different assailants. A single assailant would most likely use the same weapon, because if it worked for him once it would be likely to work again. Changing the weapon each time is a risky strategy. It would make more sense to use the tried and tested one. If the same man has committed all three murders he must be extremely dangerous indeed if he is able to wield these different weapons with equal effectiveness."

"Perhaps I'm so desperate to link the three murders that I'm determined to prove the same person is behind them."

"It's reassuring to think so, as it suggests we're looking for fewer murderers. I'm inclined to think that the same man murdered Mr and Mrs Forster. I think the original intention was to murder Mr Forster at his home along with his wife. I believe the Alfred Holland murder was carried out by a different assailant."

"Someone who was equally proficient?"

"Absolutely. In each case the culprit knew exactly what he was doing."

"So perhaps there is no connection between Alfred Holland and the Forster murders after all."

"I think not, unless you are able to find one. It may be nothing more than coincidence that the men worked in India. I have found no evidence to suggest that they knew one another."

"Alfred's sister Emma is trying to find out more," I said, briefly recounting the conversation from earlier that afternoon.

"It's encouraging that she is keen to do something to help," he replied.

"She seems reluctant to place her trust in Inspector Reeves. In fact, she seems to think I have a greater chance of solving the case than he does."

James laughed. "You probably have, Penny."

We stopped outside a small French restaurant with a blue and gold awning.

"It would be rather nice to have something to eat, wouldn't it?" said James, looking in through the window. "But I don't suppose it would be appropriate."

I sighed. "I don't suppose it would."

"When this wedding is over and the excitement has died down we'll be able to do that sort of thing again."

"I wouldn't be so sure, James. I think that once you're married things will be very different indeed."

"No, I don't think —"

"James, please don't let's argue about it. I know it to be true."

He held my gaze and said nothing further.

CHAPTER 27

"If only you had a little more height, Penelope," said my sister. "The skirts drag along the floor a little. I wonder if we could pin them somehow." She pinched some of the blue fabric and held it beneath my tightly buttoned bodice. "No, that still doesn't look right."

"Good," I replied. "I don't like this dress anyway. The lace scratches my throat."

"It's a perfectly good day dress and it cost a pretty penny."

"I'm sure it did, Ellie, and please don't take offence. I simply don't feel comfortable in it."

Eliza sighed and let the fabric fall from her hand. "That's exactly why I stopped wearing dresses like this. You can hardly do a thing in them, can you? Let's try the next one on. Burgundy and cream go so well together, don't they? There's no scratchy lace on this one, just a silk ribbon at the neck. I wore it to the Ascot Races. There's a lovely parasol which goes with it somewhere."

"I prefer it to this one," I said, fidgeting with the buttons on the bodice. "I can't even get out of this dress. I feel as though I'm doomed to wear it forever."

"Let me help you, Penelope. You seem to be making quite an effort for your meeting with this banker."

"I have to pretend that I'm a woman of means, Ellie."

She laughed.

"What's the joke?"

"The things you end up doing for your work. Earlier this year you were a maid and now you're to wear one of my dresses and put on your best airs and graces. I've practically given up trying to understand the whys and wherefores of it all."

"Inspector Blakely would like me to speak to a banker in the City to whom Mr Forster owed money."

"Mr Forster who was so tragically stabbed in St James's Square?"

"Yes."

"But that could be dangerous, Penelope! Do you think the banker might have killed the poor man because Forster was unable to repay him?"

"We don't know yet."

"You don't know, but you're still going to meet with this man? Is the inspector going with you?"

"No."

"*No?*"

"James has tried speaking to Mr Chakravarty a couple of times, but he hasn't been especially willing to talk."

"But Inspector Blakely is a police officer. He can force him to talk!"

"He would prefer to use a softer approach at this present moment."

"And you're the softer approach?"

"I suppose I am."

"How dreadful. I don't understand why you should have to do this."

"Because although Mr Fish has the Forster story now I'm

working on the Alfred Holland story, which I'm sure is connected somehow. There are too many coincidences for it not to be."

"And I suppose Inspector Blakely is indifferent to the fact that this banker could stick a knife into you at any given moment?"

"He won't do that, Ellie. Even if he's the murdering type I should think he would only do such a thing to those who cross him."

"And that's all right, is it?"

"No, but—"

"It's not safe, Penelope. You must have a man to accompany you."

"But it can't be Inspector Blakely because Mr Chakravarty has already met him."

"Then you must take George." She helped me step into the burgundy dress.

"I don't want to bother George with this."

"But the City is his purlieu. He's so familiar with lawyers and bankers and all those professional types that I think you would be even more convincing with George in attendance."

"But he cannot pretend to be my husband!"

"No, of course not, but he could accompany you as your brother-in-law. In fact, such is George's reputation in that part of London that it's very likely Mr Chakravarty has heard his name before. I think his presence will lend further credence to your *woman of means* role."

Although I did not usually enjoy the company of my brother-in-law, the thought of visiting Mr Chakravarty with an acquaintance felt surprisingly reassuring.

"All right, Ellie, just so long as you don't think he'll mind."

"Of course he won't. Now what do you think of this dress? It's still a little long, but it sits much better about the hips and the bodice is terribly pretty, don't you think?"

"Yes, I like this one."

"Good." She looked me up and down and grimaced. "You'll have to do something fashionable with your hair, but I can't think what. It's almost irredeemable."

"Thank you, Ellie."

CHAPTER 28

"Chakravarty of Change Alley," mused George as we travelled along Cheapside by hansom cab. "Hindu, I would guess."

"His grandfather was from India."

"I can't say I've encountered the man personally. He takes on private clients rather than businesses, I think. I've seen his advertisements in the *Morning Express*."

"Inspector Blakely says he'll meet us outside the Royal Exchange," I said.

"What do we need to meet him for?"

"He just wants to ensure that we're happy with the plan."

"There's a plan?"

"The plan is for us to have a conversation with Mr Chakravarty about me borrowing some money to purchase a property in Kensington."

"That's all the plan we need, isn't it? Only you're not actually going to buy a property in Kensington, are you? I understand this is some ruse to speak to the man you suspect may be behind the murder of that Forster chap."

"He might not be. I don't think Inspector Blakely considers him a suspect just yet."

"Then why are we doing such a thing?"

"To find out more about him. Any conversation you can have with him, you know, the man-to-man sort of thing, would be useful."

"Ah, yes. I understand you now, Penelope. You'd like me to talk around the topic a bit?"

"I shall try to do the same, but I suspect that Mr Chakravarty will respond more favourably to conversation with a fellow gentleman."

"Naturally." George pushed his lower lip out and nodded. "And I must say it's a rather interesting morning excursion. I barely recognised you at first in all your get-up."

I was wearing the burgundy and cream dress with cream silk gloves which buttoned up to my elbows. Eliza had also lent me a diamond bracelet and Mrs Garnett had pinned my unruly fair hair into neat curls. A small silk hat had been fastened into my hair and I had reluctantly parted with my spectacles, which Eliza had said made me look like a working woman.

Despite my short-sightedness I was able to recognise the large, columned portico of the Royal Exchange as it came into view. I made a great effort to step elegantly out of the cab once we stopped and immediately opened my fringed parasol to shield my face from the sun.

Although my bodice was tight and my skirts were cumbersome I found myself enjoying the prestige afforded me by my attire. I smiled to myself as I noticed a few heads turning in my direction.

"Penny?" James' face was a blur until he stood close beside me. He looked me up and down and grinned. "I... Well, I... I can't believe you're you!"

I felt a warmth in my face. "Is that a good or a bad thing?"

"It's... You look good. Extremely good indeed! Not the Penny I'm used to, but certainly not in a bad way."

"Left you tongue-tied, hasn't she?" laughed George. "Surprisingly well-favoured when she makes the effort, isn't she?"

The reaction of the two gentlemen made me realise that I usually neglected my appearance.

"Shall we get on with it?" I asked impatiently.

"You're here to tell us about some plan, are you, Inspector?" asked George.

"I'd like you to subtly mention Mr Forster in conversation if possible," said James.

"How do we do that when we're there to talk about a mortgage?" George replied.

"Maybe you could pretend that he's a friend of yours."

"I could try, but what if this Chakravarty starts asking questions about him? I don't know Mr Forster from a slice of cheese."

"Don't do or say anything which makes you feel uncomfortable," said James. "Chakravarty will pick up on it and suspect something. Only mention Forster if it feels appropriate to do so."

"And to what end?" asked George.

"What do you mean?" replied James.

"Suppose we mention Forster, what then? What are we hoping this Chakravarty chap will say?"

"Who can predict what he'll say? It will be interesting just to gauge his reaction."

George sighed. "It's an intriguing plan, but I suppose it's what you detectives and news reporters are accustomed to. Are you ready, Penelope?"

"Yes, I think so."

"Good luck!" said James. "And thank you both. I appreciate your help."

. . .

I took George's arm and we crossed the street before stepping into a narrow passageway. I was accustomed to London alleyways being smelly, dingy places frequented by shifty-looking people. This one was more salubrious, widening as we progressed along it and lined with attractive shops.

"This was once the home of the coffee houses," said George, swinging his cane as he walked. "Garraway's was on this corner here. And there was also Jonathan's. It's where it all began, you know."

"Where what began?"

"Trading in stocks and shares. The great men of those days came here for coffee and important discussions. What fun it must have been."

We passed a clock shop and saw a man in a top hat and a lady in a silk bustle dress admiring its wares in the window.

"Is this it?" asked George, pausing by a doorway, beside which was a brass plaque etched with the words: 'Samuel T. Chakravarty (Banker), established 1862'.

"It is indeed," I replied.

He gave three sharp raps on the door with the mother-of-pearl-encrusted top of his cane.

CHAPTER 29

Mr Chakravarty was a humourless, brown-skinned man with heavy eyebrows and streaks of grey in his wavy black hair. His collar was so tall that it appeared to dig uncomfortably into his jowls. He sat at his desk beneath a portrait of a traditionally dressed Indian gentleman, who I guessed was a family member judging by the similarity of their features.

He listened intently as George explained my proposition to borrow six thousand pounds. I nodded politely and smiled where appropriate, all the while trying to assume a self-assured air.

"Everything sounds satisfactory," said the banker once George had finished his explanation, "and I can foresee no reason why we should be unable to proceed in a straightforward manner. Have I seen you before at the Colthurst Club, Mr Billington-Grieg?"

"You may well have. I've been a member there for twelve years now."

"Eighteen myself. It's not what it used to be, but it's still an agreeable venue."

"The food has gone a little downhill since the new chef arrived."

"Hasn't it just? He insisted on engaging a new meat supplier, I understand."

"I insist on the previous one!" stated George.

"As do I. The spiced lamb served up last week was practically indigestible."

"Have you complained?"

"Oh yes, I've complained all right, but if the food doesn't pick up I shan't mind too much. It's the company I enjoy there more than anything, and the imperfections of the Colthurst are part of its appeal, wouldn't you say?"

I did my best to stifle a yawn. Although I knew this sort of conversation was important for building rapport I felt eager to move on to a topic I had a hope of contributing to.

Mr Chakravarty sat back in his chair and steepled his fingers. "As a fellow man of the Colthurst, Mr Billington-Grieg, I would consider offering your sister-in-law a favourable rate of interest."

"Would you indeed? That's very kind of you, my good man."

"My pleasure. It's something I like to offer acquaintances of mine, and in doing so I hope that it might pave the way for future business?"

"Absolutely. I'm game for anything that might help in paving the way."

"Good, good. Shall we get on with the paperwork, then?"

"Yes, let's!"

George was enjoying his conversation with Mr Chakravarty so much that he seemed to have forgotten I had no intention of going ahead with the mortgage.

"If we get on with the paperwork," I ventured, "does that mean everything will be signed and sealed today?"

"It certainly does," replied Mr Chakravarty. "You can't ask for a quicker service than that, can you?"

"May I request a day or two to consider it properly? The purpose of this meeting was really to see whether we could agree something in principle."

Mr Chakravarty's face fell.

"It is such a lot of money, you see. I become quite nervous about large sums of money!" I added with a sweet smile.

Mr Chakravarty looked at George and shook his head.

"Women, eh, Mr Billington-Grieg?"

"I've always said it and I continue to say it: they don't have the head for finance," said George, "or politics, either."

"Or the law," added Mr Chakravarty.

"Especially the law!" agreed George.

I looked from one man to the other, incredulous that my stalling comment had drawn such unjust criticism.

"Do you think it would be a good idea for me to sign the papers today, George?" I asked with an acidic tone to my voice.

My brother-in-law laughed loudly and nervously. "My dear Penelope, since you have expressed a wish to spend a day or two considering Mr Chakravarty's kind offer, that is exactly what we'll do."

"Even though I don't have the head for finance?" I was beginning to wish that Eliza hadn't insisted on George accompanying me.

"Yes, I have learnt over the years that one must always indulge a woman's whim, otherwise a fellow never gets a moment's peace."

Mr Chakravarty nodded in agreement. "Very well. I'm sure that after a day or two you will realise how favourable an offer it is, Miss Green, so I shall make a note of a few particulars and await your confirmation."

He dipped his pen into an inkpot and began to write something down. I felt inwardly relieved.

"Will you be contacting me yourself, Miss Green?"

"Yes," I replied uneasily.

George caught my eye, as if he had finally remembered why we were there.

"I say, terrible news about that Forster chap, isn't it?" said George.

I felt my teeth clench at his clumsy introduction of the topic.

"Mr Forster?" The banker looked up from his writing, seemingly baffled by the sudden change in conversation.

"The chap who was stabbed in the back in St James's Square."

"Yes, a most unpleasant business," murmured Mr Chakravarty, returning to his notes.

"Did you know the fellow at all?" asked George.

Mr Chakravarty looked up again, appearing even more perplexed. "Know him? Why should I know him?"

"Oh, I just wondered." There were beads of perspiration on George's brow.

"Did *you* know him?" asked Chakravarty.

"No, no, I didn't know the fellow. I, er, in fact I don't know anyone who knew him. But it was a terrible business as I hear that his wife was also murdered."

"I heard the same thing." Mr Chakravarty rested his pen down on his desk. "Why are you asking me about Mr Forster?"

"I was just making conversation. It's been in the papers a lot over the past few days, hasn't it? In fact, Penelope..."

I felt my heart leap into my throat as I realised he had been about to mention that I was a news reporter.

"Penelope what?" asked Chakravarty. His brows hung low over his eyes.

"Oh, nothing really. I was going to say that Penelope, my sister-in-law here, is a keen reader of the *Morning Express*. You have been following the story intently, haven't you, Penelope?"

"I have indeed."

"The *Morning Express*, eh?" replied Chakravarty. "I take *The Times* myself."

My heart thudded heavily in my chest as I realised that George was in danger of saying just the wrong thing at any moment. Although he had developed a good rapport with Mr Chakravarty, his attempts to steer the conversation had set me on edge.

"Apologies, Mr Chakravarty, for introducing a seemingly random topic of conversation," said George. "I'm a garrulous fellow and cannot help myself at times."

"No need for an apology," replied the banker. "It's just an odd coincidence, you see. The fact of the matter is that I did know the unfortunate fellow."

"You don't say!" replied George with mock surprise.

"Yes! In fact, he defrauded me."

"Oh goodness, is that so? What a dreadful thing to do. Why should the fellow wish to do that?"

"He got himself into a quagmire, that's what. And he thought he could borrow money from me to get himself out of it. I lent him some cash for a mortgage on a property that it turned out he didn't own."

"The rat!" declared George.

"I prefer not to speak ill of the dead."

"Ah yes, I apologise."

"Again, there's no need, old chap. Part of the fault must lie with me. I should have had more checks and balances in place."

"What did you do when you found out he had defrauded you?" I asked.

"I began legal proceedings in an attempt to recover the money," replied the banker. "That was the only above-board method available."

"And below-board?" inquired George.

Mr Chakravarty sat back in his chair and folded his arms. "I'm not a below-board sort of man, Mr Billington-Grieg. What are you implying here?"

"Nothing at all!"

I winced as George gave a nervous laugh.

"I hope you don't mind me saying this, sir, but I can't quite get the measure of you," said Mr Chakravarty. "One moment we're having a pleasant conversation and are about to proceed with your sister-in-law's mortgage, and the next you begin asking me all sorts of odd questions."

"I do apologise if my questions were perceived as odd, Mr Chakravarty, I'm a garrulous fellow and —"

"So you've already explained," interrupted the banker. "I've been in this business a long time, Mr Billington-Grieg, and I've learned to be wary. I admit that I was caught napping when it came to Forster, but most of the time I consider myself pretty shrewd."

My mouth felt dry. The conversation had taken a turn for the worse and I needed to stop George talking any further.

"Please blame me, Mr Chakravarty," I said. "I was talking to my brother-in-law about Mr Forster just before we stepped through your doorway, so when a natural pause arose in the conversation the murder was the first thing that came to mind, wasn't it, George?"

"It was indeed, and —"

"And although George was not personally acquainted with Mr Forster, he has been quite affected by the incident as both Mr Forster and his late wife seemed like any other middle-class couple. I believe anyone from a similar background would cast a glance at their tragic demise and wonder whether the same thing could happen to them. It's only natural."

"That's exactly my concern!" said George earnestly.

"As we have learned more detail about the case we've realised how unlikely it is to happen to us given that we aren't in such dire financial and legal straits," I continued. "Though I'm not suggesting for one minute that's why they were murdered so horribly. It's possible that in making the decisions they did they acquainted themselves with nefarious types who lived beyond the realms of the law. I'm inclined to think that an association with someone of the criminal classes may have played a part."

I took a much-needed breath and hoped Mr Chakravarty's response would be amenable.

"Most eloquently put, Miss Green," he said with a nod. "I think that's a fair assumption when it comes to Forster. And it's clearly little more than coincidence that you happened to begin discussing him while you were here. I just get a little fretful when former clients of mine are mentioned."

I felt thankful that Mr Chakravarty was momentarily appeased, but was keen to get myself and George out of his office as quickly as possible.

"It's a shame about your lost money, though," said George. "Is there any chance you'll ever see it again?"

"I'm taking it up with Mr Forster's estate," replied the banker. "I always get my money back; I make damned sure of it."

CHAPTER 30

"I don't think I've perspired so much in my entire life!" exclaimed George as we walked along Change Alley toward Cornhill and the Royal Exchange. "That was incredibly stressful, Penelope. Awful! Everything was going swimmingly until I mentioned Forster, but the chap took umbrage at that, didn't he?"

"Yes, it was rather an interesting reaction," I said. "As if he were guilty of something."

"Oh no, he couldn't have done it, could he? He's a professional gentleman."

"Professional gentlemen can be murderers too, George."

"Well, don't ever ask me to do anything like that again. It wore my nerves down completely."

"I didn't ask you, Eliza did."

"But it was your idea."

"No, it wasn't. It was Eliza's."

"I see. I shall blame her, then."

"Please do."

"I fail to understand what the aim of our meeting with him was," said George.

"As James stated, all we needed to do was gauge Chakravarty's reaction."

"He was quite defensive, I thought."

"There you go, so that tells us something."

"Such as what?"

"As I've already suggested, George, it implies that he's hiding something."

"You do realise I'll be bumping into him at the Colthurst Club now? It's all going to be terribly awkward, especially when you don't go ahead with the mortgage. How do I explain that to him?"

"Tell him I'm a flighty woman prone to whimsies and that my mind changes with the weather. Rather typical of my sex, no doubt."

"I'll use that."

James was waiting for us outside the Royal Exchange, so George and I told him how the meeting with Mr Chakravarty had turned out.

"Thank you, Mr Billington-Grieg, for involving yourself in what must seem to you a rather odd setup," said James.

"It does seem rather odd, and I can't say that I enjoyed the experience. I shall take my leave of you both now. I need to get to my office in Austin Friars and work on a government contract with one of my clients. I can only hope that I will be recovered in time for dinner tonight."

"Of course, George," I said. "Will you be dining anywhere nice?"

"The Burlington Hotel. In fact, I wonder if Chakravarty will also be attending. It's a dinner for gentlemen with interests in India."

My heart skipped a beat. "With Mr Lewis Sheridan?" I asked.

"Why, yes. How on earth did you know that, Penelope?"

"Because I need an invitation to that very dinner myself!"

George laughed. "Only chaps allowed, I'm afraid."

"Mr Sheridan is the merchant Mr Forster used to work for," I said.

"Is he indeed?" asked George.

"Yes!"

"Well, he's the chap who gifted me those Chinese vases your sister adores so much."

"You know him well, then?" I asked.

"Only through the business we've conducted with him at the law firm."

"Then you must tell me and Inspector Blakely all about him!"

"Not now, Penelope, I have work to do. And besides, I don't know a great deal about the fellow."

"Oh, how I wish I could be a fly on the wall at tonight's dinner," I said. "Do you think you could —?"

"Ask Sheridan about Forster and gauge his reaction?" replied George. "No, I'm not falling into that trap again, Penelope. Once in a lifetime is more than enough for me."

"Oh, George, *please*!"

"Absolutely not. I have no skill in such matters. I'll leave the prying to you and Inspector Blakely here. I shall be attending this dinner with the full intention of enjoying myself and hopefully acquiring a little business along the way. You'll have to find another opportunity to speak to Mr Sheridan." He doffed his hat and strode away, swinging his cane.

"I shall never understand why my sister married that man," I said to James as we watched George's retreating form.

"In his defence, I suppose we have asked quite a lot of him," he replied. "Not everyone feels comfortable asking awkward questions."

"I'd say few people are."

"Exactly, though for some reason people like you and I enjoy doing so," he said with a smile. "Don't be too hard on your brother-in-law."

"It's not just about today; I don't like him much anyway. I've told Eliza before now that I think his views are old-fashioned and bigoted."

"Let's forget about him for the time being," said James. "What we've learnt this morning is that Mr Chakravarty is rather sensitive to questions about Mr Forster. And he chose not to give much away."

"He doesn't seem to be the sort of man to give much away."

"But thanks to your work this morning I'll make a note that he's someone to bear in mind. It's possible he decided that he would only get his money back from Forster once the man was dead."

"I should think him capable of it, too," I replied. "I cannot muster any fondness for the man."

James laughed.

"What's so funny?"

"It takes rather a lot to impress you, doesn't it?"

"Not really. Just being an honest, likeable person is enough." I looked down at my lavish dress. "It's time for me to go home and change out of this now."

"Don't you want to make the most of your fine dress?" asked James. "We could find a restaurant nearby."

"Much as I'd like to, James, we can't. We discussed this only a matter of days ago. Charlotte wouldn't allow it."

"She needn't find out," he replied quietly. "And besides, there's something I need to tell you that I certainly won't be telling her about."

CHAPTER 31

J ames and I sat at a table in the corner of Leman's Dinner Rooms, which had an elegant corniced ceiling and white tablecloths. He kept looking about him, as if worried we might be seen.

I put on my spectacles so that I could also keep a lookout for anybody who might disapprove of us being seen together. I found myself enjoying the illicit nature of our lunch. It seemed that the closer James' wedding drew the more clandestine our meetings had to become.

The waiter took our order and we were soon dining on potato and leek soup.

"So what is it you needed to tell me?" I asked James. "And why can't you tell Charlotte?"

"She has a delicate disposition."

"Poor Charlotte."

"And she would probably request that I cease my detective work immediately."

"Would she? What would she rather have you do?"

"She says accountancy is a safer profession."

"She's not wrong."

"There are some days when I think that perhaps I should have chosen that path."

"Oh no, James, don't say that. Police work is in your blood, just like your father and grandfather before you."

"You're right, Penny."

"So what is it?"

"Ah, yes. I realise now that telling you while we eat may not be the best idea after all."

"But I need to know now! You can't leave me waiting until we've finished eating to find out, the suspense is too great!"

"I don't think you'll feel like that once you hear what I have to say."

"And that comment simply adds to the suspense! What's happened?"

"I received a letter in the post."

"An unpleasant anonymous one?"

"You've guessed correctly, Penny," he replied with a grin.

"We have experience of those, don't we? They're usually an indication that we're on the right track with an investigation."

"You're right, they're a very good indicator of that. And they provide a useful opportunity to identify the sender."

"Unless it's a hoax letter."

"There is that to consider, though this letter is certainly not a hoax."

"How can you be sure?" I asked.

'Because of one defining factor, which I'll get to shortly."

"So what did it say?"

"It told me in no uncertain terms to stop investigating the deaths of Mr and Mrs Forster."

"Was there a threat explaining what would happen if you didn't?"

"Not explicitly, no."

"From your description so far it sounds like a fairly

innocuous letter, but it seems to be bothering you greatly. Why is that?"

"Are you sure you wish to hear it while you're enjoying your soup?"

"James, my dinner will feel completely ruined if you don't explain to me right away what was so terrible about the letter."

"Something unpleasant was enclosed in the envelope."

I sat poised with my spoon hovering above my soup.

"What exactly?"

"A severed human finger."

My spoon fell into my soup, sending splashes all over my sister's beautiful dress.

"A *finger*?"

James nodded.

I picked up my serviette and wiped at the bodice. "*Whose* finger?" I said.

"I don't know."

"Male? Female?"

"Definitely male."

"And which one?"

"The little finger. I've had a police surgeon analyse it."

"Could he tell you anything more about it?"

"He said that it comes from an adult male who is engaged in laborious work and is likely to be between the ages of twenty and thirty."

"But who? And what has happened to him?" I shuddered. "If he's still alive he's missing at least one finger. They may have cut off more, or they might have killed the chap. Oh, it doesn't bear thinking about! Did the message say the perpetrator would do the same thing to you?"

"I suspect that was the implication."

A sense of dread turned my stomach. I looked down at my soup and realised I had completely lost my appetite.

"These people need to be caught, James. They're extremely dangerous, and they could be anywhere! They could be watching you right now!"

"That is not a comforting thought," said James, glancing around again.

"The Forsters' servants aren't safe," I said, "especially the boy. Anyone who witnessed the attacks on the Forsters must surely be at risk. Can you protect them?"

"Inspector Bowles has housed the boy somewhere. I'll ask him where he's up to with the other servants."

"These people seem well organised and ruthless," I said. "It's frightening. And to think they would send a severed finger to Scotland Yard! That just goes to show how little respect they have for authority."

"Lack of respect for authority is the least of our worries, Penny."

"What is Chief Inspector Cullen doing about it?"

"He's concerned, as is the commissioner. I've told them we need more men on the Forster case."

"It may also have something to do with Alfred Holland."

"It's possible."

"Oh, James!" I shivered. "Aren't you tempted to disappear somewhere and get away from all this?"

"On a personal level I am, but it's my duty to stay here and see this through. Please don't worry about me, Penny. I'm having second thoughts as to whether I should have told you about this."

"Of course you should!"

"Then please don't make me regret it by worrying about me. I'll be fine."

CHAPTER 32

Once home I changed out of Eliza's fancy frock and into my usual skirt and blouse. Then I stepped out in the early evening and took the underground railway from Moorgate to Charing Cross. While I had no hope of attending the dinner at the Burlington Hotel, there was another method I could employ in order to speak to Mr Sheridan. I could approach him as a news reporter.

It was a twenty-minute walk from Charing Cross to the hotel on Cork Street. I stood by the railings, close to the columned entrance, and waited for the dinner attendees to arrive. I had no idea what Mr Sheridan looked like, so I could only hope that my brother-in-law would arrive swiftly and give me a description of the man.

A four-wheeled brougham carriage drew up and the hotel footman helped a frail, white-haired gentleman step out.

"Mr Sheridan?" I said hopefully.

"What?"

"Are you Mr Sheridan, sir?"

"A who?"

The footman shouted my question into the old man's ear and the elderly gentlemen shook his head in reply.

"No, no. Not me."

I watched the footman help him into the hotel and continued the wait.

An expensive landau carriage arrived and a large man with a profusion of grey whiskers stepped out, but he wasn't Mr Sheridan either and didn't seem to like me asking the question.

"No, thank you! Not interested!" he barked.

The third carriage was an elegant, well-polished barouche with an open top. This time I recognised the occupant: a short, round man sitting comfortably at the centre of the large seat. He wore a top hat and spectacles with a high collar, black bow tie and black dinner suit. I felt sure he was the man I had seen with Mr Forster in Margaret Street the morning after Mrs Forster's murder.

"Mr Sheridan?" I ventured as he made a sprightly leap out of his carriage.

"Why, yes. What can I do for you?" He smiled.

I introduced myself. "I've been reporting on the story of Mr and Mrs Forster's death, and I recall seeing you with Mr Forster outside his home after the terrible events that occurred there."

"Yes, I was there to support Augustus. Simply dreadful, it was, and then Augustus himself just a few days later!"

I was pleasantly surprised to find him amenable and talkative.

"Why should anyone wish to do such a thing?"

"I have no idea. Mr and Mrs Forster were good friends, and this is the first evening I have been out since their deaths. In fact, I wasn't planning to come at all, but this is a long-standing appointment and I didn't wish to let Sir Archibald Duffield down as it took him a long time to get all these chaps together. And this event is quite timely as my company is currently brokering a contract with the India Office and there are some influential men here this evening who can smooth the waters where that's concerned. I start to become nervous at this stage of negotiation. Just when you think you have everything in order something comes along to upset proceedings. That's happened to me many times before, and I've learnt not to raise my hopes too quickly about such matters. This contract is one of the most important I've ever negotiated, and for Forster's murder to have taken place at a time like this..." He trailed off for a moment. "Well, it's really one of the worst things that could have happened. It's hard to keep your mind focused on business when it's distracted by grief."

"I can only imagine. What is the contract for?"

"Ah, I'm afraid that must remain top secret for now, Miss Green! I shall be making a public announcement as soon as the ink is dry, but for the time being I'll be fretting about it. Still, this evening should be quite pleasant. I'm determined to enjoy it even though it's been such a difficult week."

"There is some speculation that Mr Forster's financial difficulties may have had something to do with his death," I said.

"I couldn't possibly say. I never involve myself in the affairs of another man, and his money woes are no business of mine unless he were to make a point of discussing them with me. In the case of Mr Forster I had no inkling that his finances were in such a dire state. I knew that his company in Calcutta was struggling with its profits, but I had no idea that he was attempting to shore things up in such a questionable manner. The chap was a friend of mine and I would have happily assisted him had he asked me to. But as no request was forthcoming I assumed he was handling the matter himself, which of course he was, though not particularly efficiently."

"So you believe that this inefficient handling of his affairs may be the reason someone wished him harm?"

"Who can say?" He shrugged. "It's a possibility, Miss Green, but not a certainty. We shall have to leave all that to the detectives."

"Have they approached you yet?"

"Not yet. If I can be of any assistance I should be more than happy to speak to them, although I'm not sure I have much to add. Mr Forster stopped working for my company last summer."

"Why did he leave?"

"He wished to return to England, realising by that point, I think, that his own attempts to run a merchant company had failed. He'd tried and tried, but it wasn't to be."

"Was he happy to be returning to England?"

"Yes, I think so, but disappointed about his company. He was looking forward to living in his father's home."

"Which he wrongly believed he owned himself."

"Did he? Well, I wouldn't know anything about that. It was an extremely pleasant home in a delightful part of London, and then some murdering gang came along that evening and..." He paused. "Everything changed."

Another carriage had pulled up alongside us.

"Penelope?" said a familiar voice. "What on earth are you doing here?"

"George!" I gave my brother-in-law a broad smile. His dinner suit was a fraction too tight.

"You know Mr Billington-Grieg?" asked Mr Sheridan.

"Yes, he's my brother-in-law."

"What a marvellous coincidence!" Mr Sheridan smiled. "Good evening, sir. How are you?"

"I'm very well, thank you, Mr Sheridan. I do apologise if my sister-in-law has been troubling you."

"Not at all! I'm enjoying our conversation. She's been writing about old Forster for the *Morning Express.*"

George gave me a look which suggested he had seen enough of me for one day.

"Allow Mr Sheridan to enjoy his evening now, Penelope. He doesn't wish to be pestered by the press during his important engagement."

"Oh, I don't mind at all," replied Mr Sheridan. "I think it quite charming that this young lady is showing such concern for the fellow. I really do find it worrying that something so barbaric could happen to a couple as pleasant as the Forsters. Doesn't it bother you, Mr Billington-Grieg?"

"Yes, it does. I think it bothers many of us. I, for one, won't feel safe until the culprits are apprehended."

"Mr Alfred Holland," I interjected. "Does that name mean anything to you, Mr Sheridan?"

He gave me a puzzled look. "Holland? Alfred? No. Why?"

"He was shot dead in an opium den."

"No, I don't recall hearing anything about him. What a terrible way to go."

"He had also worked in India as an opium agent in Ghazipur."

"Really?" Mr Sheridan cocked his head to one side with interest.

"But you have heard nothing about him? I'm trying to find out whether he and Mr Forster knew each other."

"No, I don't recognise the name. In an opium den, you say? And he was an opium agent in India? It sounds as though he jumped out of the frying pan and into the fire."

"Penelope, Mr Sheridan and I must go and enjoy our evening now," said George. "Do please excuse us."

He rested a hand on Mr Sheridan's shoulder and guided him toward the door of the Burlington Hotel.

"Thank you very much for speaking to me, Mr Sheridan!" I called after them.

He raised a hand in acknowledgement and then they were gone.

CHAPTER 33

"I hope you don't mind my saying so, Penny, but you look rather pale this morning. Is everything all right?" whispered Mr Edwards.

"Oh, I'm just a little tired. Thank you for asking, Francis."

In truth, I had slept badly the previous night. Every time I had closed my eyes the image of a severed finger had swum before them. I had never felt so concerned for James before. Someone who was willing to cut off another person's finger had to be extremely barbaric. How could James, or any police officer, defend himself against something so inhuman?

"Are you sure it's just tiredness?" asked Francis. "You seem worried about something."

"It's these murders. They're so dreadful." I shuddered.

Francis sighed. "I wonder if there might be some merit in you writing for a different type of publication," he said.

"A different one? No, I couldn't possibly. I like writing for the *Morning Express*."

"But it means you have to encounter such gruesome stories, Penny. Meanwhile, there are many excellent periodi-

cals you could write far more pleasant stories for. The *Ladies'
Scholarly Repository* magazine, for example."

"I wrote articles for them during my brief hiatus in
employment at the paper last year."

"I don't recall that. What happened?"

"It was before we were acquainted with one another. I
criticised the work of Chief Inspector Cullen on a case and
he complained to the commissioner, who just happens to be
the cousin of my editor, Mr Sherman."

"Oh dear."

"I won't go into the detail now, but suffice to say that
Chief Inspector Cullen and I have never worked well
together. I have had some experience writing for other publi-
cations, but I found them all rather dull, I'm afraid."

"But surely dull is preferable to gruesome?"

"If you think about it sensibly I suppose it should be, but
there's a little more excitement with the gruesome stores,
isn't there?"

"Excitement, but also danger."

I sighed. "Yes, there is danger, but I feel I can do something with these stories. When I think about the cases I've
reported on, and particularly the ones I've worked on with
Inspector Blakely, I feel that I've helped in bringing the
perpetrators to justice. There's no chance of doing that when
you're writing about French authors for the *Ladies' Scholarly
Repository*. I know that because I've already done it."

"You have your father's sense of adventure," said Francis
with a smile.

"Yes, I think I do."

"But you must also be careful."

"I'm always careful, Francis."

"Your visit to the opium den worried me."

"It mustn't; I was absolutely fine. If there's anyone we
should be concerned about it's Inspector Blakely."

"Why him?" Francis frowned.

"It seems he has some particularly nasty people to deal with at the moment. I'm worried for him."

"Oh, you shouldn't worry about him. He can look after himself."

"I hope so."

"It's not unusual for the police to put themselves at risk in the course of their work. And don't forget that they're accustomed to dealing with nasty people."

"I know. And I know that I shouldn't be concerned."

"So why are you?" There was something unusually sharp in his tone.

"He's an acquaintance I've worked with for some time, and it's natural for me to worry about the people I know and care about. I would be just as concerned about my sister, and about you."

"Would you?"

"Yes, though your work isn't quite as dangerous as the work James does, unless a particularly heavy tome were to slip off a shelf and fall on your head!"

I had intended this comment to be light-hearted, but Francis' expression darkened.

"I shall go and see if any readers are at the desk awaiting assistance," he said.

"Is something wrong, Francis?"

"No, not at all. I'll leave you to your work, Penny."

CHAPTER 34

"So Inspector Blakely had you doing a spot of work for him, did he?" asked Edgar. "I heard about your meeting with Mr Chakravarty."

"I'm not sure what it achieved," I replied. "In fact, Mr Chakravarty is probably wondering why he hasn't heard from me about his mortgage offer."

"I wonder why Blakely didn't ask me," said Edgar. "I'm the one who's writing about the Forster murders."

Frederick chuckled. "That chap wouldn't have been fooled by you for a moment, Fish. There's no subtlety in you whatsoever."

"You don't mince your words, do you, Potter?" retorted Edgar. "I'd have been a darn sight more convincing than you. Your only attempt at undercover work was as a customer at a pie shop."

"And I played the part well."

"Not too difficult given your generous girth."

"Better a wide girth than a sheep's head."

"Oh, I have a sheep's head, do I? Well, I think you should go and boil your head, and —"

"Edgar! Frederick!" I interrupted. "There is no need to argue like schoolboys."

"He started it!" said Edgar.

"What's all this noise about?" asked Mr Sherman as he marched into the newsroom, leaving the door to slam behind him once again.

"Fish told me to boil my head, sir!" protested Frederick.

"Not a bad idea," replied Mr Sherman. "Where have you got to with the Forster story, Fish?"

"It's going reasonably well, though for some reason Blakely of the Yard asked Miss Green to do some work for him on it."

"Is that so?" asked Mr Sherman, turning to me.

I explained what had happened at the mortgage interview with Mr Chakravarty.

"I can't say that I like Blakely dragging you off on a whim to undertake investigations for him," said Mr Sherman with a scowl.

"I wasn't doing his work for him, I was merely assisting with a task he was unable to carry out himself."

"But you're not even working on the Forster story. I object to his using my staff in this manner; it's akin to my asking a detective from Scotland Yard to report on a news story."

"You should do that, sir," said Edgar.

"I'm sorry?"

"You should ask a police officer to write a news story for the *Morning Express*."

"What a ridiculous suggestion, Fish. It's difficult enough getting my own staff to do what they're supposed to."

Edgar's face coloured.

"What's your update on the Forsters?"

"The police are looking for the gang which broke into their home."

"That's the same update we had yesterday. Anything else?"

"It'll take a while for them to find the culprits, sir."

"I'm sure it will. Why don't you get down to D or C Division, or the Yard, and start asking more questions? I'm tired of you resting on your laurels in the newsroom. Police officers and the like need harassing. Miss Green may be guilty of carrying out work that is not strictly her own, but there's no denying she's out there giving chaps a difficult time until they answer her questions."

"That sort of thing comes more naturally to the fairer sex," replied Edgar.

"No more excuses, Fish. Get out of my sight and bring back something worth printing. Now, where have you got to on the Franchise Bill story, Miss Green?"

I was just about to reply when I heard a tentative knock at the door.

"Come in!" barked Mr Sherman.

The door opened slightly and in stepped Emma Holland.

"Can I help you, young lady?" asked the editor.

"My apologies for interrupting, sir, but I'd like to speak to Miss Green if I may."

"Is it regarding a story she's working on?"

"It is, sir," I replied, standing to my feet. "This is Emma Holland, the sister of Alfred Holland."

"The chap from the opium den? Please accept my condolences, Miss Holland."

"Thank you."

"You don't have long, Miss Green. I need a thousand words on Lord Salisbury and the Franchise Bill by deadline today."

Mr Sherman left the room and I moved some papers to make space for Emma to sit down. I introduced her to Edgar and Frederick, who greeted the young woman and then regarded her in respectful silence.

"Do you mind talking here in the newsroom?" I asked. "Or would you rather chat somewhere more private?"

Emma looked around. "Here should be fine."

"Don't worry," said Edgar, "I'm just on my way out. I was ordered away by the editor."

"I'll be on my way too," said Frederick. "I get nervous whenever I find myself outnumbered by women."

Once the two men had left the room Emma pulled out a book from the bag she had been carrying.

"I didn't intend to frighten your colleagues away, Penny."

"Don't worry about them. They have work to be getting on with."

"This is Alfred's diary from last year," said Emma, laying it on the table. I could see that she had marked several passages with pieces of scarlet ribbon. She turned to one of them.

"Alfred describes how he caught one of his colleagues stealing opium."

"What happened?"

"Do you recall me telling you that his job was to weigh the pots of opium when they arrived at the Ghazipur factory?"

I nodded in reply.

"As I said before, it was considered to be an important job because opium is so precious. The natives were keen to get their hands on it and had to be regularly checked to make sure they weren't stealing the product. Apparently, even fragments of storage pots were highly sought-after in the hope that there might be opium residue on them."

She turned the pages and pointed to a diary entry written in May of the previous year. "Alfred writes here that he discovered some of the papers were being altered. The opium was weighed in each district after it was harvested and then again on arrival at the factory. Alfred noticed that one of his colleagues was altering numbers on the form. It was quite a subtle change, with a single number being written on top of the original, but over the course of a few weeks he noticed these occasional corrections and the colleague's behaviour became suspicious at times."

"Did Alfred explain how?"

"It seems there was a nervousness about him. And on one occasion a bunch of keys went missing, only for this man to find them again. Alfred suspected he was behind the disappearance all along. You're welcome to read about it here; he documents the whole affair."

"Does he mention whether he reported his concerns to anyone?"

"Oh yes, he did. In the end he told someone senior and his colleague was dismissed."

"I imagine his colleague would have been quite angry about that."

"He probably was, but he was sent back to Britain so it's unlikely that Alfred ever saw him again."

"Did he name the colleague in his diaries?"

"He did, but I would need to look it up again as I can't quite remember it." She leafed through the pages. "Oh, here we are. Mawson. Charles Mawson."

CHAPTER 35

"I recall a particularly difficult Atlantic crossing in 1880 when the sea was boiling with foam," said Mr Fox-Stirling as we dined on roast chicken at Eliza's home. My sister had invited the plant-hunter and his wife for dinner to discuss the arrangements for his search.

"While one side of the ship was down in the water the other was thirty feet up in the air," he continued. "And then the side which had been thirty feet up in the air would swiftly descend and the water would sweep across the upper decks with a great splash and a roar."

Mr Fox-Stirling was a stocky, fair-haired man of about fifty. He had dominated the evening's conversation with his tales of adventure.

"Gosh, how terrifying," said Francis.

Mr Fox-Stirling shrugged nonchalantly. "One grows perfectly accustomed to it after five days and five nights."

George was present but had barely acknowledged my presence. I detected some sulkiness on his part for my appearance outside the Burlington Hotel.

"You must have suffered terrible seasickness, Mr Fox-Stirling," said Eliza.

"The secret to overcoming seasickness is to maintain a full stomach. I ate like a horse throughout the storm and suffered no ill-effects whatsoever."

"But how on earth can you even sit down to dinner when the ship is pitching about like that?" asked his silver-haired wife Margaret.

"There are ways and means, my dear. Batons are screwed onto the table, between which dinner plates are wedged with the assistance of rolled-up napkins. And the chairs are screwed to the floor. With such preparations a chap can enjoy a perfectly decent meal. My only complaint is that we had to endure pea soup three times a week."

"I think the chef did well to serve any soup at all," commented Eliza.

"Once the storm had passed the ocean was a thing of pure beauty," said Mr Fox-Stirling. "I sat on the deck smoking and watching the flying fish as the sun set."

"Flying fish?" said George. "Do they have wings?"

"Yes."

"How ridiculous!"

"It's not ridiculous, George," said Eliza, embarrassed by her husband's outburst.

"They're not *wings* as such," said Francis. "They're wing-like fins that enable the fish to glide through the air for about a hundred yards, perhaps even two hundred. They propel themselves out of the water with their tails."

"How fascinating," said Eliza. "I might have guessed you would know all about them, Francis." She gave him a warm smile. "Is there anything you don't know?"

"There must be plenty of things, I'm sure," George said gruffly.

I had been nodding at certain intervals in the conversation to feign interest, but I couldn't stop my mind dwelling on what Emma Holland had told me earlier that day. *Why had Charles Mawson failed to tell me about his time in Ghazipur?* I had asked whether he knew Alfred Holland and he had denied it. *Was he trying to hide something, or was this an innocent misunderstanding?*

"Storms threatened again as we arrived in Bridgetown on the island of Barbados," continued Mr Fox-Stirling. "However, we were safely ashore by the time they arrived. Delightful little pink houses they have there, and everyone was pestering me to buy their wares: interesting pieces of coral, lacework, jewellery and ornaments made from tortoiseshell."

I stifled a yawn and picked at the food on my plate, considering how resentful Charles Mawson must have been when Alfred Holland reported him. *Or was it possible that Charles Mawson hadn't known who had done so?* I realised I should have asked Emma for a loan of her brother's diary so I could read the account for myself. I made a note to visit her and ask if that would be possible.

"That was a first-rate piece of chicken," said Francis as he laid his knife and fork down neatly on his plate.

"Thank you, Francis!" replied my sister with a wide smile.

"It's what Napoleon had for breakfast every morning," said Mr Fox-Stirling. "Did you know that?"

We all shook our heads.

"There's a wonderful story behind it," he said. "Apparently, Napoleon would rise at any time between eight and eleven in the morning. By all accounts he wasn't a man of strict routine. He enjoyed roast chicken for breakfast each day, and this set him off thinking. He summoned his cook and asked, 'Why is it that no matter what time I breakfast the chicken is always perfectly roasted?' The cook replied, 'It's quite easy, sire. I simply put a chicken on to roast every quarter of an hour, and then there is always one which is perfectly cooked for you!"' Mr Fox-Stirling slapped the table with great mirth and there was laughter all around.

"Who ate the other chickens?" I asked.

"Napoleon's men, I suppose," replied Mr Fox-Stirling. "Or the dogs."

"Or the pigs," suggested George as the servants cleared away our plates.

"I should tell you, Mr Fox-Stirling, that I am reading volume four of *Travels, Trials and Adventure in the Andes*," said Francis.

"Are you indeed?" The explorer seemed surprised to hear that someone was reading his work. "Good man. That's most pleasing to hear."

"I'm enjoying the books immensely, and while we're between courses I should like to show you the map I've drawn." Francis unfolded the drawing he had shown me and Eliza during our boating trip. "Savanilla is at the top here, which is where you will disembark, I believe?"

"Not disembark, exactly. The ship anchors there in the delta of the River Magdalena, then a tender of some sort – usually a rickety form of marine architecture – takes the traveller on to Barranquilla."

"Ah yes. I've marked that here on the map."

Francis went on to explain the route and I watched as Mr Fox-Stirling pointedly lost interest in what he was saying. Francis also noticed and eventually tailed off.

"Maps have their uses, but I've done this before," said Mr Fox-Stirling once Francis had finished speaking.

"Francis is contributing a significant sum of money to the expedition, Mr Fox-Stirling," said Eliza.

"And money is all I require!" he replied. "I have no need for maps of a place I have been to before."

Francis looked crestfallen. "I hope you don't consider my

map to be an interference with your plans, Mr Fox-Stirling," he said. "I'm merely taking an interest in the search for Mr Green. Perhaps I can be of some assistance."

"There is no need for assistance," the explorer replied. "I know what I'm doing."

I wanted to add that he had travelled the route before and failed to find Father but decided that such a comment would only inflame the situation.

"Given the fact that Francis is contributing so generously to the search I do feel that he should have some influence as to how it is conducted," ventured Eliza tactfully.

"I appreciate the offer, Mrs Billington-Grieg, but as I say, there's no need! A chap usually hands over his money and allows me to get on with it. He knows his job and I know mine."

The room fell silent for a moment and the tension made my toes curl. I glanced at Francis' disappointed expression and wondered whether there was a risk that he might withdraw his donation.

"Darling," ventured Mrs Fox-Stirling, "don't you think that when a patron wishes to —"

"I'm fifty-three, Margaret, and I've been doing this for thirty years. I've been shot by poisoned arrows, I've saved myself from river rapids and I've been sent into a three-day trance by the juice of the Banisteriopsis Caapi vine. I don't require some young fellow to draw me a map!"

Another silence followed, and although Eliza's face remained calm I detected a slight panic in her eyes as she considered how best to calm the situation. George studied the bottom of his wine glass.

"We have plenty of time before the expedition to Colombia departs," said Eliza, breaking the silence. "Your experience and dedication is certainly respected, Mr Fox-Stirling, and likewise, Francis, your determination that the search will have a positive outcome is truly honourable. I'm certain that we can reach an agreement to marry the two —"

"I prefer not to marry things together, Mrs Billington-Grieg. I'm not a man of compromise," retorted Mr Fox-Stirling. "Call me old-fashioned if you will, but every trip I've undertaken has been done my way. That's the way it works."

The plant-hunter had bored me with his tales and his arrogance was almost too much to bear. I felt so sorry for Francis at having his well-drawn map rejected.

"It didn't work last time, though, did it?" I said. "You didn't find our father."

Everyone turned to stare at me and Mr Fox-Stirling's expression grew stormy.

"I did my best, Miss Green," he said stonily.

"Did you? You didn't even have a Spanish translator with you."

"My Spanish is perfectly —"

"I'm sorry, Mr Fox-Stirling, but it's not," I interrupted. "You admitted yourself when Eliza and I recently met with you that you didn't understand what the people in El Charqito were saying to you. They could have been telling you about Father and you would have been none the wiser."

"Penelope," warned Eliza. "I don't wish the discussion to escalate into an argument."

"I think it already has," said Francis.

Mrs Fox-Stirling looked embarrassed as her husband quickly drained his glass of wine.

Eliza summoned her housekeeper. "Skip the game course, please, and move on to pudding."

CHAPTER 36

"That didn't go terribly well, did it?" said Francis as he escorted me home in a hansom cab.

It was a warm evening and the gas lamps along Oxford Street twinkled as we passed. Although the seat was small we managed to sit at a respectful distance from one another.

"Not well at all," I replied. "Mr Fox-Stirling seems to resent any assistance with his search whatsoever."

"I used to be in awe of the chap," said Francis, "and I have enjoyed reading his books, but he was rather rude this evening, wasn't he?"

"He was, and there was no call for it, especially when you're bearing much of the cost! The man is far too arrogant for his own good. I wish someone else could look for Father instead."

"There aren't many men who would undertake the task," replied Francis. "It's frustrating as I so wish for you and your dear sister to find out once and for all what has happened to your father, and Mr Fox-Stirling isn't especially helpful. He's so insistent on doing things his own way."

"Which I don't believe is necessarily the best way," I said.

"Though he does have a lot of experience."

"Yes, but does he really possess the skills needed to find Father?"

"I had to hide my laughter when you commented quite directly that he had failed in his last mission."

"It had to be said, didn't it? There he was sitting there convinced that his way was the correct one, yet he has nothing to back the theory up with! It was rather rude of me, and now I'm worried my comments may have ruined any chance we had of him looking for Father. Eliza will scold me about it when I see her next, I know it. But I struggled to sit there and listen to him being so rude to you, and so convinced of his own methods!"

"I don't think you've ruined anything, Penny. I'm sure he will still carry out the search. The man relies on people to pay his way on these expeditions."

"In which case you'd think he would be more polite and considerate, wouldn't you?"

"Yes, you would."

"I don't want him out there looking for Father, I really don't. Ideally, I would go there myself, but I know that travel in such places is considered too dangerous for a woman."

"And we would all forbid you, Penny. You couldn't possibly put yourself at risk in such a way."

"I cannot see it being anyone's right to forbid me, but I know you, Eliza and James would nag me so much about any attempt to travel there that it would make life quite unbearable."

Francis laughed. "It's only because we care about you, Penny, besides which there is no cause for you to travel there. All you need do is find someone more trustworthy to carry out the search."

"But who exactly? You've already mentioned that not many men would be willing to undertake the task."

"Perhaps we simply need to ask around."

"We must ensure that Eliza is happy pursuing someone else first. For some time now she has been quite convinced that Mr Fox-Stirling is the only chap for the job."

"Perhaps she'll be happier to consider someone else after this evening's altercation?"

"It's possible, or perhaps she'll blame me for riling him instead. I don't think I can attend any more of these dinners; I really don't like the man. You have every right to withdraw your funding for the search, you know. He had no cause to speak to you in that manner."

"No, I want to ensure that the search goes ahead. That's the most important thing. You've waited long enough for news of your father."

"You don't have to do this, Francis. Why are you donating your money?" I turned to look at him in the dim light.

"I have an inheritance which is merely accruing interest in the bank, and I have few outgoings and a regular income from my work. At the moment the money is surplus to my needs."

"But there are many other good causes which would benefit from your money. I realise you have decided you may not need it, but there are plenty of worthy institutions that might, such as orphanages and hospitals for the poor."

"I consider your father an admirable man, Penny, and I cannot be content knowing that you and Eliza have been unaware of his whereabouts for nine years now. I want to do whatever I can to help you find out what has happened to him, not least so that you can finish your book about his life."

"It goes way above and beyond your duty, Francis."

He turned to look at me, the light from the gas lamps flickering on the lenses of his spectacles. "I hold you in very high regard, Penny. Surely you must have realised that by now? You're an honest and truthful woman, and I find you highly interesting and amusing. I enjoy your company."

I held my breath, terrified that a proposal was forthcoming.

"I have never met anyone quite like you," he continued, "though I think I may be rather foolish to hope that you might ever hold more than a passing interest in me."

"It is more than a passing interest, Francis," I said cautiously, wishing to reassure him, yet wary of encouraging him to think that I loved him.

"Really?" he asked.

"I consider you a very honourable man."

"Just honourable?"

"And clever, too, with a wealth of knowledge on all manner of subjects, which is not only useful but entertaining."

"Thank you."

"And one day you will make someone a wonderful husband."

"Someone?"

"Yes, someone."

"Not you, Penny?"

My heart thudded heavily in my chest and I turned to look at the road ahead.

"Oh, Francis, you know that I have no intention of marrying."

A long pause followed and my teeth clenched. *Had I said the wrong thing? Was I a fool for being so dismissive of marriage when a man who could potentially become my husband was sitting right beside me at this very moment?*

I felt the slightest mention that I might be interested in marrying would bring forth an immediate proposal. Up to this moment he had been carefully testing my reaction to see whether it was worth his while asking me. I appreciated the subtlety and sensitivity of his approach.

Perhaps if I had never met James I would have been encouraging Francis to propose, I mused. I knew that I had no hope of ever marrying James, but it would have been disingenuous to encourage Francis when I knew that it was James I loved.

"You deserve someone better than me," I said.

"Nonsense, Penny!" said Francis. "In my eyes there is no finer lady than yourself."

"Oh, don't say that, it simply isn't true!"

"But it is, and I won't let you tell me otherwise. I cannot deny that I'm disappointed you have no interest in marriage. Is there anything that might change your mind?"

"I don't know. The truth is that I like my life for what it already is. I may live in a garret room with my cat, but that suits me. I can't imagine owning a large house filled with staff and children. My sister has all that, yet she seems to me to have no freedom. She strives for it, of course, with her work on women's rights, and she turns heads when she rides her bicycle, but that's all she can do. As the wife of a lawyer there are expectations and she simply has to conform. At the present time my lifestyle allows me great freedom."

"But what happens twenty years from now when you may feel too old and tired to work? Perhaps you will be in need of companionship then. Would you not like children to look after you in your dotage?"

"That's certainly not a reason to have children, Francis, though perhaps I am a little foolish for refusing to consider what my life will be like twenty years from now."

"Milton Street!" the cabman shouted down into the cab through the hatch.

Francis sighed. "Perhaps you will change your mind in time, Penny. There's no hurry, is there?"

"No, I don't suppose there is."

"I should be happy to wait," he said.

I turned to face him in the gloom. "No, Francis, you mustn't wait for me to decide whether I wish to marry or not! I've already told you there are better ladies than I —"

"I refuse to believe it. I'm in love with you, Penny! I have been in love with you since you first asked me to help with that map of Colombia in the reading room!"

CHAPTER 37

I stared at Francis' shadowed face with no idea how to respond.

"I don't expect you to love me in return," he continued. "I may as well try to influence the passage of the stars. But I suspect that my affection is no secret to you, so you must surely have had some time to consider your feelings for me."

"A little," I replied. I sat there motionless, my mouth dry.

"I must admit that I thought all was lost when I saw Blakely dishonouring you in the hallway of your sister's home. I could protect you from such advances, Penny. That man will break the heart of his wife and yours as well if you allowed him to."

"I'm sure he wouldn't —"

"There's no need to defend him, Penny. While I respect his willingness to apologise for his misdemeanour he is clearly reckless when it comes to women's hearts. I'm not like that, but I shan't make a fool of myself and propose unless I can be sure that you love me in return. I'm encouraged, however, that you think me honourable, and that I might make someone a good husband one day."

"Yes, I feel sure that you would."

There was a pause, as if he were waiting for me to say more. Perhaps he hoped for an expression of affection in return. I felt a strong pang of guilt that I was unable to give him any sort of assurance.

Francis sighed. "I suppose we've really only known each other for a short while, haven't we? Perhaps I have been rather too hasty in expressing my affections, and I realise that it may be inappropriate to do so, sitting shoulder to shoulder and unaccompanied in this cab. It's not really the way I like to conduct myself. The very last thing I should want you to think of me, Penny, is that I'm taking advantage of this time alone with you."

"Oh no, Francis, I would never think that."

The hatch in the roof opened again and the cabman shouted down through it.

"You gettin' out 'ere or what? Am I goin' ter be sittin' 'ere all night waitin' for you lovebirds ter finish with yer kissin' an' cuddlin'?"

"Just one moment, please," said Francis tersely.

The hatch slammed shut again.

"I must admit that I feel rather unguarded now that I have expressed my true feelings for you, Penny," he said. "In fact, I feel rather foolish."

"No, you mustn't!" I replied. "Please don't feel foolish! I feel that your words have been extremely complimentary, and I am deeply flattered by the warmth of your affection."

"Perhaps now that I have told you how I feel this will lead to further consideration on your part. Maybe my words will have altered your thoughts on the matter just a touch. For some reason, and I know not what it might be, I felt it appropriate to speak this evening. Perhaps I shall regret my actions in the morning."

"I wouldn't want you to regret it, Francis; there really is no need." I wished I could tell him what he wanted to hear in order to ease his discomfort, but I had too much respect for him to give any false hope.

"Please excuse me, Penny, I have talked long enough. Although I could continue I don't feel that I can add any deeper meaning to my sentiment, so I shall stop there. My work is done. *Sic vita est*."

"What does that mean?"

"Thus is life."

"How profound," I replied.

"Then perhaps I should say *quidquid latine dictum sit, altum videtur*."

"And what does that mean?"

"Anything said in Latin sounds profound."

"That's the meaning?" I said, laughing. "I shall use that phrase myself."

"You should, Penny. Good night."

My mind was too busy to sleep that night.

Mr Edwards had caused quite a stir that evening: both at the dinner and then afterwards when he had accompanied me home in the cab. Although it had been obvious that he cared for me beforehand, I had still been surprised by his declaration of love. I searched my heart, willing to find some reciprocation deep down, but I could find none. *Perhaps I was still too shocked. Perhaps if I slept I would wake in the morning and discover that I could love him in return.*

It made no sense that I should love a man who was to marry someone else. I knew that I could never marry James; therefore, it made more sense to consider the man who was willing to become my husband. *Should I make that choice or continue to live my life alone?*

I also had concerns about the search for Father. *What if Francis felt so upset about the way Mr Fox-Stirling had spoken to him that he withdrew his donation?* He had assured me that he wouldn't, but after a spot of reflection he had every right to do so. I felt angry at Fox-Stirling for being so rude. He did not deserve the money we were raising to pay him. I truly disliked him for his arrogance and sense of superiority.

Added to all this, the revelation that Alfred Holland had reported Charles Mawson for altering official forms was quite shocking. *Surely it gave Mr Mawson a motive for revenge.* Mawson was the only connection I had made between Holland and the Forsters. I would have to inform the police of the development.

There was such a great deal spinning about in my head that I wanted to talk it over with someone who might understand, but the only person who sprang to mind was James. *Was Francis right about him? Would James have willingly broken my heart? He had kissed me while he was engaged to Charlotte. What did that tell me about his character?* I had told myself that the strength of feeling between us meant he had been unable to help himself, but perhaps I was wrong. *Had he taken advantage of me?*

My mattress felt uncomfortable. I tried to find a cool section of pillow to rest my cheek on, but everything felt hot and stifling. I got up, opened the curtains and pulled up the sash window, allowing the cool night air to flow into the room.

CHAPTER 38

The following morning I travelled by underground railway to Charing Cross and stopped off at a coffee stall on the Embankment. I sipped my coffee overlooking the misty river between Charing Cross Pier and the floating Cleopatra Swimming Bath. My head felt tired and heavy, but I was excited by the prospect of telling James about the connection I had made between Alfred Holland and the Forsters.

I walked the short distance to Scotland Yard, hoping that Chief Inspector Cullen wouldn't be at his desk. Unfortunately, James was nowhere to be seen when I arrived at his office, while the chief inspector was seated nearby. He looked at me over his silver-rimmed spectacles.

"What is it this time, Miss Green?"

"I've come to speak to Inspector Blakely about a link I've established between two murder cases."

"Still determined to act the lady detective, are you?"

"It was a connection I happened upon by chance, and it would be remiss of me not to inform the police of the development."

The chief inspector laid down his pen and sat back in his chair.

"Which murders are we talking about, then? I'll hazard a guess that the deaths of Mr and Mrs Forster are involved."

"Yes, and the death of Alfred Holland. It transpires that they all knew the same man."

"Did they now? And who is this gentleman?"

"His name is Charles Mawson and he works at the India Office, just a few hundred yards from where we stand now."

"And who is Charles Mawson?"

"He's a gentleman who worked in India and knew the Forsters socially from when they lived in Calcutta. I've discovered that he worked at the opium factory in Ghazipur and Alfred Holland reported him for altering information on the forms."

Chief Inspector Cullen lowered his brow. "Did he now? And how do you know all this?"

"I've been speaking with Alfred Holland's sister."

"What's her name?"

"I plan to give James all the details."

"I see. And how has Alfred Holland's sister stumbled upon this information?"

"Alfred left a diary."

Chief Inspector Cullen raised an eyebrow and took a deep puff on his pipe. "This is the chap who was shot in the opium den, is it?"

"Yes."

"He kept a diary while working in India that described how he reported a colleague for altering forms?"

I nodded.

"Presumably this colleague was altering forms because opium was being stolen," said Cullen.

"I imagine so, yes."

"So there's a written record of this, which Holland's sister is in possession of, and this chap who was reported works at the India Office in Whitehall?"

"Yes, I believe he was sent back to Britain after Mr Holland reported him."

"Yet he's somehow managed to retain employment with the India Office," commented Cullen. "How interesting. And this same chap was a friend of the Forsters. A good friend of theirs, would you say?"

"Yes. I first met him after the murder of Mrs Forster, when he was trying to find Mr Forster. When I spoke to him after Mr Forster's death it transpired that he had recently spent an evening with him at the East India Club."

"Very interesting indeed. Ah, Blakely."

I turned to see James entering the room. He greeted me with a warm smile.

"Go and have a chat with this ink-slinger somewhere private," instructed Chief Inspector Cullen. "I never thought I'd find myself saying this, but she has some interesting news for you. Make a note of everything she says, then report back to me."

"Of course, sir."

"Chief Inspector Cullen is finally taking an interest," I said as we walked out of Scotland Yard, "but we don't want him interfering, do we?"

We crossed Northumberland Avenue.

"Cullen's all right, really," replied James.

"Is he?"

"He can be abrupt, and he's rather old-fashioned, but he worked with my father for a while and had his respect."

"Is that why you're loyal to him?"

"I have to be loyal to some degree; he's my superior."

I gave an empty laugh. "In rank, perhaps, but in no other way."

"It's the way the police force is, Penny. And although he is often rude and cantankerous, he's a good detective."

"I suppose I'll have to trust you on that front. I can't say I have ever got along well with him."

"He's traditional, and when he encounters women who have a profession he struggles with the idea."

"Poor Chief Inspector Cullen," I mocked.

"I don't like the way he speaks to you," said James, "but at the same time I must respect him as a senior detective. My father always spoke highly of him."

I chose not to argue. "Why would he want you to report back to him everything I'm about to tell you?" I asked.

"The Forster murders have shocked London. It's an important case, and it would seem that you have uncovered some interesting information. Cullen's extremely concerned about the severed finger and has warned me to tread carefully, but I cannot allow such threats to stop me from doing my job, and I'm looking forward to hearing all about Alfred Holland's diary. Have you eaten breakfast yet? There's a decent eatery here on Northumberland Street."

We sat at a small table covered with a gingham tablecloth. A waiter took our order, and as we waited for our food to arrive I told James about Emma Holland and Charles Mawson. I tried my best not to become distracted by how handsome James looked. He was wearing a dark grey suit, and there was a gold tiepin topped with a star pinned to his blue tie.

"We need to see the diary," he said when I had finished. "Do you think Emma Holland would lend it to me?"

"I should think so. She'll be extremely encouraged to hear

that Scotland Yard is investigating her brother's death. She is most frustrated by the lack of progress so far."

"Before we get too excited by this development we need to establish that Charles Mawson who works at the India Office is the same Charles Mawson that Holland refers to in his diary."

The waiter brought over toast, eggs, bacon and a pot of tea.

"I'm sure it must be the same Charles Mawson," I replied, "and it would be easy to ask him given that he works so close by."

"Where can we find Mr Holland's sister and the diaries?"

"She lives in Euston. I've visited her there, so I know which house is hers."

"Have you shared this new information with Inspector Reeves?"

"No, not yet. I only spoke to Emma Holland yesterday and then the evening was taken up with a rather uncomfortable dinner at my sister's house."

"Oh dear, what happened?"

I told James about the altercation between Mr Fox-Stirling and Mr Edwards.

"That sounds very awkward indeed."

"I'm quite put off by the thought of Mr Fox-Stirling searching for Father," I said. "I can't say that I was particularly fond of him to start with, but seeing how rude he was to Francis was truly awful."

"It doesn't sound as though he deserves your patronage," said James.

"He doesn't, and I am determined to find someone else to look for Father. There must be plenty of other men who would be willing to go."

"I'm sure there will be; another plant-hunter, perhaps, or an explorer of some sort. You could try the Royal Geographical Society, or maybe the Royal Botanical Society could recommend someone."

"Good idea, I'll suggest that to Francis. He is funding most of the trip, after all."

"He thinks highly of you, doesn't he?"

I felt my face colour. "I don't know."

"I can see that he does. I wonder whether he'll propose."

"I have no wish to talk about that now," I snapped, still bristling from my discussion with Francis the night before.

James seemed surprised by my reaction. "I'm sorry, I didn't mean to discuss something so personal."

"I'd like to concentrate on these murder cases for the time being," I replied, keen to stay away from the topic of marriage. "Once you have confirmed that Charles Mawson links Holland and the Forsters this has to become one case."

"Which is what you suspected right from the beginning, isn't it?" He smiled.

"I'm always right."

"I think you are."

'I was joking; I'm nothing of the kind. In fact, most of the time I'm quite sure that I'm making all the wrong decisions."

"With regard to what?"

"Nothing I wish to discuss at the moment."

"Are you all right, Penny?"

"I'm fine. I feel a little tired after that strange evening, but I'm excited by the possible progress in these murder cases."

"Let's go and confirm it with this Mawson chap. Have you the time to accompany me?"

"I have indeed."

CHAPTER 39

"Inspector James Blakely of Scotland Yard," said James to the uniformed man at the India Office, flashing him his warrant card. "I'd like to see Mr Charles Mawson, please."

As the man went off to find him, James glanced around at the marble columns and gilded decoration. "What an impressive place this is," he whispered.

"If you're lucky Mr Mawson will give you a tour," I replied.

The uniformed man returned moments later with a slightly puzzled Mr Mawson in tow. He smiled at me, then glanced warily at James.

"How can I help you, Inspector?" he asked.

"Mr Mawson, I recall seeing you outside Mr and Mrs Forster's home shortly after Mrs Forster was tragically attacked. Is that right?" asked James.

His watery grey eyes darted between my face and James'.

"Yes, that's right, I was there. What's this about?"

"Is there somewhere more private we can talk?"

Mr Mawson glanced nervously around him. "I suppose

the council chamber might be free, we could go in there. Will this take long?"

"Hopefully not," replied James.

We followed Mr Mawson along an elaborately decorated corridor and into a large room with an impressive corniced ceiling. A large shiny table stood at the centre of the room, and full-length portraits of statesmen hung either side of the marble fireplace.

"Do please take a seat, Inspector. Miss Green."

I noticed Mawson's hand shaking as he gestured toward the chairs. *Was he worried that he had been found out?*

"I believe you spent some time in India, Mr Mawson," said James convivially as we sat down.

"Yes, that's right." He went on to tell James about his social activities there, repeating almost word for word what he had already told me.

"The Ghazipur opium factory," announced James. "Have you ever been there?"

Mawson shifted awkwardly in his seat.

"I visited a few times."

"Only visited? Did you not work there?"

Mawson scratched his temple. "I worked there for a short while."

"Did you ever come across a chap by the name of Holland?"

"No, I can't say that I did."

"Alfred Holland, the man who was recently shot in Lime-house, worked at the Ghazipur factory. Are you certain that you didn't come across him there?"

"I may have done, but the name doesn't ring a bell."

"What was your job in Ghazipur, Mr Mawson?"

"It was an administrative position. The natives are the ones who process the opium."

"But what was your actual role? What did you do there?"

Mawson sighed, seemingly reluctant to discuss it. "I weighed the opium when it arrived from the districts and was occasionally involved in the testing of its quality."

"That's interesting to hear," said James, "because I believe Alfred Holland did much the same. Am I right, Miss Green?"

"It sounds very similar to the way Mr Holland's sister described his job," I said.

"When did you carry out this work, Mr Mawson?" asked James.

"Last year for a short while."

"Can you be a little more specific? Which months were you there?"

"It was summer. March through to August, I think."

"Isn't that around the same time Mr Holland was there?" James asked me.

"Yes, I think so. He came back to Britain in August."

"How interesting that you didn't know him, Mr Mawson," said James. "Quite unusual, wouldn't you say?"

Mawson fidgeted with his hands.

"Why did you leave the factory?" James asked.

"I was asked to return to a role here at the India Office."

"Was there a reason for that?"

Only that I was told there was a job waiting for me here."

"Were you pleased to be returning to Britain?"

"Yes, I missed home, though I also enjoyed being in India."

"So no reason was given by your superiors to explain your return to Britain?"

"No."

"Are you being honest with me, Mr Mawson?"

He scowled. "Of course, why wouldn't I be?"

"I don't think you are, sir," said James. "I happen to know that there is a particular reason why you were asked to return to London. Would you care to share it with me?"

"With what consequences?" snapped Mawson. "What happens to me?"

"Why should you be worried about consequences?" asked James. "Have you done something illegal?"

"Are you here to arrest me, Inspector?"

"Arrest you for what?"

"I don't know! I don't like this probing."

"No one enjoys being questioned like this, Mr Mawson, so my suggestion is that you answer the questions honestly so they're over and done with quickly."

"Only if you can assure me there will be no consequences."

"Mr Mawson, if you have committed a misdemeanour in India during the course of your employment there then it's your employer's business, not mine. If you have committed a crime on British soil, however —"

"I have committed no crime!"

"I see."

"But I may have committed a misdemeanour," Mawson added quietly.

"Is that the reason you were asked to return?"

"Yes."

"So the matter has already been dealt with by the Indian government. What was the nature of this misdemeanour, Mr Mawson?"

"I altered the entries on some forms."

"May I ask why?"

"I was asked to do so."

"By whom?"

"A native, if you must know. He offered me money."

"And what was the chap's motive for asking you to alter them?"

"He wanted the forms altered so it appeared that the factory had received less opium than it actually had, and the difference in weight found its way into his possession. I needed the money. I had promised my mother I would send a little something home each month, and my salary didn't cover everything. I regret it all now, of course. I deeply regret my actions."

"Was this native apprehended?"

"I don't know. I was asked to leave before I could find out."

"How did your superiors find out about the form altering?"

"Someone spotted it."

"Do you know who that might have been?"

Mr Mawson glanced over at me, then back at James. "Mr Holland," he muttered.

"Thank you," said James. "We are finally making progress. So you did know Mr Alfred Holland."

"Yes."

"Then why didn't you tell us this sooner?" I asked. "I asked you about him during my last visit and you denied all knowledge!"

"Because he is inextricably linked to my shame," retorted Mawson. "If I'd admitted to having known him you would have asked about the circumstances and then this whole sorry tale would have emerged. A fellow has pride, you know!" Spots of red appeared high on his cheeks above his whiskers.

"There is no shame in admitting your mistakes, Mr Mawson," said James. "I've no doubt the Indian government dealt with you in the necessary manner."

"Indeed."

"May I ask why you have been permitted to work for the India Office after committing this misdemeanour?" I asked.

Mr Mawson coughed. "I have an uncle who occupies a senior position here, and the matter was hushed up to save face. Very few people know about it, and I'd be grateful if you didn't mention the matter to anyone."

"Your secret's safe with us, Mr Mawson," said James. "Can you shed any further light on why someone might wish Alfred Holland dead?"

"I'm afraid not."

"You have finally admitted to us that you knew him, but how well did you know him?"

"Not well at all."

"Are you being truthful?"

"Yes!" said Mawson earnestly. "He and I were quite different. He was a pleasant enough chap, but he was a good twenty years younger than me. We didn't have much in common."

"Were you aware that he was an opium addict?"

"I knew that he smoked it, but I didn't know him well enough to see that he was addicted to the substance."

"Was his work impaired by this opium use?"

"Clearly not, seeing as he was keen-eyed enough to spot the changes on the forms!"

"You must have felt some animosity toward him when he reported you."

"I did, yes, but I suppose someone was bound to spot the discrepancy before long. If it hadn't been Holland it would have been someone else. He was only doing his job."

"But his actions led to you being sent back to Britain in disgrace," I said. "That must have angered you."

"It did a little, but there was no use in me harbouring any resentment. I got off very lightly, all things considered."

"Did you see Alfred Holland after he returned to London?" I asked.

"No, the last time I saw him was in Ghazipur. I didn't realise he had returned until I heard about the death at the opium den. Even then I wasn't certain it was the same Alfred Holland."

"And you have no idea why someone would wish to murder him?" asked James.

"No, none at all."

"Did he report anyone else?"

"Not as far as I know. I hope you don't think I had anything to do with it! I was briefly angered by his actions, but I would never have considered taking revenge of any sort. I was embarrassed by what happened and wished to have it all forgotten about. Raising the matter with him would only have reminded me of my shameful actions. I'm not a vengeful man, Inspector!"

"Thank you, Mr Mawson," said James.

The man before us was trembling and pale.

The door to the council chamber swung open and a man in a top hat, monocle and dark suit stepped in.

"My apologies, gentlemen – and lady – this room is required."

"We were just finishing up, sir," said James, standing to his feet.

Mr Mawson and I followed suit.

"Thank you for your time, Mr Mawson," continued James, "and for your honesty."

Mr Mawson gave us an uneasy look as we left the room.

CHAPTER 40

"And now on to Euston, Miss Holland and her brother's diaries," said James as he hailed a cab on Whitehall.

"What did you make of Mr Mawson?" I asked once we were sitting side by side in the cab.

"I can't work out whether he was still being evasive," replied James. "He was honest with us eventually, wasn't he? But I think it likely that he's hiding something else."

"Such as the murder of Alfred Holland?" I suggested.

"I can't imagine him shooting anyone," said James, "but I suppose you could say the same thing of anyone who commits murder."

"He may also have murdered the Forsters."

"Yes, I suppose he might have."

"He's the only person we've discovered so far who knew both them and Alfred Holland."

"This is true."

"He could have hired the gang that robbed the Forsters. It's rather interesting, don't you think, that he was outside the house so soon afterward?" I said.

"It is. Perhaps if he had ordered the crime to be committed he was checking that everything had been carried out as it should have been."

"Which it hadn't, because Mr Forster wasn't at home when the gang struck. Perhaps Mr Mawson was keen to establish Mr Forster's whereabouts that morning because he wanted to finish the job."

"That's a good point."

"And he found him, of course! He spent an evening with him, and shortly after that Mr Forster was killed."

"But what could Mawson's motive for murdering the Forsters have been?" asked James.

"Money?"

"Money is a recurrent theme in this case, isn't it? Forster was short of it and Mawson was lured into committing fraud by the promise of it."

"Perhaps Mr Forster owed Mr Mawson money."

"He may have done. I think it's worth finding out a little more about their relationship."

"And the motive he had for murdering Alfred Holland had to be revenge," I said.

"He didn't seem particularly vengeful toward Holland though, did he?"

"No, but he wouldn't appear to be, would he? Otherwise we'd have been suspicious of him."

"We're suspicious of him anyway. Though I think if he felt any animosity toward Holland we'd have seen a little more of it," said James.

"Perhaps the anger has faded now that Mr Holland is dead."

"Maybe. I think there is a possibility that Mawson may have been behind Holland's death, but I'm still struggling to believe that he would actually go through with it, or even order someone else to do it. There's something rather insipid about him, don't you think?"

"Insipid or not I think there's a good chance he's behind the deaths," I said. "The circumstances all point to him. He knew all three victims, he was quickly at the scene of Mrs Forster's death and he was with Mr Forster shortly before he died. Also, he has a motive for Alfred Holland's murder. We haven't found anyone else who comes close to that."

"He's one to keep an eye on, Penny, there's no doubt about it. We'll need to be careful that he doesn't realise we suspect him in case he decides to bolt. Meanwhile, Inspector Bowles in D Division is certain that he's holding the gang members who broke into the Forsters' home."

"That's excellent news!"

"When I last spoke to Bowles they were arranging identity parades for the household staff to attend."

"Have you met any of those arrested yet?"

"Not yet, but I'll go straight to Marylebone Lane station after we've seen Miss Holland and offer Bowles my assistance. Unsurprisingly, most of those arrested are already known to the police."

"Mr Mawson might have hired them to carry out the attacks on the Forsters and Mr Holland."

"It's a possibility, but we're a long way off proving anything. I suspect the gang's motive was money; they were probably paid to carry out the murders. It's unlikely they had any personal connection to the victims."

"Which reinforces the idea that Mawson hired them."

"Either him or someone else."

The cab pulled up opposite the large Euston arch.

"Drummond Street!" called the cabman.

James paid him and we climbed out.

"Emma Holland lives at number seven. It's this one here," I said as we approached the terraced house.

The maid I recognised from my previous visit answered the door.

"Miss 'Olland ain't home," she said, "but if yer leave yer card and a message I'll pass 'em on, Inspector."

"That's a shame," said James. "What time are you expecting her home?"

"She's stayin' away overnight. She'll be back tomorrah."

"Thank you. We'll call back tomorrow," said James.

The maid closed the door.

"How disappointing," he said, "but it can't be helped. And waiting another day isn't the end of the world. Thank you, Penny, for all the work you've done so far. It has been invaluable. Would you mind accompanying me on my visit to Miss Holland tomorrow? You seem to be well acquainted with her, and I think your presence will be a great help."

"Of course."

"Good, then I shall send you a telegram in the morning. In the meantime I'll go to Marylebone Lane and meet these gang members."

"Be careful, James, they don't sound at all pleasant. They could be the ones who sent you that..." I trailed off, feeling nauseous at the thought of the severed finger.

"It may well have been them," he replied. "It's the sort of thing the ruthless men who join these gangs do. Thankfully, they're behind bars at the present time, so the worst of it is likely to be over."

"I do hope so, James."

We held each other's gaze and he smiled. "Likewise. See you tomorrow, Penny."

CHAPTER 41

"What are your thoughts on the rather disastrous events of yesterday evening, Penelope?"

Eliza was seated on my bed in her tweed cycling outfit while Tiger hid beneath it. My sister was too loud and overbearing for the cat to feel comfortable in her presence.

"I think Mr Fox-Stirling was extremely rude to Francis."

"He was, wasn't he? It seems he doesn't like anyone else to have an opinion as to how the search for Father should be conducted."

"Francis didn't even express much of an opinion; the map alone seemed to cause the man offence."

"It did indeed. I hope the disagreement won't scupper our plans for the search effort."

"Francis has every right to withdraw his funding. Mr Fox-Stirling was horribly rude to him."

"Do you think he will?"

"As a matter of fact, I don't. We discussed the possibility of finding someone to replace Mr Fox-Stirling, but I don't think Francis will withdraw his money altogether. He remains very keen for the search to go ahead."

"We have you to thank for that, Penelope."

"Me? Why?"

"Because of his deep affection for you."

I groaned in reply.

"What's the matter?"

"I don't deserve his affection, and I've told him so."

"You said that to him? Well now the search for Father may truly hang in the balance. You can't say such things to an admirer, Penelope! What on earth made you say that?"

"I simply spoke the truth. Francis is an honourable man and I told him that. I respect him too much to deceive him."

"What could you possibly wish to deceive him about?"

"I don't love him, Ellie."

"That's not so terrible. True love can take time to develop."

"So you've told me before, but I'm not sure that I believe it."

"It happened to me. Besides, it really doesn't matter that you don't consider yourself to be in love with him, as he hasn't asked you to marry him. Or has he?"

"No, he hasn't. I told him I have no wish to marry."

"Oh Penelope, you didn't!" Eliza slapped her thigh in indignation. "How could you? I wish I had given you some instruction on how to conduct yourself in conversations like these. You have said all the wrong things."

"Wrong according to whom?"

"It's just not the done thing. A lady cannot speak her mind in such a fashion. She must show that she's flattered by his attentions and at least give the chap some hope."

"Hope for what?"

"Marriage."

"But I have no wish to marry him, Ellie!"

"How can you be so sure?"

"I've already told you, I don't love him."

"Do you really know what love feels like, Penelope? I sincerely hope you're not expecting the sort of love you read about in poems and novels, because it's not like that in real life."

"I realise that."

"So perhaps you love him after all, you just don't realise it yet. That's how I felt with George. In fact, it wasn't until after Fenella was born that I discovered how I truly felt about him."

The thought depressed me. "I'm not as naive as you think, Ellie, I'm thirty-five. I'm three years older than you, remember?"

"And a spinster."

"That doesn't mean I know nothing of love!"

Eliza gave an exasperated laugh. "I hope you do marry one day, Penelope, because you will look back on this time and realise how little you knew about affairs of the heart."

I felt a sudden wrath burning in my chest.

"Don't patronise me, Ellie. It's possible that I know more about it than you and your passionless husband!"

"Penelope! How dare you —?"

I ignored my sister's shocked expression, allowing my words to flow out in anger.

"I know what it is to love someone with an intensity that cannot be quenched by reason or instruction; a passion beyond my power to control. It's the type of love I wish did not exist; a passion that can never be requited. Do you know what that feels like? Or do you only know the comfortable acceptance of a rather dull man with whom you've been ordained to spend the rest of your days?"

Eliza rose to her feet. "Don't you ever speak to me like that —"

"Why not? You think it perfectly acceptable to discuss my marital status at any time of your choosing. Year in, year out I have had to listen to your views on possible suitors and my incapacity for knowing my own mind. It's high time I asked you to listen to something similar. Have you ever considered that you didn't know your own mind when you married George?'

Eliza's mouth hung open.

"Of course you haven't," I continued, "because to consider such a thing might lead to an acknowledgement that you made a mistake, and that would be too dreadful for words, wouldn't it? I pity you being married to a man who yearns to live in a bygone era and refuses to allow his wife to pursue an employment of her own. Have you ever considered the irony of being married to a man who opposes women's suffrage when it's one of the biggest causes you champion? Is there anything you and your husband agree on?"

I stopped when I saw a tear rolling down my sister's cheek.

"Ellie, I'm sorry, I didn't mean... Here." I dashed over to a drawer, grabbed a clean handkerchief and held it out to her.

"I'm quite all right, thank you, Penelope. I have my own." She dabbed at her face with a lace handkerchief, her voice cool. "Have you finished what you wanted to say?"

"Yes, but I'm sorry. I didn't mean to upset you. I was angry and... yesterday evening was difficult, not only because of the dinner but also because Francis hinted at the question of marriage in the hansom cab and I'm really rather tired of discussing it. I didn't mean those things I said about George. It wasn't kind of me."

"This intense, unrequited love you speak of," said Eliza. "It's the inspector, isn't it?"

I nodded sheepishly.

"I knew it," she said, folding up her handkerchief. "We all knew it. I suspect poor Francis does too."

"Which is why I told him he deserves someone better than me."

"And you're right, he does."

"I'm not sure why he persists."

"Because he loves you, Penelope. And next month Inspector Blakely is to marry someone else. You need to prepare yourself and decide what you're going to do about it."

CHAPTER 42

"There really is no use in me working on the Forster story any more, sir," said Edgar as we sat side by side in Mr Sherman's cluttered office. "Miss Green has journeyed off with it like a speeding express train —"

"That's not quite true, Edgar," I protested. "I was working on the Alfred Holland story when I happened across a connection between him and the Forsters."

"And now Blakely's firmly on the case I have no chance whatsoever, do I? Everyone knows what a close acquaintance the two have."

I glanced at the clock on the wall of Mr Sherman's office. It was almost eleven o'clock and I hadn't yet heard from James about his proposed meeting at Emma Holland's home. It was unlike him to be tardy.

"If I understand you correctly, Fish," said Mr Sherman, "you're telling me that you no longer wish to work on the Forster story."

"Sir, I don't want you to consider me an idle fellow. I would gladly keep hold of the Forster story but I'm feeling the effect of Miss Green's elbows, metaphorically speaking."

"You don't half mince your words, Fish," said the editor. "What's your point?"

"As the Forsters and Holland may now be considered part of the same case it makes sense for me to have the Holland story as well, or for the whole lot to be handed over to her."

"By *her*, you mean Miss Green, I presume."

"Yes, sir. Otherwise there will be too much jostling of the elbows between us."

"That's the second time you've mentioned elbows, Fish. I get the picture."

"Mr Sherman," I said, "can I please have the story? I have done considerable work on it so far and I've also struck up a friendship with Emma Holland, Alfred's sister. In addition to that I'm on good terms with Mr Mawson, who has become central to this case and have already met with him twice —"

"I've heard enough, Miss Green, you can have the story," said Mr Sherman brusquely, looking through some papers on his desk as though keen to focus on something else.

"Really, sir? Oh, thank you!" I felt my heart skip.

"But sir!" protested Edgar. "What about all the hard work I've done on the story?"

"What hard work, Fish?"

"I've been out and about, as you asked."

"That's the problem, Fish, I had to ask you to do so. You should be able to undertake your work independently. I can't deny that Miss Green has trodden on your toes on this story, but I can't fault the woman for going out there and getting the work done."

Edgar glared at me and I occupied myself with rubbing at an ink stain on my finger.

"Go and get on with it, the both of you," said Mr Sherman.

I stood to my feet.

"But what am I to work on instead?" whined Edgar.

"I need a thousand words on the proposed rescue of General Gordon from Khartoum," said the editor. "Sink your teeth into that."

The speaking tube beside his desk whistled, and Mr Sherman answered it gruffly.

I returned to the newsroom happy that I could continue with the Forster and Holland stories uninterrupted. I had hoped a telegram from James would have arrived while I was in Mr Sherman's office, but when I went to the telegraph room and asked the messenger boy if anything had turned up he replied that it had not.

I returned to my desk and wondered what could have detained James. I thought of our meeting with Mr Mawson and struggled to believe the man had arranged the three murders. *No one else was linked to them all as he was. Surely he had played a part in it. Had Mawson sent James the severed finger?*

I was interrupted by a visitor to the newsroom, but it wasn't the boy from the telegraph room, as I had hoped. It was Emma Holland, and she appeared flustered.

"What's the matter?" I asked, trying to guide her toward a chair.

She shrugged me off, glancing warily at Frederick and Edgar.

"Shall we speak outside in the corridor?" I suggested.

She nodded.

"We've been robbed," she said breathlessly as soon as we were out of earshot. "I've just returned from a friend's house in Hertfordshire having spent the night away from home. Someone has robbed us in the night!"

I immediately thought of the gang that had targeted the Forsters' home.

"I hope nobody has been hurt," I said.

"The servants slept through it, but the burglar ransacked

my room. I don't know what would have happened had I been there!" Her hands trembled and fidgeted as she spoke.

"It's lucky you weren't. What has been taken?"

"Nothing valuable, that's the strange thing. Whoever it was knew exactly what they were looking for."

"What was that?"

"Alfred's papers! His diaries and letters are all gone!"

"Oh no, Emma, that's terrible!"

I thought of Mr Mawson. Had James or I mentioned to him that Alfred's sister had the diaries? I couldn't recall doing so. James had been keen to coax an admission of guilt from Mr Mawson without giving away too much information.

"Who knew that you had them?" I asked Emma.

"That's the odd thing; hardly anyone!"

"What about your cousin and her husband?"

"I mentioned it to them, but only in passing. I hadn't told my parents."

"So your cousin and her husband are the only people you've told."

"Apart from you, yes!" She wiped a trembling hand across her brow.

"Would you like to sit down, Emma?"

"No, I don't need to sit! Have you told anyone about my brother's diaries?"

"Only Inspector Blakely of Scotland Yard. We found a connection between your brother and Mr and Mrs Forster, who were murdered a few weeks ago. We called on you yesterday to discuss it."

"Yes, Doris told me."

"Inspector Blakely was keen to see the diaries for himself."

"What's the connection between Alfred and the Forsters?"

"It's Mr Mawson, the man your brother reported in Ghazipur for altering the forms. Remember?"

"He knew all three of them?"

I nodded. "Inspector Blakely and I met him yesterday and he confirmed to us that he had worked with your brother in Ghazipur, and that Alfred had reported him for his misdemeanour."

"Then he has to be the one who has taken the diaries!"

"You would think so, wouldn't you? However, I'm certain that neither Inspector Blakely nor myself mentioned them to him. That's what's so puzzling. I don't think I've mentioned them to anyone apart from Inspector Blakely, and having worked on a few cases with him I trust the man implicitly. Perhaps he let slip to someone about the diaries, but I can't think who."

"It must have been Mr Mawson," said Emma.

"He's the only person I can think of who had a motive for the theft, but I don't understand how Mr Mawson could have found out about the diaries unless Inspector Blakely went to see him again. That would be highly unlikely. Inspector Blakely had planned to visit you again this morning, Emma; in fact, we had both planned to do so. I've been waiting on a telegram from him to confirm a time but I've received nothing at all from him, which is highly unusual."

"So what do we do now?"

"I'm sure we can retrieve the diaries. Have you called the police?"

"Yes, a constable from Holborn Division visited and took down the particulars, though I can't say that he's treating it as a great emergency seeing as my jewellery and other valuables were left undisturbed. He didn't appear to think the theft of a few diaries was anything to worry about!"

"Whoever took them must be trying to suppress their contents," I said.

"It could be the same person who wished to silence Alfred!"

"It could well be."

Emma gave a shiver and began to pace the floor. "It frightens me to think that the man who killed Alfred may have been in my house! As soon as I discovered the burglary this morning I went out and bought a revolver. I have no wish to be murdered in my home like Mrs Forster. If anyone breaks into my house again they'll pay for it with their life!"

"Please be careful, Emma," I said. The thought of her wielding a gun while in a heightened emotional state worried me. "You need to make the police at Holborn aware of how significant this burglary is. They need to speak to the detectives working on the case across the different divisions. Better still, they need to speak to Inspector Blakely. I'll send him a telegram right away."

CHAPTER 43

I tried to work in the reading room that afternoon but found it difficult to concentrate. *Who had stolen Alfred Holland's diaries? And why had I heard nothing from James?* Emma had gone to Tottenham Court Road police station to explain to the inspector there about the possible connection between the theft and her brother's murder.

There was something meek and reserved about Francis' manner as he approached, as if he felt embarrassed about our conversation in the cab a few evenings previously. I fixed a smile on my face and tried to pretend that it hadn't occurred.

"I wonder if I've been a bit uncharitable about Mr Fox-Stirling," he whispered to me. "Although I'm keen to do what I can in the search for your father I understand, on reflection, why he might see my enthusiasm as interference. The old dog is rather set in his ways, I suppose."

He brushed his sandy hair away from his spectacles and the heated conversation with Eliza came back to my mind. *Was it possible that I could ever find Francis attractive enough to marry him?* I pushed the thought away and concentrated on the conversation.

"I don't think you've been at all uncharitable," I replied. "I think your anger was quite justified. Eliza isn't particularly happy with him either, but until we can find someone more suitable I suppose we're stuck with the chap."

Francis sighed. "Yes, I suppose we are for now. Perhaps all explorers are difficult to work with. They're accustomed to relying on their own resources and abilities without much help from others, and they're accustomed to making their own decisions."

"Perhaps my father was equally cantankerous to work with," I suggested.

"Surely not."

"I cannot pretend that he was perfect, Francis. These men have difficult decisions to make when they're on their adventures."

I thought of the massacre Father had been caught up in when he had been forced to defend himself. I had read about the event in his diaries and it still made me uncomfortable; so uncomfortable, in fact, that the only person I'd discussed it with was Eliza.

I glanced toward the door, hoping James might suddenly make an appearance as he had so often done in the past.

"Is something bothering you, Penny?" Francis asked. He was quite astute in noticing when something was troubling me.

"Do you remember researching a man named Mr Mawson for me?" I asked.

He nodded in reply.

"I think he may be a murderer."

"Really?"

"Yes, I've discovered that he had a grievance with Alfred Holland, the poor chap who was shot in Limehouse. And he also knew the Forsters. He was the man I saw hanging about after Mrs Forster's death. And now Alfred Holland's diaries have gone missing."

"From where?"

"They were stolen from the house of his sister, Emma Holland. She was trying to find out who might have borne him a grudge, and we discovered that Mr Mawson received a mention. I shall have to explain it all to you in detail at a later date. Suffice to say that after Inspector Blakely spoke to Mr Mawson the diaries were stolen. To make matters more frustrating the Holborn police aren't treating the theft as a serious crime because they're not fully aware of the circumstances. I've been trying to contact James but I've heard nothing from him. I may need to march down to Scotland Yard to find him."

I noticed Francis' face darken at the mention of James.

"Presumably he's busy working on the case."

"I suppose he must be. He was meeting yesterday with suspected gang members who were arrested on suspicion of burgling the Forsters' home. The trouble is, he received something horribly threatening and macabre in a package and I cannot help but worry about him."

"I'm sure there's no need to worry about Blakely. He can look after himself."

"But why have I not heard from him?"

"Why should you have heard from him? He's clearly busy with his detective work, and something unexpected must have cropped up. Isn't that what happens with detectives? There's always something unexpected."

"I suppose that's the nature of his work."

"Perhaps he has arrested Mr Mawson."

"Yes, that's a good point, perhaps he has. Something needs to be done about the man. He's clearly more dangerous than he first appeared."

Discussing the matter with Francis had convinced me that

Mawson was behind the murders, and that the theft of Alfred Holland's diaries was an attempt to cover up any further revelations.

"Might your conversation be carried out elsewhere?" a man with large ears sitting nearby whispered. "I'd have thought a clerk of the reading room would know better than to chatter away and disturb the work of others."

Ordinarily, Francis would have apologised to the man, but instead he glared at him. "I hope to see you again soon, Penny," he said before returning to his work.

I also glared at the man, then looked down at my notes, but my mind refused to concentrate. I knew Francis was probably right in saying that James hadn't been in touch because he was so busy with the case, but I couldn't help but wonder what was happening. *Had Mawson been arrested? Had the Holborn police recognised the significance of the burglary at Emma Holland's home?*

I gave up trying to work and packed the papers into my carpet bag. It was no use trying to stay away; I would have to go down to Scotland Yard. My mind would find no rest until I knew exactly what was taking place.

I hailed a cab on Great Russell Street. It was a brisk twenty-minute walk down Charing Cross Road to Whitehall, but a cab could manage the journey in ten. When we reached Trafalgar Square the traffic became heavier and I could hear my cab driver hollering to those around him, a sure sign that they were getting in one another's way.

As the cab tried to push its way through Trafalgar Square I began to feel sorry for the poor horse being urged to barge its way into the narrow gaps between vehicles. After a few minutes it shook its head and refused to budge, causing the cabman to lose his temper.

I pushed open the hatch in the roof. "I'll walk from here!" I called up to him.

Once I had paid my fare I stepped out of the cab and tried my best to avoid the mass of hooves and wheels as I scampered toward Northumberland Avenue. The traffic wasn't usually so bad and I began to wonder whether something had occurred. *Was this why James had yet to make contact with me?*

I was about to walk down Northumberland Avenue to Scotland Yard when I saw a group of people in earnest discussion outside the bank on the corner. By this stage I had a strong sense that something wasn't quite right.

"Excuse me," I said to a man in a top hat, "has something happened? It seems unusually busy around here."

"I heard there's been a murder," he replied.

I felt a lurch in my chest. "Where?"

"Down that way, apparently," he said, pointing in the direction of Whitehall. "I hope it's nobody important; all the government buildings are down there. It might have been an assassination!"

"I shall go and find out," I said.

The traffic stood still at the top of Whitehall and crowds filled the pavement. I pushed my way through, shouting out that I was a press reporter. James was somewhere within the crowd, I felt sure of it.

Then a terrible thought struck me and the image of a severed finger came to mind. *Could James have been the victim of a fatal attack?*

CHAPTER 44

I pushed through the Whitehall crowds with a renewed sense of urgency. I felt nauseous and tried to slow my quick, shallow breathing as I reassured myself that James could not have come to any harm. The crowds were even thicker around Downing Street, where enterprising street hawkers were trying to sell watercress, apples and song sheets. I was pushed and shoved in all directions.

"Let me through!" I shouted. "Press!"

Most people moved aside when I asked, though a few were upset by my shouting in their ears.

Just beyond Downing Street were the enormous stone buildings housing the Colonial Office, Foreign Office, Home Office and India Office, but before I could reach them a line of police constables blocked my way.

"Miss Green, *Morning Express!*" I called to them, brandishing my card. "I need to speak to Inspector Blakely of Scotland Yard!" I had learned that offering constables a specific name was more likely to give me a passage through, but on this occasion I received only blank expressions in reply.

"What's happened?" I asked.

There was no response from the constables.

"Someone's been murdered!" a woman said to me.

"But who?" I asked.

She shrugged.

I managed to shove my way along the police line, hoping I might find a constable who was more receptive. This time I decided to shout out the name of a more senior officer.

"I'm here to see Chief Inspector Cullen!" I shouted at a constable, thrusting my card at him. To my surprise, he let me straight through.

There was an eerie lull beyond the police cordon. The government buildings loomed in front of me and I realised I had no idea where I was going. I strode purposefully along Charles Street, wary that if I appeared vague in my intentions I would be asked to leave.

Where was Chief Inspector Cullen? And more importantly, where was James?

As I walked toward the side entrance to the building I grew increasingly convinced that this incident had something to do with Mr Mawson. *Had something gone wrong when James attempted to arrest him?* I shuddered at the thought. My breath felt shaky as I reached the entrance.

The constable standing guard had clearly decided there was no need to trouble me as I had already been allowed through the cordon. I explained who I was, regardless, and he nodded me on through the archway which led to the quadrant at the centre of the building. As I emerged from the archway I saw a group of figures in the middle of the sunlit, gravelled courtyard.

I stopped sharply when I saw a dark blanket covering something on the ground.

Where was James? My heart thudded heavily in my chest. I glanced at each man in turn but there was no sign of him. I looked again at the bundle on the ground. I felt sure it was the body of a man. *But it couldn't be James. Surely it wasn't James.*

A sudden panic seized me, and I struggled to breathe. I wanted to run over to them shouting for him. *Was he dead? Why had no one noticed me?*

A dreadful sickening sensation rose up from my stomach and I began to feel faint. For a moment I felt doomed to stand there for the rest of my days just watching and waiting, never quite certain whether the most unimaginable tragedy had struck or not.

"James!" His name left my lips before I had time to think about what I was saying. The men turned to stare at me, but James' face wasn't among them. A man began walking toward me, and I could see from the thick grey moustache and spectacles that it was Chief Inspector Cullen.

"Miss Green." His voice seemed distant.

My eyes were drawn to the bundle again.

"What are you doing here?" he asked as he reached my side. "How did you even get in here?"

"I came to see James," I said, still staring at the dreadful tableau in front of me.

"He's not here," he replied.

I turned to look at him, not yet able to feel relief.

"It's your chap Mawson beneath that blanket," he said.

"And James?"

"He's not here, Miss Green! But Mawson is dead; someone's taken a knife to him. Such a messy business."

He seemed bemused by my confused state. "Get your notebook out and write down the details. That's why you're here, isn't it?"

I nodded and did as he suggested.

CHAPTER 45

"There isn't much I can say about the assailant," said the uniformed man who usually guarded the door at the India Office. His name was Mr Finch, and Mr Mawson's attacker had spoken to him shortly before the stabbing.

"He was a young, smart-looking man wearing a dark suit and a bowler hat," he continued. "He was presentable and reasonably well-spoken. I had no idea he was carrying a weapon; none at all! If only I'd known I could have stopped him. We check for weapons when it's someone important they come to see, but on this occasion there was nothing to rouse my suspicions. To think I could have done something to prevent this!"

"What happened when Mr Mawson arrived?" I asked.

"The young man suggested they walk for a short while outside because there was something he wished to speak to Mawson about."

"Do you think Mr Mawson knew the man?"

"He didn't seem to from what I could glean."

"Chief Inspector Cullen tells me the man left a card with you, but he suspects that it bears a false name."

"That's correct. The card contains the name Edward Brown and there's an address on it, too. I've no doubt police officers are visiting the address as we speak, but it may be false. A murderer is hardly likely to leave his personal details at the scene of a crime, is he?"

"Did you hear any of the conversation between the two men?"

"None whatsoever. My impression is that it was a professional conversation rather than a personal one. A short while after they walked through that door over there I heard a cry from outside. Usually it's quite peaceful here, so I was quick to step outside and that's when I saw the attacker landing the last of his blows and running away. Poor Mr Mawson was lying on the ground, and initially I thought he had been struck by the man's fist. As I got closer I saw the blood and realised a weapon must have been used. Mr Mawson was still conscious at that time and I was torn between tending to him and chasing after the culprit.

"I called out for help and as soon as my colleague Mr Haynes joined me I ran out onto Charles Street. There was no sign of the man by then. He may have turned right and run into St James's Park or left and out onto Whitehall. Either way would have been a decent escape route, and I regret that I was unable to catch him. I ran into the park first, surmising at the time that he would choose that path as it would offer him more places to hide. Unfortunately, there was no sign of him. He had either successfully hidden or made his getaway.

"I summoned the park keeper at his lodge on Birdcage Walk and he helped search for the man in the park, entreating a few other men to do the same. We summoned officers down at King Street police station as well as several inspectors at Scotland Yard. To think that this terrible attack took place only a short distance from the Yard! And there's a police station just over the road!"

The mention of the Yard reminded me of James. I still hadn't been able to ascertain where he was.

"Thank you, Mr Finch," I said, "you've been most helpful. Please accept my condolences on the sad death of your colleague."

"Thank you, Miss Green. I've worked here for twelve years and never have I encountered anything like this. It's truly dreadful."

I returned to the quadrant, where Mr Mawson's body had been placed into a removal shell and was being loaded into a carriage to be taken away to the mortuary. I approached Chief Inspector Cullen, who was overseeing the proceedings.

"This is something to do with the murder of the Forsters, isn't it?" I said. "And the murder of Mr Holland. James and I spoke to Mr Mawson just yesterday, and he admitted to knowing Mr Holland. In fact, I had wondered whether he was the murderer himself. Then Alfred Holland's diaries were stolen last night and I was convinced Mr Mawson was behind that as well. Perhaps he was."

Chief Inspector Cullen scowled. "Your mind runs along at a great pace, Miss Green. I can't really keep track of what you're saying."

"But don't you see how all of this links together?"

"I believe so, but I'll need to have a proper read of the case file to understand the ins and outs of it all."

"The burglary at the home of Alfred Holland's sister Emma needs to be properly investigated," I said. "It sounds as though the police at Holborn aren't taking it seriously because they don't understand the wider implications. The man or men who burgled her home must be linked to those who murdered her brother. Otherwise, why would they steal his diaries? Barely anyone knew she was in possession of them, so that will narrow down the suspects considerably."

"You've lost me once again, Miss Green. I shall have to return to the Yard and read everything through before reaching any conclusions."

"But it's important to move quickly! Who knows when these men will strike again, Chief Inspector? I thought a number of them were already in custody as James was due to speak to them at Marylebone Lane station yesterday. Yet there has been a burglary and a murder since then! So who is behind this, and why?"

"It's a complicated case, Miss Green," the senior officer said, refusing to comment further as he lit his pipe.

We watched as the carriage left the quadrant and some members of staff from the India Office came out with buckets and mops to clean the ground.

"Where's James?" I asked. "He should be here."

"I don't know. He's clearly been detained with another aspect of the case. It's quite frustrating, really, as we could have done with having him here."

"Have you seen him at all today?"

"No."

"It's important that he's told what has happened as soon as possible. As I've said, we met with Mr Mawson only yesterday and this turn of events changes everything. He must also be informed of the burglary."

"I shall update him as soon as he returns to the Yard."

As Chief Inspector Cullen puffed on his pipe again his lack of urgency concerned me. Beyond the walls of the government offices and the police cordon hundreds of people were clamouring for news of the murder. It was my job to return to the *Morning Express* offices and write the story for tomorrow's edition, but instead I was detained here, trying to compel the man to act. It seemed an odd situation to find myself in. *Did he really plan to update James when he returned?* I felt sure he would, but his lackadaisical manner was cause for concern.

"You will tell James everything when he returns later, won't you?" I asked. "I should be happy to do so myself. If I only knew where he was I'd go and find him this very instant."

"Haven't you a news article to write, Miss Green?"

"Yes, I have."

"If I were you I'd go and get on with that."

CHAPTER 46

The thick-set form of Inspector Bowles strode into the wood-panelled waiting room at Marylebone Lane police station.

"Hello again, Miss Green."

I asked him about the gang and his left eye drifted over my shoulder as he told me he was confident all of its members had been arrested and would be up at Marylebone Police Court the following day.

"Did Inspector Blakely meet with them yesterday?" I asked.

"Yes, he assisted me with some of the interviews."

"And today?"

"No, not today."

"Have you seen him today?"

"I haven't, no."

I felt a cold sensation grip my heart. *Something wasn't right.*

"I've been trying to make contact with Inspector Blakely all day and have been unable to find him," I said shakily. "I assumed he was here with you."

"I haven't seen him since yesterday afternoon."

"Did he tell you what his plans were once you had concluded the interviews?"

"Not in any great detail. He explained to me about the chap who knew the Forsters and the unfortunate individual who was shot inside the opium den."

"Did you realise that first chap was murdered today?"

"Was he indeed? I heard there had been a murder in Whitehall but I wasn't aware of the fellow's identity. Goodness! That's rather perturbing."

"I don't know whether Inspector Blakely knows about it yet. He seems to have completely vanished."

"He explained something to me about diaries. They belonged to the opium den fellow, is that right?"

"Yes, and they've been stolen, but I'm not sure Inspector Blakely knows about that yet either. So much has happened and he's the only one who can pull all these strands together, but he's nowhere to be found! I'm beginning to worry."

"I'm sure there's no need, Miss Green."

"But he received a threat! Did he not mention that to you?"

"No, he didn't, but a threat isn't unusual in our line of work."

"This one was... Perhaps he'll tell you more about it himself. These men you've arrested were hired by someone to burgle the Forsters' home and then kill them, weren't they?"

"Undoubtedly."

"Who could it be?"

"They haven't been forthcoming, but we'll get it out of them before long."

"For a short while I wondered whether it could have been Mr Mawson, but now that he's been murdered I'm beginning to doubt it."

"Perhaps it was and someone has exacted their revenge on him. We'll get to the bottom of it, just you wait."

"I hope so, but it's difficult to see how at the moment. Your division is working on the murder of Mrs Forster, C Division is investigating Mr Forster's murder, K Division is looking after the Holland investigation and A Division is now involved in the murder of Mr Mawson. Not to mention E Division, which is looking into the theft of Alfred Holland's diaries. It's becoming incredibly complicated!"

"You're right when you say that we need Inspector Blakely to pull it all together."

"And he's nowhere to be found! These men you're holding, do they have accomplices who may still be at large?"

"It's highly likely they do, Miss Green."

I shuddered. "Where are they from?"

"From?"

"Where do they live? Gangs usually have a territory."

"I don't believe it's that sort of gang, Miss Green. This is simply a band of miscreants which commits burglaries and possibly far worse atrocities. Its members are not precious about territory."

"But you must have taken down their names and addresses."

"I have done, yes, and most of them are from the East End."

"Specifically?"

"Spitalfields, mainly, and a few from Whitechapel."

"Is that where you found them?"

"Whitechapel's H Division found them there. They have been known to the police for some time. A description of the gang had been circulated to all divisions; I believe Inspector Blakely did that. H Division picked them up in and around Commercial Street."

"Could they have sent a message to their accomplices after you had arrested them?"

"I would highly doubt it."

"Who has visited them?"

"Their lawyers and a few family members."

"They could have passed messages on to their accomplices using any of those people! Suppose they ordered someone to hunt down Inspector Blakely yesterday?"

"I consider it extremely unlikely."

"Extremely unlikely, but not impossible."

"It wouldn't happen."

"But it's not impossible, is it?"

"I suppose it isn't impossible, no."

"So there's a chance that a member of this gang you've arrested could have sent a message to an accomplice to take care of Inspector Blakely?"

"I've never known it happen before."

"But it could have, couldn't it?"

"Please stop worrying, Miss Green, I'm sure Inspector Blakely is absolutely fine."

I left the police station and walked along Oxford Street toward Regent Circus in a despondent mood. *Should I visit James' home and check in on him?* I desperately wanted to but feared another frosty reception from Charlotte and her mother.

Perhaps the reason for his absence was a personal one, I mused, feeling a brief glimmer of hope that the wedding had been called off and James had been facing the aftermath of that decision. Then I felt concerned that perhaps something had happened to a friend or relative and taken him away from London. I felt sure that James' absence had to be personal, and that he would contact me as soon as he was able to. I took comfort from the fact that his colleagues didn't seem a bit concerned about him.

I hailed an omnibus and began my journey home, reassuring myself that James couldn't have possibly come to any harm. My mind returned to the puzzle of Mawson's death. *Who had wanted him dead, and why? Had he taken Alfred Holland's diaries or had someone else done so?*

"You have a visitor, Miss Green," Mrs Garnett said as soon as I stepped in through the front door. "She's been here a while and is waiting for you in the parlour."

"Miss Holland?" I asked as we walked toward the back of the house. "Has something else happened?"

"No. Who's she? What's happened?"

"Forget that I mentioned her. Who is this visitor?"

"A lady by the name of Miss Jenkins."

The name initially meant nothing to me. As we stepped through the door of the parlour I desperately tried to think of a connection between her and the Forsters, or with Alfred Holland.

A fair-haired woman with a wide, apple-cheeked face gave me a muted greeting as I entered the room.

It was James' fiancée, Charlotte.

CHAPTER 47

Charlotte and I held each other's gaze, the same question resting on our lips.

"Have you —?"

"No, have you?"

"No."

"He's been missing since yesterday evening!" cried Charlotte. "I just know that something terrible has happened to him!" She clutched a damp handkerchief in one hand.

I sat down at the table across from her. "I'm worried too, but there must be an explanation. I've been looking for him today, and if it's any consolation his colleagues aren't particularly concerned. They all seem to think he's busy working on the case somewhere."

"But he always gets in touch!"

"You're right, he does. I was due to meet him this morning to visit the sister of one of the murder victims but heard nothing from him. I'm sure he's all right, though."

"How do you know that?"

"I wish to remain hopeful." I thought of the severed finger and realised how unconvincing my words sounded.

"So what do we do?" asked Charlotte. "I've called at the police station closest to his home, but I'm not sure what they'll do. James *is* the police!"

"I'm sure there must be something we can do." I had no idea what, and found myself wondering why I was attempting to reassure Charlotte when I was just as worried about James myself.

"How does an officer of the law simply vanish?" asked Mrs Garnett. "Perhaps he has been kidnapped."

Charlotte's face crumpled.

"We don't know, Mrs Garnett," I said, "and we need to be careful about idle speculation. There's no use in frightening ourselves with unlikely possibilities."

"But she might be right!" said Charlotte.

"And she might be wrong," I replied. "When did you last see James?"

"The day before yesterday. He was supposed to take the train down to Croydon yesterday evening to discuss our meeting with the vicar of St John the Baptist church, as we're meeting him this Saturday. It's only five weeks until our wedding!"

"Yes, I know. But he didn't come down to Croydon?"

"No, he didn't turn up! I assumed his work had detained him, but he always sends a telegram when that happens and we received nothing. I sent him one this morning and I must confess that it was rather a scolding note, which I bitterly regret because it now appears as though something has happened to him. I didn't realise, you see. I thought he had forgotten all about our arrangement, but he never forgets things like that as a general rule."

"Something has detained him, there's no doubt about that," I said. "But let's not assume that it's anything awful. Where have you looked for him today?"

"I called at his home and there was no answer. I spoke to

his neighbours and they hadn't seen him all day. I called at the police station in St John's Wood and then at Scotland Yard, but there wasn't really anyone at the Yard to speak to. They were all involved with a murder that had happened close by, apparently."

"That's right, it was Charles Mawson. I managed to get to the murder scene, but James wasn't there. I asked Chief Inspector Cullen if he had seen him but he hadn't."

"I've sent telegrams to all his family and friends," said Charlotte, "and no one has heard anything from him."

I felt a sickening turn in my stomach once again.

"And then I thought I'd come and see you," continued Charlotte. "James had told me you lived in Milton Street, so I knocked on a good number of doors before I found you. I had hoped you would know something, but I see that you're also worried about him and now I'm exceptionally concerned. Where is he? How can he have simply disappeared?"

"There must be an explanation," I said, aware that I was stating the obvious. "And we *will* find him."

"But how?"

"I don't know yet, Miss Jenkins."

"Don't worry about formality at a time like this. Call me Charlotte."

My mind turned over and over. I couldn't think where to begin looking for James.

"Where do his parents live?" I asked.

"Wembley. They replied to my telegram saying they hadn't heard from him, and now they're also concerned about his whereabouts. I didn't want to trouble them because I knew they would worry."

"And you went to the police station?"

"Yes, the one on New Street near James' home. They told me they'd look out for him, but we need more than that, don't we? We need someone to search for him. What if he's in the river?"

My stomach turned once more. "No, he couldn't be. It's impossible."

"He could have fallen in, or perhaps someone pushed him! It would take days to find him if so. Perhaps he'll be washed up at Wapping or Rotherhithe. He told me that's where many of them end up, at the bend in the river."

"Don't talk like that!" I snapped, startling myself with the sharpness of my voice.

Charlotte was silent and wide-eyed.

"You mustn't think like that," I said soothingly. "Please don't do it. It's too upsetting to even consider. I'm sure we can find him, and don't forget that he usually has his revolver with him, so he can defend himself. We may be worrying unduly; he might simply have got caught up in a tricky aspect of a case he's been investigating. He'll turn up safe and sound overnight, and then all this worry will have been for nothing."

"Perhaps he's having second thoughts," suggested Charlotte.

"About what?"

"About the wedding."

"No, I'm sure that he isn't."

"Perhaps he no longer wishes to marry me and has taken himself away so the wedding has to be called off. Perhaps he didn't know how to break the news to me so he's run away to hide somewhere!"

It was a thought I briefly consoled myself with, and I felt a pang of guilt for doing so.

"Nonsense, Charlotte, he would never do such a thing. It's getting quite late in the evening now, so let's just hope that he isn't missing for a second night. I think you should return to your parents' home in Croydon, and I'm sure he will send word there as soon as he can."

"And what if he doesn't?"

"Then tomorrow we must begin our search in earnest. I don't quite know where to begin, but I'll have a think about it this evening. Perhaps you could consider anyone else we might be able to contact."

"I will." Charlotte nodded her head and then began to sob.

For a moment I watched her, unsure what to do.

I had grown to dislike this woman who constantly kept me and James apart, but I had only met her twice before and I didn't know her personally at all. In front of me now I saw a woman crying for the man I loved.

I felt a lump rise into my throat. I wanted to cry like Charlotte but I couldn't. Her tears were permitted because James was her fiancé, while any tears of mine would need to be shed in private. Seeing how desperately upset she was, I got up from my chair and rested an arm across her shoulders.

"James wouldn't want you to be sad like this," I said. "I know it feels as though you haven't heard from him in a long while, but in reality it's only been twenty-four hours. I feel certain that you'll hear from him soon. Come now, you should be at home. Would you like me to accompany you?"

I struggled to believe I had just offered to accompany Charlotte all the way to Croydon.

"No, I'll be fine." She wiped her face.

"Which train station will you travel from?"

"London Bridge."

"At least allow me to accompany you there."

"I shall be fine, thank you Penny, I'll travel there by cab. It will be quite quick from here." She dried away the last of her tears.

"Would you like a spoonful of Dr Cobbold's Remedy?" asked Mrs Garnett, who had been fidgeting with some vases behind me in a bid to overhear our conversation.

"No, thank you. I shall be all right."

"A wise decision," I said to Charlotte. "It's rather unpleasant."

"But it works!" said Mrs Garnett indignantly.

"Let's go and find a cab," I said. "You don't want to leave it too late."

By the time Charlotte and I stepped out onto Milton Street she was quite composed. The sun hung low in the sky.

"Thank you, Penny." She stood slightly shorter than me, her eyes wide and blue. "I never thought I'd... I don't know if this is the right thing to say or not, but I never thought I would encounter you in this way. James has spoken about you a great deal and I admit there have been times when I... when I would rather not have heard about you. I hope you're not offended by my words."

"Not at all," I said quickly, wishing to put her at ease. I held out my hand for a passing hansom cab, which stopped close by.

"Thank you. And thank you for being so kind to me this evening. I'm sorry I got so upset about all this."

"It's completely understandable, Charlotte. It would only have been a matter of time before I'd come calling at your door. I'm pleased we've been able to share our concerns with each other, and although I don't know what's happened to James I feel sure that he will be all right."

"Oh, I hope so, Penny. Thank you again."

She climbed into the cab.

"Send me a telegram if you hear from him," I said, "either to my home or to the *Morning Express* offices."

"I will do. Let me give you my address," she said, opening her bag. She pulled out a card and handed it to me. "You can send a telegram to my parents' home."

"Thank you, Charlotte. Have a safe journey home, and hopefully we'll receive good news tomorrow."

"I hope so." She waved as the cab pulled away and I felt guilty about my duplicity. I had done what I could to comfort her, yet the poor woman had no idea how I truly felt about her future husband.

CHAPTER 48

Although the reassurances I had given Charlotte were heartfelt I could find no comfort in them that night. I lay awake in bed and then sat at my writing desk with the curtains open so I could watch the stars twinkle above London. It was a warm, restless night. Tiger prowled in and out through the window and I tried to imagine every possible scenario to account for James' disappearance.

I prayed that all my worry was in vain, and that I would receive a telegram from either James or Charlotte in the morning to tell me he was safe. It was the only possible outcome I could bear to consider.

But what if no telegram arrived? What was I to do if there was still no news of him by midday? Could I endure another day of not knowing what had happened? The longer he was missing the more likely it was that he had come to serious harm.

Images of the severed finger sprang to mind, and as I tried to push the thought away Charlotte's voice came into my head: *Perhaps he'll be washed up at Wapping or Rotherhithe. He told me that's where many of them end up, at the bend in the river.*

I decided to make myself a cup of cocoa, pacing my room

while I waited for the water to boil. I felt exhausted as my mind swung uncontrollably between thoughts of hope and deep anguish.

I had to do something to find James, but where could I start?

Once I had made my cocoa I sat at my desk and readied myself with a pen and paper. The only useful thing I could manage was to begin writing everything down.

I sipped at the warm, sweet cocoa and a sense of calm descended upon me. I had to make the most of the moment to write my thoughts down before the next wave of panic set in.

Was James' disappearance associated with the case he was investigating? That seemed like a safe assumption.

The murder of Mrs Forster had been carried out by a gang, some members of which were now in custody at Marylebone Lane police station. James had spoken to them on the day of his disappearance and had failed to keep his appointment with Charlotte that evening in Croydon. I felt sure the gang had accomplices who were still at large, and the possibility that the gang had ordered an attack on James was possible, despite Inspector Bowles considering it unlikely.

There was a remarkable similarity between the murders of Mr Forster and Mr Mawson. Both men had been stabbed in a public location. Mr Mawson's killer had deliberately sought him out at the opium den and Mr Forster's killer had done likewise at the East India Club. *Could the same man have carried out both murders, and did he have a connection to the gang who were already in custody?*

If it was the same killer I had to assume that he knew the gang because Mr Forster's murder had presumably been planned alongside Mrs Forster's. The gang had failed to find Mr Forster on that first fateful evening, so an accomplice had been sent after him. If that same accomplice had killed Mr

Mawson he was still at large and might have harmed James. I shivered at the thought.

The day before James' disappearance we had met with Mr Mawson, who had only realised at the end of our meeting that he might be considered a suspect in the murder of Mr Holland. Had he become so concerned by the idea of James suspecting him that he had ordered someone to attack him? If he had ordered an attack on Mr Holland it was likely he would do the same to James. But if so, why was Mr Mawson now dead?

I felt convinced that Mr Mawson had arranged the theft of Mr Holland's diaries, as there was no doubt that they contained incriminating accounts of his time in Ghazipur. But I still couldn't recall us having mentioned Mr Holland's diaries to him.

So who actually knew about the diaries?

Emma Holland had shown me one in the newsroom. I recalled that Edgar and Frederick had scarpered by that point, but questioned whether my memory was accurate. I could remember her showing me the mention of Charles Mawson and felt sure that at that time we had been the only two people in the newsroom. *But had Edgar or Frederick somehow overheard us and told someone about the diary? If they had, why?*

The only other occasion on which I could recall discussing the diaries with Emma was in the tea room at Anderton's Hotel. It was there that she had first told me about their existence and I had advised her to read them. *It was possible that someone had overheard us, but who? Surely no one had expected to see us there as our meeting had been quite spontaneous.*

Emma had told me that her cousin and her cousin's husband also knew about the diaries, but the chances of this knowledge reaching the ears of an unscrupulous person seemed slim. *Perhaps Emma had told someone else about the diaries.*

Or perhaps James had mentioned them to the gang at Marylebone Lane police station.

As I wrote all this down and drew lines connecting the names and times I began to feel even more confused. What I saw on the paper before me was a tangled web, and somehow James was caught up in it.

I sat back in my chair feeling defeated. There had been four murders, one disappearance and a burglary. I was trying to make sense of it all but was getting nowhere.

I saw a faint glow above the rooftops on the horizon as the summer sun heralded the start of a new day. *Was James safe? Would I see him today?*

I couldn't sit around waiting for him; I had to do something. All I could think to do was pay a visit to Scotland Yard and find out whether his colleagues had any idea of his whereabouts.

During my last visit to the Yard Chief Inspector Cullen had begun to show some interest in the case. I recalled him smoking his pipe as I told him about Charles Mawson, and how he had known the Forsters and Holland. The chief inspector had raised an eyebrow when I mentioned Alfred Holland's diary.

That was something I'd forgotten. *I had told Cullen about the diary.*

Could a senior detective at Scotland Yard be behind the theft of Alfred Holland's diaries?

CHAPTER 49

I left home that morning having received no reassuring telegram from Charlotte. My heart felt heavy and I imagined hers feeling much the same. I travelled by underground railway from Moorgate to Westminster Bridge and arrived at Scotland Yard shortly before nine o'clock.

As I climbed the stairs to James' office I hoped beyond hope that he would be sitting at his desk. When I walked into the office I could barely bring myself to look at his empty chair. A chill ran through me.

Chief Inspector Cullen didn't seem remotely surprised to see me.

"Inspector Raynes is looking after the Mawson murder," he said, leafing through some papers. "You'll need to speak to him about the details."

"Thank you, sir, I will do," I replied. "Have you heard from Inspector Blakely?"

He glanced at the empty desk. "No, not yet. We're looking into it."

"What are you doing about his disappearance? What do you think has happened to him?"

"I really don't know, Miss Green. The chap must have been caught up in some bother."

"Do you know what sort of bother?"

"No, I don't."

"Because as far as I knew he was busy working on the Forster case. What else might he have got himself caught up in?"

"That's what we're trying to establish."

"You know about the severed finger, don't you?"

"Yes, we know all about that."

"It was presumably sent to him as a warning, and now the person who sent it appears to have gone one step further."

"It may not be that simple."

"None of it is *simple*, Chief Inspector!"

"There's no need to be curt with me."

"I didn't sleep last night, and yesterday evening Inspector Blakely's fiancée Charlotte visited me. She's terribly distraught about his disappearance, as are his parents. He's supposed to be getting married in five weeks' time! Everyone is beside themselves with worry."

"I'm sure they are, Miss Green. Inspector Blakely's colleagues are also concerned, and I'm a little bothered that one of my best detectives has not been seen for almost two days."

"What exactly are you doing about it?"

He sighed and regarded me over the rims of his spectacles. "We're looking into it, as I've already explained. It's unfortunate timing as we've had a sequence of horrendous murders, not least the dreadful business at the India Office yesterday."

"But surely the same people are behind all these tragic events?"

"Are they? That seems rather a grand assumption to make,

Miss Green. It's not how we approach things here at the Yard."

"Why should someone wish to steal Alfred Holland's diaries?"

Chief Inspector Cullen shook his head as if he had just been boxed about the ears. "They've been stolen, have they?"

"Yes!" I went on to explain how Emma Holland's home had been burgled.

"I see," he said when I had finished giving my explanation. I detected a slight smile beneath his thick moustache. "Perhaps Blakely has made off with them!"

"Is that supposed to be a joke?" I snapped.

"It was to begin with, but on reflection it's an interesting thought. We know that he wanted to read the diaries, and it must have been frustrating for him to discover that Emma Holland was not at home when you called there together. So instead of going to meet his fiancée that evening he hatched a plan to break into Miss Holland's home and steal the diaries. Having successfully carried off the theft he has chosen to lay low for a few days."

"James would never do anything like that!" I said scornfully.

"How do you know?"

"Because I know James. He wouldn't break into a house and frighten people. Besides, he didn't need to. Our plan was to meet Emma Holland the following day and look at the diaries then."

"Perhaps you don't know Blakely as well as you think you do."

"I know him well enough to know he would never behave in such a way."

"Sometimes detectives need to behave in unpredictable ways to pursue a successful outcome in a case."

I paused for a moment, struggling to comprehend what I

was hearing. *Could there be any truth to what Chief Inspector Cullen was saying?* It was certainly a reassuring explanation for James' disappearance, but I simply couldn't imagine him doing such a thing. It didn't seem right.

"I don't believe it," I said.

"I shouldn't like to believe it either," he replied, lighting his pipe. "But as a detective myself I know that I must consider all the possibilities, and one of those possibilities is Inspector Blakely behaving out of character. It would be a mistake to presume that everyone is completely predictable."

"Someone threatened Inspector Blakely," I retorted. "Someone committed the dreadful act of severing a man's finger from his hand. That person is capable of extreme violence, and I for one am incredibly worried about James. It would be a mistake to console yourself with the theory that he stole something and is in hiding. He's in danger, and the longer it takes us to find him..." I trailed off momentarily, mindful of what had happened to Charles Mawson only the previous day. "They have to be connected to the gang Inspector Bowles of D Division is holding at Marylebone Lane. Have you spoken to him?"

"Inspector Raynes has."

"Is Inspector Raynes carrying out the work Inspector Blakely had been doing?"

"For the time being, yes. You'll probably want to go and bother him now."

"Sometimes I find your manner quite offensive, sir."

"Offensive is a strong word, Miss Green."

"I recall you describing me as an ink-slinger with ideas above my station. You accused me of distracting Inspector Blakely from his work and threatened to have a word with Mr Sherman about my conduct."

"I don't see the need to haul all this up now, Miss Green.

We have a detective missing and a lot of work to do. Now go and bother Inspector Raynes, as I've already suggested."

"Did you order those diaries to be stolen, Chief Inspector Cullen?"

He removed his pipe from his mouth. "What a preposterous question! Why on earth would I do such a thing?"

"Because barely anyone else knew of their existence, sir."

"That's the only reason you have for accusing me?"

"At the moment, yes, but something doesn't seem quite right to me. You seemed completely unconcerned by Inspector Blakely's disappearance yesterday —"

"I was distracted by an horrific murder!"

"And there doesn't seem to be a great urgency about the search for him today."

"I would get a darn sight more done if you weren't here pestering me, now leave this office at once! He pointed a large forefinger at the door.

"What's going on, Chief Inspector? Do you know something you're not telling me?"

"I said *get out*!"

Not wishing to rile him any further, I did as he asked.

CHAPTER 50

After an unenlightening conversation with Inspector Raynes, who turned out to be a tall detective with a long nose, I headed over to the reading room. Perhaps I had hoped James would come and find me there as he had done on so many occasions.

I sat at one of the desks, removed some papers from my bag and placed them in front of me. I had an update from Inspector Raynes to write up, but it provided scarcely any new information.

"Penny!" whispered Francis. "How are you?"

The question sent an involuntary tear rolling down my face. Another followed and then several more until it felt impossible to stop them.

"I'm sorry," I replied, getting up from my seat and dashing toward the door.

Francis followed me out onto the steps of the British Museum, where I stopped and drew in great gulps of air.

"What has happened?" he asked. "You seem distraught."

He pulled a neatly folded handkerchief from his pocket and handed it to me. I pulled off my spectacles, mopped my face with it and began to feel faint. I sank down onto one of the steps.

Francis sat down beside me.

"Penny?"

"It's James, he's missing!"

"Missing?"

Between sobs I explained the events of the past few days. His brow furrowed as I spoke.

"There must be a simple explanation," he said when I had finished. "James can't have come to any harm, I feel sure of it."

"I hope not. But these people... they don't care about anyone. Four have already been murdered, and then there's the finger. Someone cut off a finger, Francis!"

He sighed and shook his head. "Grotesque."

"They won't hurt James, will they? We would know if he'd been murdered, wouldn't we? Much like Mr Mawson at the India Office. They would have attacked him in a similar way, wouldn't they? They must be holding him somewhere, but hopefully he's unharmed. I cannot bear the thought of someone hurting him. If anything happened to him I would hold myself accountable!"

"Why should you do that? It's not your fault. Being a detective is a dangerous job. You and I both know that, as does James."

"But we would know if they had hurt him, wouldn't we?"

"I should think so, yes. Although hearing no news is concerning, we can also be encouraged by it. We must remain hopeful of his safe return."

"Where can he be, Francis? Where is he right at this moment? I cannot bear it any longer. I just need to know!"

The tears overwhelmed me again and Francis sat close by as I bent my head into my knees and cried. He gently wrapped an arm across my shoulders, his presence instantly warm and comforting.

The tears eventually stopped, but my body felt heavy with exhaustion. I leaned against Francis' shoulder and we sat there together for some time.

Once I had recovered I put my spectacles back on and looked down at the steps, remembering it as the place where James and I had first met one foggy day in October. He had been investigating the murder of Lizzie Dixie and asked for my help. I smiled as I remembered how I had considered him a nuisance at the time.

I raised my eyes to the railings which ran along Great Russell Street and looked beyond them to where the Museum Tavern sat on the corner of Museum Street. The pub had been our meeting place so many times, and now those days seemed to be confined to the past.

Would I ever see James again?

Another loud sob erupted from my chest.

"Are you all right, Penny?"

"I'm not, Francis. I wish there was something I could do, but I feel completely helpless."

"I'm sure if you put your mind to it you'd think of something. Just remember all those problematic cases you've assisted James with in the past."

"Only it's rather different when you're involved in it, isn't it?"

"You've been involved in each and every case, Penny, you make it your business to be. That's why you're so good at what you do."

"Thank you, Francis. I appreciate the compliment, but I wish I shared your confidence. These events feel completely beyond my control. I simply cannot see a way out."

"Perhaps Blakely went to Bognor Regis for the sea air."

"Shush, Potter," said Edgar. "You'll make Miss Green feel even worse."

I sat at the typewriter staring silently at the keys in front of me. According to the clock on the newsroom mantelpiece it was almost three o'clock and there had still been no word from James.

The door slammed, and I tried my best to finish the sentence I had begun typing about five minutes previously. For a few minutes I had felt overcome by the urge to sleep, and there had been moments when I hadn't been sure whether I was awake or dreaming.

"Miss Green?"

"Yes, sir?"

Mr Sherman stood by my side. "So you did hear me?"

"Yes."

"Eventually! I said your name three times."

"Did you, sir? I'm sorry, I really don't know what I was thinking about ..."

"Blakely, no doubt."

"I'm worried about him."

"I'm not surprised. Once you've finished your article you should go home and take some rest."

"It's difficult to rest when my mind is so busy."

"That doesn't mean you shouldn't try."

"He'll turn up, Miss Green," said Edgar. "He wouldn't want you worrying about him like this. The chap has everything under control, I feel sure of that."

"Did you know anything about Alfred Holland's diaries?" I asked Edgar.

He shook his head. "No."

"Did you know about them, Frederick?" I asked.

"Know about what?"

"The diaries Alfred Holland kept? Did you see his sister bringing one of the diaries here?"

"No, should I have? I think we were on our way out when she visited."

"That's my recollection," I admitted.

"Why do you ask, Miss Green?" asked Edgar.

"Someone stole the diaries from her," I said, "and the person who did so must be connected in some way to Alfred Holland's death. And possibly to the murder of the Forsters and Charles Mawson."

"Please go home and rest, Miss Green," said my editor. "Leave the case for the police to work on, and if there's any extra reporting required over the next day or so I can ask one of these chaps to do it. You'll come down with a fever if you don't stop thinking about all this. Ask that landlady of yours to keep an eye on you for a day or two."

"I'm fine, Mr Sherman, and I don't need a rest."

He stared at me and said nothing.

"But I'll do what you ask given that I probably don't have any choice in the matter," I added.

He gave me a brief smile. "Very good, Miss Green."

I left the offices a short while later and stepped out into Fleet Street, where a light drizzle was beginning to fall. Although I had no inclination to rest I knew the advice everyone was giving me made sense. I looked out for the next omnibus which would take me in the direction of the Bank.

A few yards away a woman was glancing up at the buildings as if trying to read the signage on them. She wore a pale blue dress and looked familiar somehow.

"Charlotte?" I asked.

CHAPTER 51

"Oh, Penny! Thank goodness I've found you. For a moment I couldn't remember the name of the newspaper you worked for. The *Morning Express*, isn't it? My mind feels so muddled."

Charlotte's face looked more drawn than usual, and I suspected that she hadn't slept either.

"Is there any news?" I asked.

"None." She sighed. "I've been sitting at home with Mother and Father for much of the day, just waiting to hear something. I sent a telegram to the Yard and received a reply telling me to remain where I was in case James gets in touch."

Charlotte's hat and hair were damp with rain. I pulled an umbrella out of my carpet bag and opened it out over both of us.

"I visited the Yard this morning and spoke with Chief Inspector Cullen," I said. "They're looking for James and he isn't too concerned yet, so we should take comfort from that."

There was no comfort to be found in Cullen's actions, but

I had no wish to let Charlotte know that. For some reason I still felt the need to reassure her.

"I suppose they know what they're doing, don't they?"

"Yes," I replied, but I could tell that she had noticed my less-than-convincing expression. "I'm assuming you came to Fleet Street to find me."

"I did! I hope you don't mind. As I said, I've spent much of the day sitting at home, and by this afternoon I feared I would be driven mad by all the waiting and not knowing. How long will it go on for?"

"I wish I knew."

"I thought I'd come and find you, Penny, because there must be something I can do, mustn't there? I really don't know what, but I'm aware from what James has told me that you usually find a way of making things happen."

Charlotte's expression remained hopeful.

"James may well have overstated my capabilities," I said. "I've never been in a situation before where someone I care... someone I *know* has gone missing in this way. I've never been so worried before, and although I have tried to reassure myself that James will return to us unharmed, I really don't know what to do. I'm sorry, Charlotte, but I feel quite lost at the moment. I have no suggestions at all."

"But you must! You have to! I came here full of hope that you'd have at least one idea of what we could do to find him. You're a news reporter, and you've been to all sorts of places and done all kinds of things. You've helped James solve some of his cases. Please, Penny, I realise you're tired and upset, but I know you can do something about this. I'm here to help you. We can do it together. We have to!"

I knew Charlotte would never have approached me if she had an inkling that I had kissed her future husband. I looked away, worried that she would somehow read what I had done in my face.

I looked along Fleet Street in the direction of home and knew that if I returned there I would only be pacing the floor of my room, and that sleep wouldn't come easily. Like Charlotte, I knew my mind would find no rest unless I was doing something about James' disappearance.

"There's one place I can think of," I began.

"Where?" I looked at Charlotte's young, hopeful face and felt concerned that she had probably never been anywhere remotely unpleasant in her life.

"The East End."

Her hopeful look faded slightly, as I had expected it would.

"Inspector Bowles of Marylebone Lane police station is holding a gang there who are suspected of breaking into the home of Mr and Mrs Forster."

"She was murdered there, wasn't she?"

"Yes, sadly the gang attacked Mrs Forster in her bed. I know that James helped interview the gang at Marylebone Lane station on the day of his disappearance. Inspector Bowles told me a few of them had been arrested around Commercial Street. I have a suspicion that a few of their acquaintances may still be in the area."

Charlotte's eyes grew wide with worry.

"You think we should go to the East End to find members of the gang? But what does that have to do with James?"

"I'm wondering whether the gang he spoke to wanted to exact some sort of revenge on him. They may have asked an accomplice to —"

"To do what?" Charlotte's eyes widened even further.

"I'm sure he's fine, Charlotte. They may have detained him somewhere, but let's go and see what we can find out from H Division at the station on Commercial Street."

"The gang are holding him, is that what you think?"

"It's a thought, that's all. I really don't know what else to try."

"Then let's go."

"Are you sure you're happy to do this?"

"We have to do something, don't we?"

The journey to the police station at the north end of Commercial Street took about twenty minutes in a hansom cab. As we travelled I tried to explain the case to Charlotte.

"Goodness, it all sounds rather confusing," she said. "James had told me a little of it, but I try to discourage him from talking about work too much. I think it's important for him to forget about it now and again, and to enjoy other aspects of life. I'm not very successful in stopping him, however. He can become terribly distracted by it. He's often scribbling down little notes to himself or pondering over something. He did seem unusually distracted in the lead-up to his disappearance."

When Charlotte talked about James I felt envious. I wished I could have spent those moments with him instead of her, and I would never have tried to discourage him from talking about his work. I understood how a case could occupy one's mind night and day, and for a moment I imagined what it would be like if James and I were married. We would have discussed cases for as long as we liked, whenever we wanted. And then I wondered whether that was necessarily a good thing.

Although I felt envious of Charlotte I also felt sympathy for her. I knew exactly how she felt, and I could see that she was relying on me to make her feel better. In her hour of need she had turned to me for help. I realised that my motivation for helping her was partly driven by guilt.

The police station on Commercial Street was a large,

wedge-shaped building with a lower storey clad in stone and two upper storeys of red brick.

"I hope they can help us," muttered Charlotte as we stepped through the door.

A young, wiry police sergeant was chatting to the desk officer as we walked in. I introduced Charlotte and myself.

"Have you heard about the disappearance of Inspector James Blakely?" I asked the police sergeant.

"Can't say that I have," he replied.

"But you're aware that Inspector Bowles is holding some men from this area at Marylebone Lane police station?"

"Ah yes, the men who burgled the Forster home in St James's Square. I helped Bowles with that. I rounded many of them up personally. I'm Detective Sergeant Harrison." He had a thin, clean-shaven face and keen brown eyes.

"I was wondering whether the men being held by Inspector Bowles have any acquaintances in this area," I asked.

"Yes, everyone knows them around here."

"I suspect the men you arrested may have instructed someone to harm..." I glanced warily at Charlotte "...Not harm, necessarily, but somehow detain Inspector Blakely. I think someone in this area may have had something to do with his disappearance."

"Do you want me to find out for you?"

"We would be extremely grateful for anything you could do to help. We're desperate for news."

"Has Scotland Yard not asked for your help in finding him yet?" asked Charlotte.

"No, there's been no word from the Yard about the inspector. Never mind, let's go and find him, shall we?"

"You make it sound so easy, Sergeant," she replied.

CHAPTER 52

Sergeant Harrison skipped down the steps of the police station and we followed him at a brisk pace down Commercial Street, which was thronging with people despite the rain. A crowd had gathered outside a music hall, readying themselves for an evening of entertainment. The taverns were busy, and the costermongers were desperately trying to sell off the last of their wares for the day. A quick glance down the side streets revealed numerous rundown lodging houses, cramped houses and littered courtyards. Dirty-faced children played in the street, skipping out of the way of carts and barrows just in time.

We reached the junction with Hanbury Street and Sergeant Harrison led us up to a large, noisy pub called The Golden Heart. Without hesitation he pushed open one of the doors and we followed him inside, where loud voices and tobacco smoke filled the air.

A number of the men inside seemed to recognise the sergeant, and they parted to let us through. Charlotte and I ignored the leers and suggestive comments.

We walked through a door to a smaller bar, and Sergeant

Harrison made straight for a table of lean, grimy-looking men with slack jaws and hard, narrow eyes. Their expressions suggested a deep dislike of him. For an uneasy moment we surveyed each other, and one of the men lifted a clay pipe to his mouth. My eye was drawn to the movement, and then I spotted something unusual about his hand.

The little finger was missing.

"Him!" I cried, pointing at the young man. "He must know something!"

To my astonishment, Sergeant Harrison swiftly grabbed the young man by the ear and hauled him up off his stool.

"Out the back," he ordered.

He dragged the man out through a small door and into a foul-smelling yard with a high wall. The man's friends cackled as we followed the pair.

"Get orf!" protested the man as Harrison continued to pull at his ear.

"It's not necessary to hurt him," I said.

"Oh, but it is, madam, it is," replied Sergeant Harrison. He sneered at the young man as he addressed him. "Introduce yourself to these nice ladies."

"Tommy," he replied through gritted teeth.

"Now then, Tommy, would you happen to know anything about the inspector from the Yard what's gone missing?"

"No."

"Are you sure?" Sergeant Harrison pulled harder on the lad's ear, which made him yelp.

"Perhaps if you let go he'd be more inclined to answer," I said.

Sergeant Harrison glared at me for interrupting.

"There's only one way of dealing with men like this," he barked. "Now what can you tell me about the inspector?" he said to Tommy.

"Nuffink!"

Voices rose up from beyond the high wall, and Charlotte and I exchanged a worried glance. The place made me anxious, and the bullying behaviour of Sergeant Harrison did nothing to put my mind at ease.

"What has happened to your finger?" I asked Tommy.

"I ain't sayin'."

"Did someone cut it off?" I asked. "Do you know what they did with it?"

"Why do you want to know that?" Sergeant Harrison asked me.

"Inspector Blakely received a severed finger in the post," I replied. "Perhaps it belonged to Tommy."

"Someone sent James a *finger*?" exclaimed Charlotte in abject horror. I had forgotten she had not been informed of the development. "In the *post*?"

"The Yard receives quite a lot of odd things in the post," I said, trying to lessen the impact of this new revelation.

"I realise that, but a finger? Was it this man's finger?" she asked.

"That's what I should like to know," I said. "Because if it is, he can lead us to the people who threatened James and are presumably responsible for his disappearance."

"I see." Charlotte's face had turned pale.

"Heard from your friends in Marylebone Lane, have you?" Sergeant Harrison pulled even harder on Tommy's ear, causing him to howl with pain. "Did they send you a message?" he demanded.

"Stop it!" shouted Charlotte.

"I've got to make him talk, madam."

"Not like this," she said. "He's already had his finger cut off, show the man some sympathy. Perhaps we could ask him nicely —"

Charlotte was interrupted by a cackle of laughter from Sergeant Harrison.

"Ask him nicely, Miss Jenkins? Does this man look like the sort of man you can speak nicely to? He can hardly string three words together, let alone understand questions other people put to him."

"If he's of no help to us, please stop hurting him," I said.

"I didn't say he was of no help. His brother Blinker's a member of that gang down in Marylebone Lane."

"I don't know nuffink about wot 'e done!" Tommy protested.

I wondered whether Tommy's brother had removed the finger. More voices could be heard from the other side of the wall.

"Do you know who ordered the gang to carry out the attack on Mr and Mrs Forster, Tommy?" I asked.

"I don't know nuffink, like I said!"

The situation was becoming quite frustrating. Even if Tommy knew something he evidently wasn't going to share it with us.

A shout came from beyond the wall and suddenly there was a loud smash behind Sergeant Harrison. A flash of flame rose up and spread across the yard. He let go of the young man and lunged toward the door of the pub.

Charlotte screamed. I grabbed her arm and pulled her along behind me in pursuit of Sergeant Harrison. Inside the pub, people leapt to their feet as they realised something serious had occurred.

There was no sign of Tommy or his friends.

"We need to get out of here!" I called to Charlotte.

"Fire!" someone shouted, prompting a rush to the street outside.

Elbows were shoved into my shoulders and face. I fought to push through the smelly, unwashed crowd. I couldn't see past the men in front of me, and for a moment my feet left the floor as I was carried by the mob. A sensation of panic rose from my chest into my throat, and my breath felt constricted. I stumbled as my feet returned to the ground and I fought to stay upright, terrified that if I fell I would be trampled upon.

Just as I was beginning to think I would be confined to this interminable crush forever I found myself outside on the damp, filthy pavement, gasping for air. People stumbled all around me.

"Charlotte!" I called out.

I looked around frantically, trying to catch a glimpse of her pale blue dress. I eventually found her slumped against the wall of the pub, where a sunken-cheeked man with an eyepatch was trying to make her acquaintance.

"Charlotte, are you all right?"

"Penny, thank goodness!" She took my hand and stood to her feet. "What happened in that yard? Where did those flames come from?"

"I'm guessing it was lit paraffin in a bottle. We heard those voices on the other side of the wall, didn't we? They must have been Tommy's friends."

She nodded.

I turned to see a dozen or so police officers dispersing the crowd with their truncheons raised.

"So what do we do now?" Charlotte asked.

"I really don't know."

CHAPTER 53

"It's no enormous surprise to find you at the centre of this debacle, Miss Green," said Chief Inspector Cullen as we stood in the parade room at Commercial Street police station.

Sergeant Harrison had found Charlotte and me outside the Golden Heart pub and escorted us back to the police station in the interests of our safety.

"I find your comment rather uncharitable, Chief Inspector," I retorted. "Miss Jenkins and I were merely conducting some enquiries about the possible whereabouts of Inspector Blakely."

"Which ended up causing a full-scale riot in London's East End!"

"That was not our fault! There is clearly great antagonism between H Division and some of the people who live here, and we merely found ourselves caught up in it."

"There's no antagonism, Miss Green," corrected Sergeant Harrison. "They understand we're in charge and sometimes they get a little lively."

"You need to return home, Miss Jenkins," said Chief

Inspector Cullen. "You're making a big mistake having anything to do with this ink-slinger. In fact, you probably don't need me to tell you that; you've no doubt realised it for yourself by now."

"I want to know where James is," protested Charlotte, "and I asked Miss Green for her help!"

"You should have asked the police," he replied, "not some news reporter."

"I did ask the police," she replied, "and they've done nothing! *You've* done nothing! That's why I thought Miss Green was my best hope."

"You're overestimating the woman's capabilities."

"What exactly are you doing to find Inspector Blakely, Chief Inspector?" I asked. "Someone must be holding him somewhere, and this someone has to be connected to the case he's working on. D Division already has some of the men in custody, so why aren't you arresting more and questioning them?"

"We're doing what we can, Miss Green."

"I don't think you are, and that's why Miss Jenkins has asked for my help. She and her family are desperate for news, yet they've received no assurance that anything is being done. One of your colleagues is missing and you don't seem the least bit concerned about it."

Chief Inspector Cullen sighed. "It's almost eight o'clock in the evening and you ladies should be in the safety of your homes."

"Is there something you're not telling us, Chief Inspector?" I asked bluntly.

"Of course not. And even if there was I cannot publicly state something which might prejudice the investigation. You're a news reporter, Miss Green, so it should come as no surprise to you that I have no wish to divulge the details of everything I'm working on."

"I have no interest in publishing any of this in the newspaper! My concern for Inspector Blakely is of a personal nature, and Miss Jenkins is his fiancée. Don't you see how important any information you might have on his whereabouts is to her? I demand you to tell her something – anything – which could allay her fears. She and Inspector Blakely are to be married in just a few weeks' time, and she needs to know that matters are in hand for his safe return. How will she even be able to sleep at night otherwise? If you wish to tell her something in private I can leave this room in order for you to do so. Surely you can see how trying this is for her."

"You misunderstand me," he said. "I did not intend to suggest that I know anything, but merely to clarify that if I did I wouldn't necessarily, as a matter of course, share that information with you. Now go home, Miss Green, before you say something you later regret."

CHAPTER 54

Mrs Garnett's knock woke me the following morning. A heavy sleep had finally descended upon me in the early hours and my head ached as I opened my eyes.

"Telegram!" she called out, pushing an envelope beneath my door.

I leapt up to read it, hopeful of good news. My head span with the sudden movement and I stumbled as I picked the envelope up from the floor.

The telegram was from the *Morning Express* offices:

Miss Holland begs meeting with you.

The telegram was dated the previous evening. I had returned home so late that I hadn't noticed it waiting for me on the hallway table.

I hurriedly dressed and fed Tiger some sardines. After eating them she curled up on my bed to sleep while I left the house and dashed to Moorgate station, from which point I could take the underground train to Gower Street station near Euston.

I couldn't think why Emma wished to see me, but I was desperate for news of any sort. I wanted something – no matter how small or irrelevant – which would hopefully lead me to James.

"Penny, are you all right?" asked Emma as she welcomed me into her home. "You're not unwell, are you?"

"No, I'm quite well, thank you. I must confess that I haven't eaten a great deal in the past few days. I've been rather distracted."

"Come and sit in the dining room. We've only just finished breakfast, so I'll ask Doris to bring up some fresh toast and eggs."

I felt the need to explain my tired appearance, so I told her about James' disappearance and of my fruitless search for him.

"How terrible! I suppose we usually assume that detectives never come to any harm. They somehow seem infallible, don't they? You must be extremely worried."

I nodded. "I have to remain hopeful and determined. I don't trust Chief Inspector Cullen, his superior at the Yard. I think he's withholding something from me."

"That other chap was murdered, wasn't he?"

"Which one?" I asked, buttering a slice of toast. I suddenly realised how hungry I was.

"The man Alfred mentioned in his diaries. Mr Mawson."

"Yes, it was a dreadful attack. I interviewed a member of staff at the India Office who had spoken to the perpetrator shortly before he carried out the act. It's just awful. I cannot make head nor tail of what's been happening these past few days. Have the Holborn police been of any help with regard to the theft of your brother's diaries?"

"None at all."

She sighed, and I felt disappointed that she appeared to have nothing new to tell me.

"I think the man who attacked Mr Mawson could be the same man who murdered your brother," I said. "Inspector Raynes at Scotland Yard is looking after the case. Has he spoken to you?"

"No, I haven't heard from him. Perhaps he's planning to."

"I hope so. I should like to know where your brother's diaries have got to. They clearly contained information someone wished to remain hidden."

"Yes, they contained quite a few damning accusations. I don't know how true it all is, but I have no reason to believe that Alfred would lie."

"Just the accusations regarding Mawson, or others as well?"

"Alfred was also caught up in something. I was too upset when I saw you last to explain what else I had read."

"Did you manage to read much of the diaries before they were taken?"

"I got as far as July, but I hadn't found the chance to update you. I visited your offices yesterday evening in the hope that I would catch you just as you finished work for the day."

"I was already heading for the East End with Charlotte Jenkins at that time. What exactly was Alfred caught up in?"

"After Mawson was dismissed a man approached Alfred. It seems he told him in no uncertain terms that because he had caused Mawson's dismissal Alfred would have to take his place."

"Oh dear. Did your brother say who the man was?"

"No, I don't think he knew his name, but he wrote that the chap was a native."

"And did Alfred agree to the man's request?"

"No, he declined. He explained that many forms had to be completed when the opium arrived from the districts, and that other people oversaw the filling out of these forms. He made it clear that the opium pots were locked away as soon as they arrived and told the man he couldn't agree to such a thing.

"But it seems the native didn't give up. He made a second approach and Alfred refused once again. Then he approached him a third time and it seems his manner became more threatening. He told my brother he would inform the factory that Alfred was stealing opium from them, which was untrue of course, if Alfred wasn't acquiescent. He also offered him money, and in the end I think Alfred was worn down by it all."

"So Alfred began stealing opium from the factory?"

"Yes, just as Mawson had."

"And was he found out?"

"I presume that was why he returned to England. By then he was using opium regularly, and I don't think he ever recovered from the shame of what he had done."

"Did he write in any detail about the people for whom he was stealing?"

"He was trying to find out more. In the last entry he wrote that he was about to question the native man who met with him once a week. They had begun to get along quite well, and Alfred seemed to think he had gained the man's trust."

"So it's possible Alfred did find out more and wrote about it in his diary?"

"Yes, although unfortunately I didn't get as far as that part before the diary was stolen. There was a mention of some sort of unofficial trade with China."

"Presumably illegal trade, away from the jurisdiction of the Indian government."

"I can't say that for certain, but his diary certainly implied it."

"Anyone obtaining and selling opium in that way must be making good money as they would avoid paying tax to both the Indian and Chinese governments."

"I imagine so, though I really don't know enough about it."

"Your brother and Charles Mawson found themselves caught up in the trade of stolen opium. I wonder if Mr Forster also had a hand in it. That may be the connection between their deaths."

"I suppose it could be. But how can we prove it? And how do we find out who killed them?"

"I think it has to be the person who didn't want Inspector James Blakely to find out. It must be the man behind James' disappearance."

CHAPTER 55

"I'm convinced that Chief Inspector Cullen of Scotland Yard knows more than he is letting on about Inspector Blakely's disappearance," I said to Mr Sherman in his office later that morning.

"What makes you so sure?"

"I have deduced it from the way he conducts himself; from the things he says and the things he doesn't say."

"If he does know something I'm sure he must have an extremely good reason for withholding it."

"But not from Inspector Blakely's fiancée. The woman is beside herself! Poor Charlotte. Chief Inspector Cullen won't even tell her what he knows."

"Perhaps he doesn't know anything more."

"I am certain that he does!"

Mr Sherman sighed. "You're simply assuming."

"I have never liked nor trusted the man."

"That's where the root of this sentiment lies, isn't it? You assume that he's up to no good because you've never trusted him."

"We need to find Inspector Blakely urgently. Charlotte is desperate with worry."

"As are you, no doubt."

"Yes, I am! If Chief Inspector Cullen would only tell me what he knows I could help him."

"You need to leave all this to the Yard."

"But I don't trust the man"

"What would you have me do about it?"

"We need to publish a story about Inspector Blakely's disappearance and hope that someone reading it will come forward with useful information. And I'd also like you to speak to your cousin."

"Commissioner Dickson?" Sherman sighed again.

"Yes, your cousin is the chief inspector's superior, after all. He can wring the information out of him!"

"It's not my job to get involved, Miss Green."

"But we have to do something. Chief Inspector Cullen soon got himself involved when I wrote that article about the wrong man being hanged for the Doughty Street murders. He used the relationship between yourself and Dickson to have me suspended me from my job."

"So getting Dickson involved again is your opportunity for revenge."

"Of course not! I just want someone to ensure me that the chief inspector is being quite honest about Inspector Blakely's disappearance."

"Surely it's not a question of who's being honest. The important point is that the chap's found, isn't it? I'm sure Cullen has no interest whatsoever in complicating the case. He'll be doing his best to ensure the safe return of his colleague, and his methods are not for you or me to question, Miss Green. I certainly can't use my familial relationship with the commissioner to ensure that Cullen is doing his job properly! I can understand your frustration, but there's a limit to what I can do. You must trust the Yard to find their man. You may not agree with the way Cullen conducts himself, but he's worked for the Metropolitan Police for more than thirty years. On this occasion I insist that you defer to his considerable experience."

My jaw was clenched tightly as I left the editor's office.

"I thought you were supposed to be resting at home, Miss Green," said Edgar.

"I cannot rest while Inspector Blakely is missing," I retorted.

"If you're working today perhaps you would like to pursue one of the news stories Sherman has dropped on me and Potter," continued Edgar. "We have far too much to do."

"Maybe later," I replied, packing my papers into my carpet bag. "There's someone I have to go and see."

My brother-in-law worked at a law firm in the narrow, cobbled thoroughfare of Austin Friars in the City of London. He appeared surprised, and slightly displeased, to see me.

"Penelope I'm extremely busy. You mustn't make a habit of disturbing me at work."

"I think this is the first time I have ever disturbed you at work, George."

He sat in a large office with mahogany wainscoting and red-and-gold flocked wallpaper. A leather easy chair beside the fireplace looked particularly comfortable and I could picture him having an afternoon rest in it.

"Although I welcome you here as my sister-in-law, I'm aware that you're currently acting in your capacity as a news reporter and that I am here in my capacity as a lawyer —"

"I won't detain you for more than a minute, George. Please can you tell me where I might find Mr Sheridan?"

"Oh no, Penny, I cannot allow you to go pestering that man again. Both he and I are working extremely hard on the contract with the India Office, and negotiations have reached the most critical stage."

"Yes, he mentioned that contract to me when I last spoke to him. However, I'm sure he won't mind speaking to me again. He was quite amenable outside the Burlington Hotel last week."

"He's a busy man, Penny."

"We're all busy, George. Where's his office?"

His mouth open and closed, but no words came out. He seemed torn between telling me and keeping the information to himself.

"It's in the City, isn't it?" I said. "It can't be far from here. Just tell me and then I'll be on my way."

"What are you going to ask him?"

"About Mr Forster. I have reason to believe that he may have been caught up in something illegal, and I should like to find out whether Mr Sheridan knows anything more about it."

"Mr Sheridan certainly won't know of any illegal activity! He's one of my most prestigious clients, and if he finds out I've sent you to his door —"

"He won't find out."

"Can you promise me that?"

"If I had really wanted to find out where Mr Sheridan's office was I could have researched his company's address in the records kept at the British Library. I came here because I assumed it would be quicker."

"You're going to tell him that you searched for the address of his company at the British Library?"

"Of course! Your name won't come into it, I promise. Now where is he?"

"You mustn't pester him."

"I won't! I have a single question to put to him about Mr Forster, and that is all. This is important, George. You heard about the murder in Whitehall, didn't you?"

"Yes, a shocking business, that is."

"Indeed it is, and I intend to find out who's behind it."

CHAPTER 56

"Mr Sheridan doesn't see visitors without an appointment," said his secretary, Miss Wainman.

She was a plump lady in a dark stuff dress. Its hem skimmed the shiny floor of a large hallway in which white pilasters supported an elaborate plasterwork ceiling. A glittering chandelier was suspended over our heads and on the wall a flattering portrait of Mr Sheridan hung next to a large map of India.

"I realise he would prefer me to have made an appointment," I said. "However, I spoke with him just the other evening and I only wish to ask him a quick question about Mr Forster."

After my protracted conversation with George I was growing tired of people being obstructive.

"Please, Miss Wainman," I continued, "can't you at least let Mr Sheridan know that I wish to have a quick word with him? Then perhaps he can decide for himself whether he wishes to speak to me or not."

"He employs me to make these decisions for him."

"Perhaps you could remind him that he spoke to me

outside the Burlington Hotel last week. I'm sure he'll remember."

At that moment a door at the far end of the hall opened and a young man with a dark moustache stepped out. He acknowledged me with a nod.

"May I have a word, Miss Wainman?" he asked.

They both looked at me as if waiting for me to leave, but I stayed put. *If I left, how would I ever find out any answers about Mr Forster?*

"I'm here to see Mr Sheridan," I explained to the young man.

"I see, well I'll leave you in the capable hands of Miss Wainman," he replied.

I was about to argue with her further when the short, round form of Mr Sheridan stepped through the door.

"I forgot to say, Grieves... Oh, hello, Miss Green. What can I do for you?"

To my relief he gave me a warm smile. I was impressed that he had remembered my name from our brief meeting.

"Good morning, Mr Sheridan. I realise this is probably an inconvenient time, but I should like to ask you a quick question about Mr Forster if I may?"

He checked his pocket watch. "I only have a few minutes. What's happening with the investigation into his murder?"

"I wish I knew, sir."

"Bear with me one minute, Grieves. Just wait here while I speak to Miss Green."

"You've heard about the dreadful murder of Charles Mawson, I presume?" I said as he bid me sit on a velvet chair in his capacious office. Sunlight streamed in through a row of tall windows.

"I have indeed. What an awful situation."

"Do you remember me asking you about Alfred Holland?"

He paused for a moment. "I think so... Yes, I remember now. This was before the dinner at the Burlington Hotel, wasn't it? You asked me about Mr Forster and then Mr Holland."

"I have discovered that both Mr Mawson and Mr Holland worked at the Ghazipur opium factory."

"Did they indeed?"

"And they both stole opium from the factory."

"Really?" Mr Sheridan raised an eyebrow. "How ever did they manage that? There are so many checks and balances in place I would have thought it impossible."

"They falsified records."

"Goodness me!" He sat back in his chair. "Both were caught and subsequently murdered."

"It has to be the reason they were murdered, doesn't it?"

"When you put it like that, I suppose it does. Presumably the Indian government took a rather dim view of their behaviour."

"Yes, more so with Mr Holland than with Mr Mawson. Apparently, Mr Mawson had an uncle at the India Office who arranged employment for him there. Both men were coerced into stealing and Holland was apparently approached a number of times. He only agreed to it when he began to fear for his life."

"Oh dear, that is terrible."

"The opium the men stole was part of an illegal trade, and I'm wondering whether Mr Forster might also have had something to do with it."

Disappointingly, Sheridan shook his head. "Oh no, never."

"Are you sure? It might explain why all three men were targeted."

"No, Mr Forster wasn't the type to get involved in anything like that."

"He had money troubles, did he not?"

"He did, and perhaps if he had got involved in something of that ilk his money troubles might have been solved!" Mr Sheridan gave a congenial laugh. "I apologise, that was rather flippant of me. No, he liked to do things properly. He wouldn't have got himself mixed up with stolen opium, that's for sure. It's far too dangerous."

"Are you quite sure about that?" I asked, disappointed that my theory had not been confirmed.

"Quite sure, Miss Green. He worked for me for a number of years and also ran his own merchant company for a time. You and I know that it wasn't successful, but he tried. It's a shame he wasn't particularly good at managing his money. That's ultimately what led to his downfall."

He observed my downcast face. "I apologise that I haven't told you what you wished to hear, but if there's anything else I can help with at any time do just ask. I want to find out what happened to the poor man just as much as you. In fact, I'm considering putting up some money through Scotland Yard to offer a reward for any information that leads to an arrest."

"I'm sure that would be of great help. Thank you, Mr Sheridan."

CHAPTER 57

"I wondered whether I would see you again, Miss Green," said Mr Chakravarty. He sat back in his chair and regarded me with a slight sneer. "Your attire is quite different today from when we last met. I hope you're not still expecting the mortgage offer to stand."

"Mr Chakravarty, I'd like to explain —"

He held up his hand to stop me. "There's no need; I know you're a news reporter with the *Morning Express*. I can't say that I understand what that charade was all about with Mr Billington-Grieg, but as there was no attempt to rob or defraud me I can only view it as a harmless waste of time."

"I wish to apologise for being deceitful."

"Is that why you've come to visit me today? Did your conscience get the better of you?"

"Partly yes, and —"

"You want something from me."

"I came here to ask you a question."

"What sort of question?"

"Regarding the late Mr Forster."

"I recall some gauche enquiries being made about him

during your last visit. What makes you think I want to talk about the man? The sooner I can forget about him the better."

"I wish to confirm something I have learned about him."

"And you believe that I can fulfil your wish?"

"I hope so."

"And you think I would be happy to do so after you and your brother-in-law sat in this very room last week and told me a tall tale about requiring a mortgage?"

"I apologise —"

"You wasted an hour of my time. That hour could have been spent with someone who had legitimate business with me."

"I regret what happened, Mr Chakravarty, and I must ask you to forgive me."

He gave a dry laugh. "If only you could have seen what an unconvincing duo you made! The pair of you were incredibly nervous, no doubt aware of the poorly devised plan you had come here to execute. Why couldn't you speak to me directly as a news reporter?"

"I thought you might refuse to talk to me."

Mr Chakravarty laughed again. "The irony is that you have now come to me as a news reporter anyway. Don't you see how foolish you look, Miss Green?"

I felt tempted to lay part of the blame at James' feet, but as he wasn't present to defend himself I decided to accept the criticism as it was presented to me. I sat in my chair and listened patiently to Mr Chakravarty, aware that I had little chance of getting what I wanted from him until he had said his piece.

"I've done business with a lot of scoundrels, and over the years I've learned how to spot them. Forster caught me out, but on the whole I pride myself on being able to discern those who are genuine from those who are not."

"Then why didn't you confront me and Mr Billington-Grieg at the time?"

"It would have been an embarrassment, wouldn't it? I try and avoid uncomfortable confrontations wherever possible. I've learned that it's often better to allow my enemies to think they've got away with something."

"I wouldn't wish you to consider me an enemy, Mr Chakravarty."

"Then don't lie to me, Miss Green."

"I shan't lie to you again."

"Good, though I'm sure you're only saying that because you want something from me."

"I wish to ask you a question because I'm trying to find out why four people with links to India have been brutally murdered within the past few weeks. I'm also trying to find my colleague, Inspector James Blakely, who has been missing for three days. My question to you will be quick and simple. If you have no intention of answering it please say so now and I'll make my enquiries elsewhere."

I could tell that while Mr Chakravarty had no wish to help me he couldn't help but feel intrigued.

"I'm rather busy at the present time," he said.

"Then I shall take my leave of you. I apologise for wasting your time further," I said as I rose from my seat.

"What was your question, Miss Green?"

"Do you mean to answer it?"

"I can't say either way until I know what the question is!"

It felt as though the conversation were turning into a game. I sat down again.

"I have reason to believe that Mr Forster may have been involved in the illegal trade of opium."

"On what grounds?"

"I heard it from someone who worked at the Ghazipur opium factory in India."

"Someone who knew him?"

"Of sorts. To your knowledge, was his merchant company involved in the procurement of stolen opium?"

Chakravarty paused to light his pipe.

"I made enquiries about the man after I realised he had defrauded me. The enquiries I made would seem to support your suggestion."

"So I'm right! He had an arrangement with certain workers in Ghazipur that they would supply him with opium, which he then sold illegally to buyers in China?"

"I didn't get into the detail, but I discovered enough to realise that the man was up to no good. I should have made my enquiries before lending him the money, but I let my guard down. There was something rather disarming about the man; he was quite likeable. I should have been more careful."

"Are you familiar with Sheridan and Company?" I asked.

"I am indeed."

"I spoke with Mr Sheridan this morning and he thinks Forster's murder must be connected to his financial difficulties. However, I'm inclined to think the illegal opium trading could have been the cause. Engaging in such an activity is likely to have brought him into contact with unscrupulous people, isn't it?"

"Indeed."

"So which do you think it is?" I asked.

"What do you mean?" Mr Chakravarty regarded me with a cool expression, giving nothing away.

"The money trouble or the illegal opium: which was the motive for his murder?"

"I have no idea, Miss Green. The police will find it all out, no doubt. Ultimately, it doesn't really matter. What's important is that Forster's misdemeanours caught up with him in the end."

CHAPTER 58

I t was late afternoon by the time I entered the reading room. During my omnibus journey I had pondered the information everyone had given me that day. If Augustus Forster, Alfred Holland and Charles Mawson had all been involved in the theft of opium, a single motive for their deaths appeared to have made itself clear. The motive for Mr Forster's death appeared to have been extended to Mrs Forster even though she was likely to have been innocent of any involvement in her husband's affairs.

I couldn't understand why Mr Chakravarty was so sure that Forster had been involved in illegal opium dealing when Mr Sheridan was certain that he hadn't. Sheridan had known Forster better than Chakravarty, so it made sense to believe his words. And Chakravarty had a motive for wishing Forster harm for defrauding him. I deduced that he might have been keen to support the idea of an alternative motive to deflect attention away from himself.

"Penny, how are you?" whispered Francis once I was seated at a desk. "I've been so worried about you."

"There's no need to worry about me," I replied. "Worry

about James instead; there is still no word on his whereabouts."

"Is there not?" Francis' face grew more sombre. "I'm sure Scotland Yard are doing all they can to find him."

"Actually, I don't think they are," I said. "I have an odd suspicion that Chief Inspector Cullen is hiding something from me, and I don't know why. I've told him he needs to tell poor Charlotte, James' fiancée, what he knows. It's dreadful for her to have to sit around waiting for news."

"And for you, I imagine."

"For all of us! You consider James a friend, too, don't you?"

Francis exhibited an odd expression. "Of sorts," he replied.

"But it's poor Charlotte who's suffering the most," I said, keen to pretend that I didn't care as much for James as she did.

"Yes, I feel dreadfully sorry for Charlotte," he said.

Francis' manner seemed slightly offhand. *Was it possible that he had realised how deeply worried I was about James?* I decided to change the subject.

"I think I've found a motive for these dreadful murders," I said, "but there are still a few matters that are confusing me slightly. I shall have a read through some copies of *The Homeward Mail* and see if I can find any more mentions of Mr Forster, Mr Mawson or Mr Holland in there."

"Of course!" Francis seemed cheered by the opportunity to help. "Which year in particular?"

"1883 again, I think, and particularly the summer editions. I know we've looked through them already, but there must be something we've missed. I want to find out if Forster got himself into any trouble in India. I've met someone who says he did and someone who says he didn't; I don't know who to believe. If *The Homeward Mail* cannot tell me I shall have to visit the India Office again and ask there."

"No, don't go near the India Office, Penny. Not after that terrible murder."

"I shall be fine, Francis. No one will be bothered with me."

It wasn't long before I grew tired of leafing through page after page of *The Homeward Mail*. I could find no further information on the three men. I decided to call on Chief Inspector Cullen again and find out what he was doing in the search for James.

I walked down the steps of the British Museum and stepped out onto Great Russell Street, looking for a hansom cab to hail. The evening was sunny and uncomfortably warm. I crossed the road to find a cab travelling in the right direction. I had almost reached the Museum Tavern when I felt a sharp grip on my right arm. I tried to pull away, but the grip tightened.

"Ow! Get off!" I shouted.

I turned to see a man in a dark suit and a wide-brimmed hat, which partially obscured his face.

"Silence, Miss Green, I have a gun. Just do what I say and you won't get hurt."

CHAPTER 59

The man with the gun pushed me forward and stayed close behind me. I tried to sneak a look at his face.

"Look where you're going, Miss Green, I'm warning you."

He marched me past the Museum Tavern and left into Museum Street, then left again into a narrow, dingy street. I knew we were parallel to Great Russell Street and at the rear of the elaborate buildings which lined it.

My heart pounded. *How could I get away? Did he intend to shoot me if I tried to escape?* I thought of the severed finger James had been sent. If this man had something to do with that I would need to be extremely careful.

I thought of the description given of the villain who had attacked Mr Mawson and Mr Forster. The man holding my arm was remarkably similar. *Was he the one who had shot Alfred Holland?* He had a calm, professional demeanour, as though this was the sort of thing he did every day.

We passed a man sleeping in a doorway and a four-wheeled carriage awaited us up ahead. My heart thudded heavily. *I was about to be driven to an unknown location.*

"You won't hurt me, will you?" I asked as we neared the carriage. "Please don't hurt me."

"Keep quiet, like I said."

Another man wearing dark clothing and a dark hat waited beside the carriage. He opened the door.

"Get in," he ordered.

I was pushed forward and forced to climb up into the carriage. I did as I was told, my legs trembling. All the while I was considering how to escape. *Surely there would be an opportunity to get away.* As I stepped up into the carriage I lunged for the door handle on the opposite side.

"Stop there, Miss Green, or I'll shoot!" came the order from behind me.

I reluctantly did as I was told, and as I turned I saw the second man pointing a gun at me.

"All right, I won't try anything," I said reassuringly, desperate for him to move the direction of the barrel away from me.

"You'd better not."

He lowered the gun and the two men climbed inside the carriage.

I sat down on the sprung leather seat. "At least tell me who you are and what you want with me," I said. "Can you please explain?"

"This is the third time I've asked you to remain quiet, Miss Green," said the first man, "I'm beginning to find you troublesome. Take this as your final warning."

He sat next to me and nodded at the second man, who was seated opposite. The second man pulled a black hood from his pocket, leaned forward and placed it over my head. The black cloth had a musty smell and completely obscured my vision.

"Not a word more from you, Miss Green," said the second man.

What I guessed to be a piece of twine was placed around my neck, tightened and knotted. "And don't you try taking this off," he continued. "If you mess this up it'll be a long time before anyone finds you."

I swallowed nervously, staring at the black material before my eyes. I gripped the carpet bag on my lap and resolved to remain silent. One of the men knocked on the side of the carriage and we pulled away with a lurch.

CHAPTER 60

I strained to listen to the sounds beyond the carriage window as we travelled, hoping that I might gain some clue as to my whereabouts. We moved slowly to begin with, no doubt hindered by the traffic around us. I heard church bells strike five o'clock and the sound of hooves, carriages and voices. My travelling companions remained silent.

After twenty minutes or so our pace quickened, and I assumed this meant we were leaving the centre of London. We continued at this pace for some time, and I guessed we were on a long, straight road. There was still occasional street noise beyond the carriage window, but it had certainly grown quieter. I wanted to ask how long the journey would take but felt too frightened to speak.

The carriage stopped for a short while and then took a couple of sharp turns. I imagined we had crossed a major road junction. Then I heard the sound of trains, some moving at a slow speed and then a much faster one. *We were obviously close to a main railway line, but which one?*

We sat in silence for what must have been about an hour.

The carriage eventually stopped and one of the men commanded me to climb out. I felt relieved that the journey had ended but anxious about the fate that awaited me.

One of the men held my arm as I clambered out of the carriage. There was paving beneath my feet, but I could hear little other than birdsong. I wondered whether anyone else could see me and what they would have made of the sight of two men and a woman wearing a hood over her head if so.

With the firm hand still on my arm I was marched swiftly toward a doorway.

"Mind the step, Miss Green," said one of the men.

The warning came slightly too late and I stumbled over it. I felt floorboards beneath my feet and then a door was closed behind me. The only sound was footsteps on floorboards, and I felt as though I were in an enclosed space, perhaps a house.

"Sit down," said one of the men.

I had no idea where there was a seat. I resisted when he gave me a shove, then fell back into a chair.

My breath was coming quick and fast. I felt more frightened now that I was behind a closed door. *What were these men planning to do to me? What did they want? Would they harm me?* My mind spun with fear. I tried to calm my breathing and clutched hold of the bag on my lap. *Surely if these men wanted to rob me they would have taken it by now.*

I wasn't even sure whether there was anyone else in the room. *Had they left me there alone?* I hadn't heard a door open or close.

"What do you want?" I asked as bravely as I possibly could. My voice sounded weak and there was a slight echo, as if the room was sparsely furnished.

I heard some muttering and then I jumped as I felt hands touching the rope around my neck. Someone was untying it. Then the hood was hauled off my head, pulling at my hair and spectacles as it was yanked away.

I squinted, my eyes unaccustomed to the light streaming through the curtains that partially covered a window in front of me. As my eyes adjusted I saw that I was sitting in an empty living room with only a fireplace and a few chairs in it. The two dark-clothed men stood near the fireplace, neither of them looking at me. They appeared to be waiting for someone.

I held my breath. *What was about to happen? Was I to be shot?*

Hearing footsteps beyond the door, I turned to see who it might be.

Into the room walked Chief Inspector Cullen.

CHAPTER 61

Unusually for the chief inspector, he smiled at me.

"Don't worry, Miss Green, you're safe now."

Warm relief flooded over me. I was out of danger, but the situation still made no sense.

"Why did these men treat me in such a rough manner?" I asked. "I was terrified they would hurt me!"

"We had to do it to keep you out of harm's way," he replied. "Far better this than what might otherwise have happened to you."

"What might have happened to me?"

He dismissed my question with a wave. "You're much safer now, Miss Green, believe me."

Anger welled up inside me. "But I don't understand," I said. "There was no need to scare me as you did. If I was in danger all you needed to do was explain that to me! To have me snatched off the street and a hood tied over my head was completely unnecessary."

"I could have explained the danger to you, but you wouldn't have listened to a word of it," he replied. "Sometimes a sudden shock is needed."

"Was there any genuine need to frighten me like that? Did your men really have to cover my face and head? I feared for my life!"

"The intention was to frighten you a little, Miss Green, as we needed you to comply. Had my men asked you politely you wouldn't have come, would you?"

"I cannot say that I agree," I spat. "Who are these men, anyway?" I gestured animatedly toward the pair standing impassively beside the fireplace. "Are they police officers?"

"Do calm down, Miss Green, we're merely keeping you safe. You don't stay in one place for long, do you? Yesterday you were hassling gang members at a pub in the East End, and how many people have you spoken to today? I counted at least four: Miss Holland, Mr Billington-Grieg, Mr Sheridan and Mr Chakravarty. And a visit to the reading room, too."

"You've been following me," I snarled. "How *dare* you!"

"Someone needed to keep an eye on you."

"Don't you have more important things to do than follow me around?"

"Oh, I didn't do it personally, I have men to do that for me."

I felt foolish to have been so preoccupied with my work all day that I hadn't even noticed anyone following me.

"Whose side are you on?" I asked.

Chief Inspector Cullen laughed. "There's no question of *sides*, Miss Green, I'm merely managing the rather difficult situation we have found ourselves in. Now that you're here, everything will calm down a little. The situation has become rather out of hand in recent days."

"Let me rephrase my question," I said.

"I'm sure there's no need."

"Would Commissioner Dickson approve of the work you're doing?"

Chief Inspector Cullen scowled. "Sometimes unconventional methods need to be employed. The commissioner trusts me to make the right decisions."

"But what are you doing about the murders? And about Inspector Blakely?" I demanded, jumping onto my feet.

"Sit down, Miss Green," snapped Cullen. "Can you make me a promise?"

I reluctantly sat down. "It depends what it is."

"If I tell you where Inspector Blakely is will you leave the business of these murders for me to sort out?"

I stared at him as I began to grasp the meaning of his words. "So you *do* know more about James' whereabouts than you were letting on!"

"Will you promise to leave these murders to me and my men to handle?"

"What do you mean *leave them to you*? Does that mean I'm no longer allowed to report on them?"

"Exactly that, and you're to stay away from everyone who has the remotest connection to the victims."

"But I cannot agree to such a thing! I promised Emma Holland I would help her!"

"There's nothing you can do to help her, Miss Green."

"Someone broke into her home!"

"Let me allay your fears. It was on my orders that someone broke into her home and stole her brother's diaries. She and the other members of her household were not in danger at the time, and neither are they now."

"You ordered the diaries to be stolen?"

"They contained secret information."

"Secret for whom?"

"You let me worry about that, Miss Green."

"But I don't understand. Why couldn't you just have asked her for the diaries? In fact, Inspector Blakely had planned to ask her for them himself."

"It would have been dangerous for them to officially be in

the possession of the police. Blakely would have been targeted as soon as he had hold of them. He simply had no idea what he was getting himself into."

"Then tell me where he is!"

The chief inspector did not reply. Instead, he nodded to one of the men, who promptly left the room.

"Are we agreed that you will keep out of this whole business, Miss Green?" he asked.

"I cannot understand why you would ask me to do such a thing. There have been four brutal murders and you're expecting everyone in London to simply look away."

"That's not what I expect. I am merely asking you to occupy yourself with something else at the present time. This is too dangerous for the likes of you."

"What do you have against me, Inspector?"

"You know that I'm not a man to mince my words. I've told you enough times that I consider you an interfering ink-slinger. If you were a man you'd have had the sense to steer clear of all this, but being a woman you can't see any sense at all. It's a dangerous combination. Now this is my last warning, stop your work on this story."

Footsteps neared the door again and one of the dark-suited men returned to the room followed by another man.

It was James!

CHAPTER 62

I leapt to my feet and James' eyes locked with mine.

"Penny," he said quietly with a nod. There was a darkness around his eyes and he was unshaven. His dark grey suit was creased in places, as if it were the only clothing he had worn for the past few days.

"Are you all right, James?" I asked, stepping closer. "I've been so worried!" I wanted to embrace him but didn't feel comfortable doing so in front of Chief Inspector Cullen and his accomplices.

"I'm fine, thank you." His voice was unusually formal. "How are you?"

"Surprised to be here, but extremely relieved to know that you're all right. It has been a strange few days."

"Reunited at last!" said the chief inspector with a grin. "You'll have missed each other a great deal, no doubt. I apologise that the situation has called for this, but sometimes desperate measures are required. This isn't the first time I've had to undertake something so clandestine, and it won't be the last. But we'll get the better of these people eventually. All that's required at the moment is a little patience while they decide how to react to our latest move. I feel certain that everything will be restored to a perfect equilibrium before long."

"I'm sure it will, sir," said James.

"Good. I've explained to Miss Green that she must keep away from anyone with a connection to the murder victims. This will be extremely important now that we're reaching the most critical stage of this investigation. You'd be impressed by how much she's moved about today, Blakely. She has visited Miss Holland, Mr Billington-Grieg, Mr Sheridan and Mr Chakravarty."

"That sounds just like Penny," said James, giving me a weary smile.

"It does indeed," said Chief Inspector Cullen, "but she'll end up becoming the next victim if she's not careful. I didn't want another death on my hands, and I'm sure you wouldn't have been too happy about it either, Blakely. Now that you're both out of harm's way I shall sleep a little easier tonight. Do please excuse me, I have to get back to the Yard for the next stage of the investigation. How I wish you could accompany me, Blakely, but sadly it's too risky."

"What is the next stage?" I asked.

"You'll find out soon enough, Miss Green. I shall update you once this whole messy business is over."

He quitted the room, leaving me and James in the company of the two men who had kidnapped me from the street. James pulled up one of the chairs and sat beside me.

"I'm still struggling to believe you're really here," I said. "I can't tell you how worried I've been, not to mention Charlotte. We tried everything we could think of to find out what had happened to you."

"You and Charlotte?" A bemused smile spread across James' face.

"She's been so worried, James. I wish we could tell her that you're safe."

"I'm certain we will be able to reassure her soon. How is she?"

"Extremely concerned about you. She'll be so happy to see you again. How did you get here? What happened?"

"The Yard received a series of threats. The severed finger was only a small part of it."

"What sort of threats?"

"Cullen intercepted a number of them, some of which were aimed at my family."

"You received threats against your family?"

"The Yard did. I was kept from seeing them, as I'm told they were too distressing. The finger was bad enough."

"Chief Inspector Cullen told you all this?"

"Yes, and he persuaded me to hide away here for a few days in the interests of my family's safety. I couldn't breathe a word of it to anyone in case those who had issued the threats found out."

"So you have to stay here until the threat has disappeared?"

"And presumably the same applies to you, Penny."

"I'm not aware of anyone having threatened me. Chief Inspector Cullen told me I was in danger, but I'm not sure whether I believe him or not. I can understand why he feels the need to protect you, but why me? He doesn't even like me."

James gave the dark-suited men a quick glance, which reminded me that everything I said would likely be reported back to him.

"Tell me what has been happening, Penny," said James.

The light in the room began to fade as I spent a good few

minutes telling James all that had occurred in the time since he had been away.

"Cullen told me about the Mawson murder," he said. "It helped me accept that I was better off out of the way. These people are extremely ruthless."

"Chief Inspector Cullen seems to think you would have put yourself in even more danger had you borrowed Alfred Holland's diaries," I said. "No doubt it was dangerous for Emma Holland, too, and that's why he had to take them. But you can't stay here, James, not when your family and Charlotte have no idea what has happened to you. It's not fair on them. Have you asked if you can leave?"

"A number of times, but Cullen told me it's not safe. If I let anyone know where I am it would put them in danger. I'm desperate to get out of here, but I cannot risk my family being harmed or losing my job. I suppose Cullen knows what he's doing. He has been in similar situations before."

"Has he?"

"Apparently so."

"Where are we, exactly? Do you know?"

"On the Haringay Park Estate in North London."

"I know it now. We're just north of Finsbury Park, aren't we? Many new homes are being built here."

"And this is one of the most recently built properties. The Metropolitan Police has a few houses like this to keep people safe when necessary."

"Were you also kidnapped from the street?" I asked.

"No!" James gave me a look of incredulity.

"So you weren't brought here under duress with a hood tied over your head?"

"Fortunately, no." His face grew increasingly alarmed. "Is that what they did to you?"

"Yes." I glared at the two men in the room with us. "What sort of police officer orders people to do such a thing?"

"It was utterly despicable to treat you in that manner, Penny. I had no idea."

"Do you believe everything Chief Inspector Cullen tells you?" I asked James in a low whisper.

"I have done until now. Most of it, anyway. I don't see why he should have any cause to be untruthful to me, but I don't understand why he would treat you in this manner either. No one deserves to be frightened like that."

"He told me that sometimes a sudden shock is needed."

"For what purpose?"

"To invoke fear and compliance, would be my guess."

One of the men glanced over at us, as if he didn't like the fact that I was whispering.

"We're much easier to control when we're frightened, aren't we?" I continued. "I think Chief Inspector Cullen exaggerated the danger so that he could get you out of the way."

"To purposefully stop me investigating?" whispered James. "But why should he want to do that?"

The suspicious man got up from his chair and walked over to us. "No whispering," he said, "I need to hear every word you're saying. Either speak up or I will insist on silence."

James and I glared at him.

"So you came here after you met with the gang at Marylebone Lane station?" I asked James.

"Yes. Cullen arrived there just as I was finishing my meeting with them and Inspector Bowles. He explained that the Yard had received a threat directed at my family and that, for my safety and theirs, he had decided I should come and stay here for a few days. I didn't want to come, of course, but he assured me that it would only be for a short while."

"It's been three days now. Has he told you what he's doing about the murders?"

"He says the Yard has to tread carefully because of the danger we are all in."

"It sounds as though he's not doing a great deal."

"Of course he's investigating. He simply said that we need to tread carefully."

"Whatever that means. Now he's supposedly managing the next stage of the investigation, yet we've no idea what that means either. We're powerless, James. The pair of us can do nothing at all. Have you tried leaving this place?"

"Not yet. I've been trying to remain on good terms with Cullen, but I'm beginning to lose my patience. I asked if I would be able to leave today and he replied that a complication had arisen. I suspect now that he was referring to you."

I laughed. "*I'm* the complication?"

"It seems that way." James smiled. "Aren't you always?"

I lowered my voice to a whisper, though I knew I wasn't supposed to. "I feel sure that Chief Inspector Cullen has no intention of letting us go any time soon. We have to escape."

"Have you forgotten what I told you?" said the man, getting to his feet again. "We'll have silence now."

James and I exchanged an exasperated glance.

I waited patiently for the man to return to his seat before looking up at James again.

"We need to escape," I mouthed silently. "Tonight."

CHAPTER 63

A stout lady named Mrs Walker arrived at the house a short while later with a meal of bread and cold tongue. I tried to engage her in conversation while she made coffee.

"Inspector Cullen's paid me to come 'ere and 'elp as 'e needs it," she said, refusing to give anything more away.

After our meal James retired upstairs to his room and I was shown to a room at the back of the house. It contained a table and a settee, which was to serve as my bed for the night. Mrs Walker gave me a blanket and told me she would return to the house early the following morning and bring me a basin and a jug of water so I could wash.

I lay down on the settee, covered myself with the blanket and listened to the sounds of the house. James was in a room upstairs but I didn't know where the two men were. I presumed they also had rooms upstairs. *Was this place a safe haven offered for my protection? Or was I being held prisoner?* I wasn't entirely sure.

It was apparent that James still trusted and respected

Chief Inspector Cullen. He demonstrated a level of respect for the man that I had never shared.

Perhaps the chief inspector was managing the situation as best he could, but I felt suspicious of his motives. Maybe I was wrong to doubt him, and perhaps I didn't fully understand the loyalty and duty felt among police officers, but something about my current situation felt wrong. Chief Inspector Cullen was trying to control me, and I felt sure that he was also trying to control James. He had assumed we would be happy to stay in this house together, apparently safe from the dangers outside, but I knew that I had to leave, either with or without James.

There was a large sash window in the room. A little while after darkness had fallen I got up and tried to open it. To begin with the frame wouldn't budge, but it eventually gave way with a judder that shattered the silence. I quickly returned to the settee, my heart pounding in my throat, and pulled the blanket back over me.

I heard footsteps on the floorboards upstairs and held my breath, wondering if I would hear one of the men coming down the stairs. After a short while the steps subsided and silence returned to the house.

I would have liked nothing more than for James to escape with me, but it seemed too risky to go upstairs. *What if I disturbed the men who were supposedly guarding us?* My escape route was just yards away. I didn't want to leave James behind, but at least I knew that he was unharmed and I could share this good news with Charlotte. I would also have a chance to find out exactly what Chief Inspector Cullen was up to.

I estimated that half an hour had passed before I attempted to open the window again. I wondered if the men took turns to watch over us, working in shifts. I could not simply assume that everyone in the house was asleep.

I approached the window once again, slowly pushing it

open to avoid making such a dreadful noise. It juddered slightly a couple of times, so that I had to stop and hold my breath for what seemed like minutes at a time as I listened out for footsteps. The frame was eventually raised high enough to allow me enough space to climb through. I peered outside and saw what appeared to be a small garden. Beyond it I could see the outline of rooftops against the night sky.

Now was my chance.

I went back into the room to fetch my bag and listened for a few more minutes. I had hoped James would come to find me, but I could only suppose that he was already fast asleep. I felt consumed with guilt about leaving him behind, but once I had made my escape I could send help. I felt quite certain that Commissioner Dickson would not agree with Chief Inspector Cullen's methods once he discovered what was happening.

I groped around in the dark for my carpet bag, then walked back over to the window.

Was I making a mistake escaping like this? Were there greater dangers beyond my temporary prison?

I carefully climbed out of the window and stepped into the dark garden. I felt grass underfoot as I crept toward the boundary walls. I had no idea how tall they were, but I knew that I wouldn't feel at ease until I was safely away from this place.

It was then that I heard the frame of the window I had just climbed out of move, as if someone had pushed it open just a fraction wider. I remained as still as a statue, desperately holding my breath.

There was no further sound. Whoever it was had determined to move as stealthily as I had.

Could it be James?

A sharp shove to my shoulder knocked me to the ground.

I tried my best to stifle a cry as my assailant emitted a grunt of pain.

"Penny?" came a whisper from nearby.

"James! I'm here!" I whispered back. I tried to suppress the laughter rising into my throat, partly from relief and partly from fear.

"I think they're on to us; we have to move!" came the reply.

"I don't know how we can get out of here!" I whispered in return.

I turned and saw a lantern shining in the room I had just escaped from.

"Oh James, they're coming!"

"Follow me!" he hissed.

"I can't see you!"

I groped around for his hand and eventually found it, gripping my fingers tightly around his. He pulled me up from the ground and I followed blindly in his footsteps, tripping over tussocks of grass along the way.

"Oi!" came a voice from behind us.

I felt my stomach jump up into my chest and willed my legs to move more quickly than ever before as I followed James into the darkness.

"There must be a wall or a fence somewhere!" I whispered.

"Here it is," said James. In one swift movement he gripped my legs just above the knees and propelled me upwards. It was all I could do not to cry out in surprise.

"Can you get over it?" asked James, staggering forward a step.

I reached out and felt bricks beneath my fingers. Stretching upward I could feel the top of the wall. "Yes! Yes, I can!"

I tossed my bag forward into the darkness and heard it

land reassuringly on the hard ground over on the other side of the wall. I grabbed the top with both hands while James pushed my legs up.

"What about you?" I whispered back to him.

"I'll manage it," he replied. "I think it's about six feet. Just get over and I'll be right behind you."

I clambered awkwardly over the wall, my skirts getting in the way. I landed uncomfortably on the other side, falling heavily onto my elbows and back. Above me I could see the outline of the wall and a silhouette of James as he gripped the top of it with his arms.

"Blakely!" came a shout.

James' silhouette came into sharp relief as a torch was shone onto him from behind.

"James!" I reached up and seized one of his arms to help pull him over. It was imperative that the men on the other side of the wall were given no chance to pull him back down.

James reached out a hand and I grabbed it. He had managed to get most of his body onto the top of the wall, but appeared to be flailing.

"Pull on my arm, Penny!" he called down. "They've got my leg!"

He began to thrash about wildly, and I could only guess that his foot had made contact with one of the men because there was a cry of pain and then James came tumbling down onto my side of the wall.

"Are you all right?" I asked him, tripping over my bag.

"I think so. Let's move!" He jumped onto his feet and grabbed my hand again.

"This seems to be a passageway," he said. "I've no idea which direction we should take."

One of the men had reached the top of the wall and was shining the lantern down on us. I gripped my bag in one hand and James' hand in the other.

"Let's go!" he said, taking the lead.

The light from the lantern showed that the passageway ran between the gardens of a row of houses. With the two men still clambering over the wall behind, we ran as fast as we could until we reached the street.

I could only see the dark outlines of houses on one side of the street, but the sky had opened up over the other half.

"This is where they're building the new homes," said James.

I heard footsteps behind us. "They're catching us up!" I whispered.

"This way!" he said, pulling me toward the undeveloped side of the street. "They've built the road and the pavement, but not the houses as yet."

The road began to climb steeply.

"Couldn't you have chosen the downhill way?" I commented between gasps.

"I think our men have gone that way," he said, pausing and looking back down the street. We could still see the lantern light, but the men did not appear to be heading in our direction.

"It always pays to take the trickier route, Penny," he said, laughing breathlessly. "They've assumed we were heading down to the houses."

I also began to laugh as relief took hold of me.

"Where are we now?" I asked.

A brisk wind whipped around us and I noticed we were still holding hands even though there was no longer any real need.

"I think we're close to Green Lanes."

"What does that mean?"

"If we follow the road south we should hopefully reach civilisation, otherwise known as Finsbury Park."

"And south is which way?"

"Luckily, it's a clear night tonight, though it would help if the moon was out." I could just make out James' face looking up at the stars in the gloom.

"I think if we continue along this road it should join up with Green Lanes," he said. "Turning to the right will take us south."

"You can tell which direction we need to take just by looking at the stars?"

"Sometimes. It depends on the time of year. It's something my father taught me during my boyhood."

"Well it's certainly coming in useful now," I said. I glanced behind us and saw that the lantern light was even smaller than before. "Hopefully we've lost them now."

"Hopefully."

"I'm glad you came with me, James. I felt it was too dangerous to try to find you before I left."

"It was! Those men were very close behind us. I stayed awake knowing you would try to make a dash for it."

"I'm worried, though. You'll most likely lose your job for defying Chief Inspector Cullen."

"Probably, though I'm more concerned for my family than my job."

"Oh dear, yes. I hope we can keep them safe."

"The only way to do that is to find out who is behind all this. We need to put a stop to them before someone else gets hurt."

We continued to make our way up the hill, still hand in hand.

CHAPTER 64

After a short walk down to Finsbury Park we managed to hail a lone cab on Seven Sisters Road. James checked his watch by the light of a gas lamp. It was almost two o'clock.

"We should be able to find something to eat at one of the cafes that open early near the markets," said James. "How about Billingsgate?"

"That sounds good," I replied, "and it's near the offices of Chakravarty and Sheridan in the City."

The streets were deserted as we travelled toward Billingsgate with the horse progressing at a brisk trot.

"I need to speak to both Chakravarty and Sheridan," said James. "One of them believed Forster had not been caught up in any trouble and the other believed he had, is that right?"

"Yes that's right. I'm sure one of them must know something. Coincidentally, my brother-in-law is doing some legal work for Sheridan on a government contract, so it might also be worth speaking to him."

"We need to speak to as many people as possible, Penny, and we need to find out what Cullen is up to. When he first asked me to stop working on the case I believed what he had told me about the threats to my family. I felt certain at the time that he had my best interests at heart, but now I'm not so sure. It's difficult because I have always held the man in such high regard, but the manner in which he has treated you is unforgivable. I fail to understand how he can justify it."

"So maybe he didn't have your best interests at heart at all. Perhaps he was merely trying to keep you away from the investigation for his own convenience."

"I'm inclined to think that's the case. It sounds like he's caught up in something, doesn't it?"

"I believe so. I've never trusted him, as you well know."

Fish porters were already moving busily around the arched brick edifice of Billingsgate Market as they unloaded carriages piled precariously high with crates and baskets of fish.

After we had paid the cabman he pointed us in the direction of a pub, which happened to be open despite the ungodly hour.

James and I weren't the usual clientele at this time of day and a few heads turned as we walked into the Blue Boar. We sat down and were soon served with kippers, toast and coffee.

"Did you notice the telegraph office opposite the market?" I asked James. "You must send a telegram to Charlotte as soon as it opens."

"I will."

"She'll be so relieved that you're safe. She has had such a dreadful time."

"Four nights is a long time to be away."

"And no news; nothing at all! Chief Inspector Cullen could at least have reassured her or even explained what had happened. That's what I don't understand about him. He was so tight-lipped about the whole matter."

"Before I carry out my investigations today I need to

understand what the motive behind each of the murders was," said James. "Firstly, there's poor Mrs Forster."

"Presumably targeted because of her husband."

"You haven't come across any information that suggests she might have got herself in any trouble?"

"None at all."

"So we think Mrs Forster was sadly murdered because she happened to be Mr Forster's wife. The gang came for both of them but Mr Forster wasn't there that evening. Forster himself was chased down outside the East India Club in St James's Square. Mr Chakravarty suggested he may have been caught up in the trade of stolen opium, did he not?"

"That's right, although Mr Sheridan refuses to believe it."

"So Mr Forster worked for Mr Sheridan for a number of years without any bother."

"It seems that way."

"But he got into trouble with Mr Chakravarty for securing a mortgage advance on a property he didn't own."

"That's right."

"So Mr Chakravarty could have arranged Forster's murder as an act of revenge?" said James.

"Possibly."

"Then there's Mr Holland, who was caught stealing opium."

"He stole it under duress. His intentions were honourable to begin with, given that he had reported his colleague Charles Mawson."

"Mawson was dismissed for stealing opium after Holland reported him."

"Yes, and for a while I thought Mr Mawson had arranged to have Mr Holland murdered out of revenge for what he had done."

"But then Mawson was murdered."

"Yes, in a similar manner to Mr Forster," I said.

"But Mawson still could have ordered Holland's murder."

"Yes, he could have done."

"Perhaps Mawson was murdered in revenge for what he had done to Holland. This case can become confusing quite quickly, can't it?" James sighed.

"It certainly can. My theory is that Mr Holland and Mr Mawson were both murdered for stealing opium."

"It's an odd motive, though. They didn't cause anyone any personal harm, and both were punished by their employer."

"Perhaps they were murdered to ensure that they remained silent," I suggested.

"Yes, I like that theory. Someone didn't want them to talk."

"And that same someone didn't want anyone finding Mr Holland's diaries. This is where I don't understand Cullen's involvement. He said he had arranged for the dairies to be stolen because they contained secret information. How did he know what the diaries contained? He also said that it would not have been good for them to officially be in the possession of the police. Who was he protecting?"

"I'm still holding out hope that he has a suitable explanation for his actions."

A horrible realisation gripped me as I sipped my tea. "Chief Inspector Cullen said the contents of the diaries were secret, but Emma Holland has read some of them! She told me about the thefts carried out by her brother and Charles Mawson. If Cullen went to the trouble of having the diaries removed, what will he do about Emma when he realises she has read some of them?"

"Perhaps he has assumed that she won't cause any trouble."

"She's desperate to find out who murdered her brother. She will most certainly cause trouble if no progress is made on the case."

"Then we must keep an eye on her," said James.

"Perhaps Chief Inspector Cullen will have a couple of men put a hood over her head and whisk her off to North London," I scoffed. "That seems to be his manner of dealing with these situations."

"He's probably found out that we've escaped by now," said James. "He won't be happy about it."

"Good," I said. "It's about time someone stood up to him."

"But we don't have much time. We need to work quickly before he realises what we're up to." James checked his watch. "Fortunately, it's not long until the telegraph office opens, so I shall soon be able to send a telegram to Charlotte. After that we'll go and see a good friend of yours at the City of London police."

I groaned. "Not Chief Inspector Stroud?" I had come across him before while reporting on the death of Richard Geller at the medical museum inside St Bartholomew's Hospital.

"I'm afraid so, as I shall need him to lend me some men. I will have to bring in Chakravarty and Sheridan so they can be interviewed."

"What about Chief Inspector Cullen?"

"I'll have to bring both men in before he finds out what we're up to."

CHAPTER 65

Once James had sent Charlotte a telegram we made the fifteen-minute walk to the red-brick headquarters of the City of London Police headquarters in Old Jewry. Large, grey-whiskered Inspector Stroud was initially reluctant to help, still clearly resenting the manner in which James had wrested the Geller case from him. However, he begrudgingly agreed to allow a sergeant and a constable to accompany us once James had explained what he planned to do. With the two police officers in tow we made our way to Mr Chakravarty's deposit bank in Change Alley.

The City was fully awake by this time, the pavements filled with smart-suited men hopping off omnibuses and striding in through the imposing stone facades of banks and offices.

While we walked, James explained the case to the two police officers, both of whom wore the gold-buttoned uniform of the City of London Police. Sergeant Coutts was about thirty with neat brown whiskers, while Constable Ellis was a younger man with a long face and a black moustache.

. . .

Mr Chakravarty was occupied with a client when we arrived at his office in Change Alley. After a short wait we discovered that he was in a bad temper.

"Is this regarding that Forster chap again?" he fumed. "I wish I'd never set eyes on the man, I really do. I lost a lot of money to him, and now even after his death I'm being hounded." He paused and pointed a finger at me. "I've told this news reporter everything I know about him, and that was rather magnanimous of me given the circumstances in which we first met. The woman lied to me, Inspector!"

"I take full responsibility for that, Mr Chakravarty," James replied. "It was all my idea."

"It was a ridiculous idea! Call yourself an inspector of the Yard, do you? This is not how I expect Scotland Yard to conduct itself. And what are you doing in the company of a news reporter in the first place? Her kind are not to be trusted."

"You may also notice that I'm in the company of two other police officers," said James. "Please mind your manners, Mr Chakravarty."

"Don't patronise me, Inspector, I know full well how to mind my manners. What do you want?"

"I should like to request that you accompany Sergeant Coutts here to the police station in Old Jewry. I plan to interview you there later this morning."

"Are you arresting me?"

"No, this isn't an arrest."

"Then I respectfully decline."

"In which case I should be forced to arrest you. I'm giving you the opportunity to attend the police station voluntarily, Mr Chakravarty."

The moneylender laughed out loud. "But if I don't go I'll be arrested? That doesn't sound very voluntary to me, Inspector."

"You're right, it's not. But your reputation is at stake, and a voluntary attendance will surely sound better to your clients than an arrest."

Mr Chakravarty gave this some thought. "I can't disagree with you on that front, Inspector, but what am I supposed to have done? You don't think I murdered that chap and his wife, do you?"

"I don't know yet."

"Do you consider me a suspect?"

"Until you're able to clear up a few matters for us, yes."

"You think I bludgeoned the man's wife, then stabbed him in the back? Do I look like someone who would do such a thing?"

"No, but you could have paid a gang to do it."

"I wouldn't waste my money, especially having already lost so much on the man! What would I have to gain by murdering him?"

"I can't be sure until we've talked about it in greater detail. Revenge, perhaps, or maybe you were hoping to reclaim your losses from his estate."

"Believe me, Inspector, I have better ways to spend my time. I may be angry that he defrauded me, but I know how to write off my losses. It's part of the job."

"Good, then please accompany Sergeant Coutts to the station and I shall meet you there shortly," said James. "I just have one other matter to attend to first."

"It will be interesting to hear how Mr Chakravarty conducts himself during his interview," I said to James as we made our way to Sheridan and Company in Lombard Court with the young constable following closely behind.

"It will indeed. I can't work the man out at all."

"I can imagine him being cold-hearted enough to organise a murder," I said.

Lombard Court was only a short walk from Change Alley, and I could see that the young constable was impressed by the opulent decor of Sheridan and Company.

"Mr Sheridan is currently unavailable, Inspector," said Miss Wainman.

"Can you tell me when he might be able to make himself available?"

"He's not in the building at the present time."

"You didn't answer my question, Miss Wainman. When will he be available to answer a few of our questions?"

"I'm unable to say, Inspector, as I don't know when he'll be back."

James placed his card on her well-polished desk. "When he returns, can you please ask him to attend Old Jewry police station as a matter of urgency?"

"I will do."

"Have you seen him at all today?"

"Briefly, but then he went out somewhere. He doesn't always tell me what he's doing."

"It really is urgent, Miss Wainman. I expect to see him at Old Jewry later today. If he doesn't turn up we'll have to arrest him, and I'm sure that would cause great embarrassment for the man and all his colleagues."

She nodded in reply.

"Constable Ellis and I had better go back to Old Jewry now and speak to Chakravarty," said James as we stood on Gracechurch Street. "I'm not sure what we'll get from him;

the chap seems quite impenetrable. If all goes to plan Mr Sheridan will join us there very soon."

"I'll go to Euston," I replied. "I'm growing increasingly worried about Emma Holland. I still don't understand why Chief Inspector Cullen wanted those diaries."

"I plan to deal with Cullen once I've spoken to Chakravarty and Sheridan. You don't need to have anything more to do with the man, Penny, especially after the way he treated you. I intend to make a formal complaint to Commissioner Dickson about it."

"Thank you, James."

"You can leave this with me now. Hopefully the case will be solved by the end of the day."

"Good luck."

We parted at the junction of Gracechurch Street and East Cheap. I made my way toward Monument Station, from which point I could travel by underground railway to Gower Street.

"Penny!" I heard a shout from behind me and spun round to see James running straight at me. "I've changed my mind, I'm coming with you! I've left Constable Ellis waiting for Sheridan when he arrives. The train to Euston will be too slow; let's hail a cab."

CHAPTER 66

"What made you change your mind?" I asked James as the cab travelled along King William Street in the direction of the mayor's residence, Mansion House.

"I feel nervous about letting you out of my sight at the moment," he replied. "And like you I wish to make sure that Emma Holland is all right. I haven't met her yet, but the fact that she knows something about those diaries undoubtedly puts her at risk."

"Thank you for coming with me," I said with a smile, "especially when you have so many other things to be doing at the moment."

"Hopefully this won't take long. My only regret is that I haven't brought my revolver with me. Cullen asked me to hand it over to him at the house in Haringay. Let's just hope that I shan't need it."

Emma's maid Doris answered the door and instantly recognised us from our visit the previous week.

"Crikey, Miss 'Olland's popular today," she said. "She's got visitors at the moment, but I can pass a message on for yer."

"We'd prefer to wait if that's all right," said James. "Will she be long?"

"'Opefully not."

We stepped into the hallway and I saw that the door to the parlour was closed. I noticed two top hats and a bowler hat on the hallway table. There was a cane in the umbrella stand bearing a familiar mother-of-pearl top.

"You can wait in the back room if yer like," said the maid. "Miss 'Olland's just in the parlour."

"Thank you," said James.

"The cane in that umbrella stand looks familiar," I said quietly as we walked toward the back room. "My brother-in-law has one just like it."

"The same brother-in-law who has been doing legal work for Mr Sheridan?"

"Yes." My heart began to pound, and I stopped sharply in the hallway. "It couldn't be him, could it?"

"Excuse me," James called out to the retreating form of the maid. "Is Miss Holland's visitor Mr Sheridan, by any chance?"

She turned in surprise.

"Yeah, d'you know 'im?"

James strode back toward the parlour.

"Inspector?" called the maid.

I followed in James' footsteps. He pushed open the door without knocking and I stepped into the room close behind him.

There was a stunned silence as Mr Sheridan stared at us from an easy chair beside the fireplace. On the other side of the fireplace sat George, and on the settee next to Emma Holland was Chief Inspector Cullen.

He regarded us with a deep scowl.

"Have you never been taught to knock at a door before opening it, Blakely?"

CHAPTER 67

Emma Holland gave me a nervous smile, but I could see how intimidated she felt sitting alone in the room with three gentlemen.

"May I ask what your business with Miss Holland is, sir?" James asked Chief Inspector Cullen.

"None of your business, that's for sure. Leave us in peace, Blakely, I'll deal with you later."

"I would hazard a guess that you're discussing Alfred Holland's diaries," continued James. "Are you trying to find out what Miss Holland knows?"

Emma Holland gave a slight nod, clearly too nervous to speak.

Mr Sheridan stood to his feet and held out his hand for James to shake.

"It's a pleasure to meet you... Inspector Blakely, is it?" he said. "And I've had the pleasure of meeting Miss Green before. Miss Green, you're well acquainted with your brother-in-law Mr Billington-Grieg, of course! We have ensured that Miss Holland has legal representation during this interview, so all is being conducted properly. I asked Mr Billington-Grieg to accompany us and advise her accordingly."

"Advise her on what, exactly?" asked James.

"She's being interviewed by a police officer, and I wanted to ensure that everything was carried out in the proper way."

I stared at George, who looked distinctly uneasy.

"There's no need to explain yourself any further to this junior detective, Mr Sheridan. He was just about to leave," said Chief Inspector Cullen, "along with his scribbling friend."

"Aren't you wondering how we got here, Chief Inspector?" I asked. "The last time I saw you was late yesterday afternoon at a house in North London. Your men snatched me from the street and took me there blindfolded."

Emma Holland gasped.

"I suppose you hoped I would remain there as some sort of prisoner," I continued. "You had already managed to persuade James that it was too dangerous for him to leave."

"And I can see that the foolish man paid my advice no heed."

"You tried to keep Miss Green a prisoner, Chief Inspector Cullen?" asked Mr Sheridan with a shocked expression.

"Not a prisoner... she's exaggerating. It was for her own protection, but like Blakely she has chosen to ignore the advice of a senior detective with more than thirty years' experience in the Metropolitan Police. Now take yourself and this wretched woman out of here, Blakely. We need to resume our conversation with Miss Holland."

"They can stay," said Emma, her voice wavering. "This is my home and I say they must stay and tell me why they were taken to a house in North London."

"You can listen to whatever they have to say for themselves, Miss Holland," he said, "but I fear they will paint a ridiculous picture of misery designed to elicit your sympathy.

They cannot understand the complicated lengths a police officer must occasionally go to during the course of his work."

I quickly explained what had happened to Emma, and I could see that both Mr Sheridan and George were clearly surprised.

"That's dreadful, Penny!" said Emma.

"What did I tell you, Miss Holland? This story was designed to pull at your heartstrings," said Chief Inspector Cullen.

"And all of it true," I added.

"Well, it's a step too far, I should say," Mr Sheridan stated emphatically. "Not your finest hour, Cullen."

The chief inspector glared at him in response.

"What is your concern with Alfred Holland's diaries, sir?" James asked him.

"As I've explained to Miss Green, they contain secret information that must be contained."

"Secret in what sense?" asked James.

"In the sense that it could fall into the wrong hands."

"And which wrong hands did you have in mind?" James probed.

"I feel no need to explain the details of my investigation to the likes of you."

"Do you have any ideas about these wrong hands, Mr Sheridan?" asked James.

"None, I'm afraid."

"May I ask what your interest in Alfred Holland's diaries might be?"

"Don't answer that, Sheridan. Let me deal with this man," Cullen said, standing to his feet and striding over to James. "Consider yourself dismissed, Blakely. Your services are no longer required by the Yard."

"What is the reason for my dismissal, sir?"

"For your continual disobedience. The Metropolitan Police has no need for men like you."

"I obey orders when they're given in the true spirit of policing, sir."

"You cannot pick and choose which orders you obey," spat Chief Inspector Cullen.

"I believe I can when those orders come from a superior who fails to act in the best interests of his profession."

"How dare you suggest such a thing!"

"It has taken me a long time to believe it, but sadly I see now that it is true. You've done all this to cover up for the perpetrator of these dreadful murders. You have no interest in anyone being brought to justice; instead, you have tried to remove the very people who have come closest to the truth. Now you're threatening an innocent woman who just happened to read her brother's diaries in order to understand why he should have met with such an horrific and untimely death."

Chief Inspector Cullen laughed. "You've spent far too much time with this reporter. That sounds like the sort of story she'd concoct for her newspaper!"

"Do you deny it, sir?"

"Of course I deny it! Now give me your warrant card. You no longer have the authority to execute the duties of a Metropolitan Police detective."

James stared back at him. "I refuse, sir."

"You cannot refuse this order, Blakely!" Chief Inspector Cullen's reddened face was just inches away from James' and I feared the senior officer would strike him. He was a strongly built man.

"Inspector Cullen, old chap," said Mr Sheridan, standing to his feet. He appeared quite diminutive in comparison. "I fear that matters are getting a little out of hand. I feel this sort of altercation should never take place in the presence of ladies. Shall we save it for later? I'm quite happy to leave Miss Holland's home now. I think we're finished here."

The chief inspector took a step back and jabbed a finger at James. He was quaking with rage. "You'll regret this, Blakely. I shall ensure that you never work for any police force again!"

James cleared his throat. "I'm still unclear," he said calmly, "as to why Mr Sheridan should be interested in Alfred Holland's diaries."

"Mr Sheridan told me he had never heard of Alfred Holland when I spoke to him outside the Burlington Hotel," I said.

Chief Inspector Cullen paced the floor, his fists clenched. "Don't respond to a single word these two put to you, Sheridan! *He* is no longer a police officer, and *she* will no longer have a job by the time this day is through. I had her dismissed before and I'll do it again!"

"I think it is time for me to leave. Thank you for your time, Miss Holland," said Mr Sheridan, giving Emma a polite bow.

"Why are you interested in Alfred Holland's diaries, Mr Sheridan?" James asked again.

Chief Inspector Cullen bared his teeth.

"Did you know Alfred Holland after all?" continued James. "He stole opium for Mr Forster, didn't he? And Mr Forster worked for your company."

"Perhaps I can explain all this to you another time, Inspector Blakely, without your hot-headed superior present," said Mr Sheridan curtly.

"Hot-headed?" snarled the chief inspector. "You wish to resort to petty insults after all I've done for you?"

Mr Sheridan smiled politely. "Thank you for your help, Chief Inspector Cullen," he replied. "Our meeting here is concluded, and I'm quite sure this nice young lady no longer wants us cluttering up her home."

"You haven't answered Inspector Blakely's question," said Emma, rising to her feet. "Why are you so interested in my brother's diaries?"

"Ask *him*," said Mr Sheridan, pointing at Chief Inspector Cullen. "*He* took them!"

Emma turned to face James' superior, her mouth opened wide in shock. "You broke into my home and stole them?"

"Not personally, Miss Holland," said Chief Inspector Cullen irritably. "It was important that they didn't fall into the wrong hands. I took them under orders from Mr Sheridan."

"Gentlemen, now is not the time to be trading accusations," said George. "I think this matter should be discussed at a later date when everyone has calmed down."

"Your client is doing rather a good job of making me appear to be the guilty party, Mr Billington-Grieg," said Chief Inspector Cullen. "I took the diaries on the orders of Mr Sheridan, and I also tried to get these two out of the way" – he gestured toward me and James – "on the orders of Mr Sheridan."

"How much was Sheridan paying you, sir?" asked James.

The chief inspector spun round angrily. "*Paying* me? What are you talking about, Blakely?"

"You must have received a decent sum to go to such great lengths to cover up Sheridan's crimes."

Mr Sheridan laughed. "And what crimes might those be?"

"The murders of Augustus and Olivia Forster, Alfred Holland and Charles Mawson."

Mr Sheridan shook his head. "Oh dear! I see that Cullen here was right about you all along, Blakely. You really don't have a clue, do you? Forster got himself into terrible debt, Mawson was a thief and Holland was an opium addict. All three got themselves into tricky situations and only have themselves to blame for their inevitable demise."

"No one ever deserves to be murdered," I hissed, "and you've forgotten about Mrs Forster, who was entirely innocent of any wrongdoing!"

"She was indeed innocent, and her death was extremely tragic," replied Mr Sheridan. "You're speaking as though I had something to do with it."

"Oh, but you do," said James. "With your company about to sign a lucrative contract with the India Office you needed to ensure that no one had a chance to make any trouble for you. It wouldn't do, would it, to be found guilty of trading in illegal opium?"

"The trading activities of my company are perfectly legal, Inspector Blakely. Or perhaps I'm mistaken in addressing you as *inspector*. I believe Chief Inspector Cullen has just dismissed you from the Metropolitan Police."

"Once the commissioner has been made aware of the arrangement between yourself and Cullen it will be he who leaves the force, not me," retorted James.

Mr Sheridan laughed. "At this present moment I'm not convinced either of you has any authority. Come on, Mr Billington-Grieg, it's time we were on our way."

I could see George hesitating. "I'm not really sure what's going on here," he said. "I think I shall return to my office."

"Nonsense, man, you're coming with me," said Mr Sheridan. "There's a good deal still to do."

James moved to block the doorway, standing directly in their path. "Mr Sheridan, I am placing you under arrest."

CHAPTER 68

"Leave him alone, Blakely!" threatened Chief Inspector Cullen.

James simply ignored him.

"*Arrest* me?" asked Sheridan with a smile. "On what possible grounds?"

"You arranged the murder of your former colleague Mr Forster, who handled stolen opium from the factory at Ghazipur while working for your company. Not only were you aware of this work, but it was carried out at your request. It was your company that smuggled the stolen opium into China."

"What nonsense!" Sheridan said with a chuckle.

"Unfortunately for you, Forster was clumsy," continued James. "He was careless in his financial affairs, and no doubt with the stolen opium. I'm sure that once you realised how risky he was you arranged for him to be sent back to England and out of your way. It should have been easy to forget all about him, but when the possibility of a contract with the India Office came your way you realised the existence of this man could cause serious problems. If the India Office learned about your company's illegal dealings the contract would never have gone ahead. That's when you approached a notorious gang to dispose of him. Never quite sure how much Mrs Forster knew of her husband's illicit dealings you decided to be rid of her for good measure. After the supposed burglary and tragic murder of his wife you were among the first to console him, but you were also keeping a close eye on the man as he had foiled your initial murder attempt."

Mr Sheridan folded his arms and smirked at James. "What an interesting storyteller you are, Blakely! Do go on."

"Don't give him the time of day," said Chief Inspector Cullen.

"No, I must say that I'm interested to hear the rest of his tall tale. Imagine how ridiculous it'll sound in court!"

"It won't even get to court," said the chief inspector.

I stole a look at George, whose face had paled.

"A few days later your hired gang caught up with Mr Forster and he was stabbed in the back in St James's Square," continued James. "It was a dreadful murder, which shocked London. However, getting rid of Forster didn't eliminate your problems. Two other men knew about the stolen opium, and you thought it possible that they would begin speaking of it. Mr Holland had discovered what you were up to, and when he reported Mr Mawson for stealing you had no choice but to recruit him. Using a combination of money and threats you had him falsifying forms, just as you had paid Mr Mawson to do. I haven't yet had a chance to read Alfred Holland's diaries, but I understand from what Miss Green tells me that he was trying to identify who he was stealing the opium for. Isn't that right, Miss Holland?"

Emma nodded. "Yes, and he became quite friendly with the native gentleman he always dealt with, hoping that he could find out some clue from him with regard to what was happening to all the opium he stole."

"And perhaps he was successful," said James. "It explains why there was suddenly so much interest in his diary. It's the secret information Cullen was trying to keep hidden. Perhaps you can tell me, sir, if Sheridan and Company was named in Mr Holland's diary?"

Chief Inspector Cullen stared at James but said nothing.

"More nonsense," Mr Sheridan chipped in. "Is your story almost at its conclusion, Blakely?"

"Almost," said James. "Murdering these men to keep them silent was always going to cause a stir, and that's why you employed the services of Chief Inspector Cullen. I don't know how long you've been acquainted, but you knew him well enough to judge that he might be persuaded to hush up the investigation in return for payment. In theory it was easy to hush up because the men doing the dirty work were merely men you employed. No doubt they were also persuaded, through a combination of fear and bribery, to remain silent when questioned by the police. I daren't speculate on where they obtained a severed finger from, but we'll get to the bottom of it.

"Poor Mr Mawson's time on earth was always going to be limited. Although his superiors had found out what he was up to and he was duly returned to England, it would only have been a matter of time before the trail led back to you.

"As for Mr Holland, the man's circumstances had taken an unfortunate turn and you assumed few people would miss him when he was shot dead at the opium den. However, you didn't account for the bravery and determination of his sister, Miss Emma Holland, who did all she could to find out who had killed him. Fortunately, her brother had left some detailed diaries, which no one knew existed until Miss Holland mentioned them to Miss Green.

"Miss Green was also determined to find out who had killed Mr Holland, and in good faith she mentioned the existence of the diaries to Chief Inspector Cullen, who did what he needed to do to take them into his possession. I'm sure they contained all manner of incriminating evidence, which Cullen has presumably destroyed by now. Fortunately, Miss Holland had read some of the diaries and found out enough to enable Miss Green to make the connection between the victims. This, Mr Sheridan, is the reason you're here with this imposter and your trusted legal advisor today. You wished to find out what Miss Holland knew. I don't like to think what might have happened if Miss Green and I hadn't arrived when we did."

"I would have made sure the young lady remained unharmed," said George shakily.

"Would you indeed?" said James. "Are you sure about that? As Mr Sheridan's lawyer you surely had some idea what your client was up to."

"I cannot be certain that your account is accurate, Inspector Blakely," George replied. "Nothing has been proven at this stage."

"It will be in due course," said James. "In the meantime, I think you've been rather short-sighted in your choice of client. Or perhaps the money you were set to make from his lucrative contract with the India Office was enough for you to turn a blind eye?"

"Now that's unreasonable, Inspector. I would never ignore actions that were clearly illegal."

"It's all nonsense anyway, Billington-Grieg," said Sheridan. "Now, out of my way, Blakely."

"I'm afraid I cannot do that. I must detain you, sir."

Chief Inspector Cullen marched over and shoved James aside. "Let the man out of here!" he shouted. He pulled a revolver from beneath his jacket and pointed it at James.

CHAPTER 69

With a horrible lurch in my stomach I realised James was still unarmed.

"Thank you, Cullen," said Mr Sheridan, opening the parlour door. "Come on, Billington-Grieg."

I could see that George had no idea what to do. Following Mr Sheridan would mean that he was associating with a known criminal.

Emma leapt to her feet. "Put your gun away, Chief Inspector!" she shouted. "You have no right to brandish a weapon in my home!"

Chief Inspector Cullen turned to face her. "I would advise you to remain calm, Miss Holland."

"Then put your gun away immediately."

"I'm simply trying to prevent one of my officers from making a mistake."

"I don't think he's making a mistake at all. From what I read in Alfred's diary Inspector Blakely's theory sounds entirely plausible."

He pointed the gun at her. "You know too much, Miss Holland." He exchanged a glance with Mr Sheridan that made my blood run cold.

"No!" I said. "No, you mustn't harm her!"

Mr Sheridan gave Chief Inspector Cullen an almost imperceptible nod. Emma ducked down, as if trying to avoid the shot which was sure to come. I looked at the revolver in Cullen's hand, knowing that if I made a swift move toward it he could shoot at any one of us before I reached him.

Emma stood again and I saw that she also had a gun in her hand. It was pointed at Chief Inspector Cullen. I could only guess she had kept it in a stocking holster.

"Miss Green will recall me telling her that I was determined to defend myself after my brother Alfred was murdered. I always feared that the man who killed him would also come after me. How right I was."

The senior officer was startled. "Put the gun down!"

"No, this is *my* home! You drop *your* gun." She took a step toward him.

"Just do the right thing, Cullen," said Mr Sheridan. "We agreed it, didn't we?"

A deafening shot rang out and I saw Chief Inspector Cullen crumple to the floor. James leapt over to him and I heard the injured inspector cry out.

Emma had a wide smile plastered across her face, still pointing the gun at him. "I got him!" she said. "I aimed for his leg and I got him!"

I was relieved to see James wrenching Chief Inspector Cullen's gun from his hand. He lay on the floor groaning with pain, blood beginning to seep through his trouser leg. Emma turned her attention to Mr Sheridan, who had frozen beside the door with a look of horror on his face. George was quivering beside the bay window.

Emma pointed the gun at Sheridan. "You killed my brother," she snarled.

Sheridan turned and ran out of the room, but Emma immediately gave chase.

"Miss Holland!" shouted James, following her into the hallway. "Put the gun down!"

Mr Sheridan was already at the front door.

"Let me arrest him, Miss Holland, and he'll be put on trial," pleaded James. "Let a judge and jury try him!"

"Give him a chance, you mean?" she cried. "He didn't give my brother a chance!"

She was gripped with anger and I could understand her yearning for revenge, but I knew this wasn't the right way to exact it.

"Put the gun down, Emma!" I cried, running toward her.

Mr Sheridan had opened the front door and was descending the steps with Emma in hot pursuit.

"No, Miss Holland!" said James, still giving chase. "You might harm an innocent person!"

I heard another gunshot and winced. I prayed that Emma and James were both all right. Then I heard laughter.

I stepped outside to see Mr Sheridan writhing in pain on the pavement.

Emma was laughing gleefully. "I got him, too! Now I just need to finish him off!"

"Please, Miss Holland," said James. He handed me Chief Inspector Cullen's gun and began to wrestle with her. "You've done enough. Give me the gun!"

"No! I won't rest until he's dead!" she shrieked.

"He'll be punished, you wait and see," said James.

There was another loud bang and James staggered backward.

"No!" I screamed. "Stop!"

"Just let me do this!" snarled Emma, her eyes black with fury.

I could see that James was unhurt but had placed himself

between Mr Sheridan and Emma. "I forbid you to shoot this man," he called to her. "He needs to face the law courts!"

Sheridan lay on the ground, groaning and clutching at his stomach.

"Get out of my way!" shouted Emma.

"Emma, please," I said as calmly as I could manage. "Please stop this now."

I glanced down at Cullen's gun in my hand. *Should I threaten her with it?*

Emma sensed my movement and pointed her gun at James.

"Don't!" I screamed.

"I told him to get out of my way, but he refused," she replied in a flat-sounding voice.

She pressed her finger down on the trigger.

CHAPTER 70

I squeezed my eyes shut and a heavy wave of despair washed over me.

There was nothing more I could do.

I prayed that James would leap out of the way, or that Emma would miss her shot. But just as I had finished preparing myself for the worst I realised nothing had happened.

I opened my eyes again and saw Emma still trying to pull the trigger, which appeared to be jammed.

As I stepped forward and snatched the gun from her she gave me a startled, bewildered look, as though she hadn't noticed me there.

"Well done, Penny," James said, swiftly arriving at my side.

I handed both guns over to him.

"You almost got yourself killed!" I cried. "Why try to defend an evil man like him?" I pointed toward the prostrate form of Sheridan, who still lay moaning on the ground.

"I understand why Miss Holland is upset, but she cannot act as judge, jury and executioner," said James. "I told her this man needs to go to trial, as does Cullen."

I turned to face Emma. "You were about to kill James after everything he's done to help!"

"I didn't mean to... I didn't want to, but he wouldn't get out of the way. I'm sorry, I..."

Tears began to pour down her cheeks and I turned away in anger. Both James and Emma had acted foolishly, and for some odd reason I also began to cry.

"Penny," James said, resting a hand on my arm. "It's over. Everyone's still alive."

"Everyone apart from Emma's brother," I said. "And the Forsters. And Mr Mawson."

"Sheridan will pay for his crimes," said James, "and so will the gang he hired. We did it! Now let's find a doctor to tend to these injured men."

"I don't think we should be in any great hurry to do so," I replied.

CHAPTER 71

"I hope you don't mind us calling in on you unexpectedly, Penny, but I wanted to thank you personally for all your help," said Charlotte Jenkins. Her blue eyes were bright and smiling, and she clung to James' arm as the pair of them stood in Mrs Garnett's hallway. "Without you I don't know whether I would have seen James again."

"I think you're exaggerating a little, Charlotte. I didn't exactly rescue him."

"You encouraged me to see through Cullen, Penny," said James. "I trusted him and you didn't. You were right."

"I'm sure you would soon have realised."

"You must accept our gratitude," said Charlotte, "there is no need for modesty. You were of great comfort to me while James was missing and did everything you could to find him again. And here he is!" She looked up at him and beamed.

I forced a smile, knowing I had sought James for my own sake rather than Charlotte's. However, it seemed that I could no longer do any wrong in her eyes.

"I shan't let you out of my sight between now and the wedding!" she said to James.

He gave her an awkward smile. "I'll still have to go to work, Charlotte."

"Then I shall come too!" she said with a giggle. "Either that, or we'll have to stop you doing this dangerous police work altogether. Perhaps you could find yourself a nice quiet job."

"Such as working in a library?" suggested James, giving me a knowing glance.

"Yes, a library. That would be perfect!" said Charlotte. "Penny, would you like to join us for dinner this evening? There are some pleasant supper rooms on Fore Street, if I recall, and my mother will accompany us. She's waiting outside in the carriage."

The thought of spending an evening watching James being simpered over by his fiancée left me feeling cold.

"Thank you for the invitation, Charlotte, but I'm rather tired. Perhaps another time."

"Of course, I understand. We will most likely be married by then!"

The sympathy I had felt for Charlotte during James' disappearance had evaporated. I found myself disliking her smiling, apple-cheeked face and her dark green satin dress with a renewed intensity.

James and I held each other's gaze for a brief moment and I wished I could tell him what a grave mistake he was making. I felt angry as he stood in front of me, his arm linked through Charlotte's as though he were quite devoted to her.

"Enjoy your evening," I said curtly, "I need to get some rest." I turned to ascend the stairs.

"Goodbye, Penny," said James.

I turned around to look at him and saw that his brow was creased with concern. His eyes silently conveyed that there were countless words he wished to say.

You've made your choice. Those were the only words I had for him now. I hoped my eyes expressed the sentiment.

"Goodbye, James."

I turned on my heel and climbed the stairs up to my room.

CHAPTER 72

"Y ou haven't told anyone that George is staying with his brother, have you?" whispered Eliza as we strolled beneath our parasols beside the Serpentine in Hyde Park.

"No."

"His parents must not find out. We just need a short while to fully understand what has happened, as he really didn't know what he was getting himself mixed up in. He's terribly upset about the whole affair, but I still don't know what to make of it. To think that he consorted with a man as evil as Mr Sheridan! It's terrible, it really is. George has always been such a law-abiding individual, and I'm terribly shocked that he could be associated with a murder case. Do you remember those beautiful Cantonese vases Mrs Lennox admired at our meeting? It transpires they were a gift to George from Mr Sheridan. It's disgraceful! I've asked the housekeeper to remove them, and I cannot bear to have George in the house at the moment. I feel so angry and ashamed."

"There's no suggestion that George knew about the murders Mr Sheridan orchestrated," I said.

"No, but it doesn't look good, does it? The police are still talking to him. In fact, Inspector Blakely has been talking to him. You will ask James to go easy on him, won't you? George simply isn't used to being questioned by the police and I'm worried he'll say something he'll regret."

"I'll speak to James when I see him next, but I don't know when that will be. Besides, George is quite capable of looking after himself. He's a lawyer."

"You're right, I suppose he is. But he isn't at his best when he feels wrong-footed."

"Perhaps he should be more discerning about the clients he does business with, in that case."

"Oh Penelope, have some sympathy!"

"I have sympathy for you, Ellie, but none for your husband, I'm afraid. He got himself into this and he'll need to get himself out of it again. I have every confidence that he'll manage it. He has friends in all the right places."

"Oh, he does, yes. Particularly at the Colthurst Club."

"There you go, then. In the meantime, look after yourself and the children."

"To think that Mr Sheridan bribed a senior officer at Scotland Yard!" continued Eliza. "I would never have thought that possible, would you?"

"Nothing surprises me about Chief Inspector Cullen," I said. "I'm looking forward to reporting on his trial even more than Mr Sheridan's."

"By the expression on your face, Penny, I'd say that you were gleaning some sort of distorted pleasure from seeing these men punished."

"Not distorted, Ellie, it's a natural pleasure. I enjoy seeing people pay for their crimes. I think I finally understand why James risked his life trying to keep Mr Sheridan alive."

. . .

We caught up with Francis at the boathouse.

"All the boats are out at the moment," he said. "The chap thinks it will be about a ten-minute wait."

He wore a pale grey suit and a straw boater hat. The summer sunshine had given him a light dusting of freckles across his nose and cheekbones.

"That doesn't matter," said Eliza. "We can continue our walk for a little while and return here later. Does that sound all right, Penelope?"

"I'm happy with that, Ellie."

Francis and I exchanged a smile. This was the first time I had seen him since Chief Inspector Cullen had abducted me from the street close to the British Library. Although it had only been a week since then it seemed far longer. I thought he looked quite handsome and felt pleased to have this opportunity to deepen our acquaintance a little.

He gazed out over the lake and fidgeted with his collar.

"Are you all right, Francis?" asked Eliza. "You seem rather preoccupied."

"I am a little, if truth be told. I wonder if I may... This slight pause in proceedings gives me an opportunity to..." He turned to face me. "Penny, may I speak with you alone for a moment?"

"I suppose so, yes," I replied.

I glanced at Eliza, who gave me a hopeful smile.

"Eliza, I do apologise," said Francis. "I hope you don't consider me rude wishing to speak to Penny alone, but there is something I should like to say and it will only take a moment."

"Take all the time you need, Francis," she said with a grin. "I shall walk another lap of the Serpentine."

"Oh, we shan't be that long," said Francis.

"There's no hurry!" Eliza called over her shoulder as she strode off.

Francis watched as she walked away, and I noticed him swallowing nervously.

Now mark my words, Eliza's voice sounded in my head. *As soon as Inspector Blakely is married Mr Edwards will surely propose.*

I also swallowed nervously, realising the moment had arrived, albeit a few weeks earlier than she had predicted.

"Shall we?" suggested Francis, gesturing toward a path which led away from the lake.

"Of course." I smiled, my heart thudding in my chest.

"I can't say that I enjoy such conversations," said Francis, "but sometimes they're quite necessary. I'll try to get to the point as quickly as I can."

What would my reply be? Would I be making a big mistake if I said yes? Would it be polite to ask him to allow me time to consider his proposal?

Either way, I knew that I couldn't turn him down with a simple no. He had given me plenty of time to prepare for this moment, yet I felt less prepared than ever.

"I hope you haven't forgotten our conversation in the hansom cab that evening following our dinner with Mr Fox-Stirling," continued Francis.

"Of course not."

"As I look back on it now I feel rather embarrassed that my words were so direct, but I stood by them then and I stand by them now."

"Thank you, Francis, I'm grateful to you for expressing yourself so honestly that evening. You shouldn't feel embarrassed, and I should like to say in return that I —"

Francis held up his hand. "Please don't consider me rude in interrupting you, Penny, only I'm finding this conversation rather difficult, and it's taken me a little while to ready myself for it. Would you mind hearing what I have to say before you respond?"

"Of course." I smiled, feeling some sympathy for him. I wanted to make it as easy for him as possible.

Did this mean I was ready to accept his proposal?

He stopped beside a beautifully scented rose bush and took a deep breath.

"I should like to remind you, Penny, how much I care about you. Please remember that."

"Of course, Francis."

"Good, because that is very important to me. The strength of my feelings for you has caused me to make a decision." He scratched his chin. "I must take action, and I hope you will feel pleased about it."

"I hope so." I looked into his green eyes and realised I was holding my breath.

"I plan to travel to South America in search of your father, Penny."

I continued to hold my breath, unsure as to whether I had heard him correctly. "But you can't!" My voice sounded strained.

"Can't?"

"You want to look for my father?"

He nodded.

"But it's dangerous!"

"I don't care, Penny. I am anxious to find him."

"You wish to leave London? Leave the country?"

"I will have to if I'm to look for your father."

"But I never thought you would want to. I thought —"

"Thought what? Did you think I had planned to say something different?"

I nodded, and a rush of embarrassment washed over me.

"For a time I thought I would, but I have come to realise that it wouldn't be the right thing for me to do. I tried to convince myself that you were blameless when Inspector

Blakely kissed you, but in truth I think you wanted it to happen."

A surge of heat rushed to my face. "So you're leaving?"

"I wish to do something interesting and rewarding. I have no desire to spend the rest of my days in a library hoping that one day you might agree to marry me."

"But I haven't known you for long, Francis. Maybe a little more time —"

"It's not a question of time, Penny. You're in love with Inspector Blakely, and I cannot compete with him for your affection. I don't know what will happen once the chap is married; perhaps your feelings for him will change. But even if they did and you wished to marry me I would always know that I was your second choice."

"You deserve better," I said, my voice choked with emotion.

"You've told me that before, and I have come to believe that you are right. I wish to marry someone who loves me just as I love her."

"I hope you find her, Francis."

"So do I, Penny."

THE END

THANK YOU

༺❧༻

Thank you for reading *Curse of the Poppy*, I really hope you enjoyed it!

Would you like to know when I release new books? Here are some ways to stay updated:

- Join my mailing list and receive a free short mystery: *Westminster Bridge* emilyorgan.com/westminster-bridge
- Like my Facebook page: facebook.com/emilyorganwriter
- Follow me on Goodreads: goodreads.com/emily_organ
- Follow me on BookBub: bookbub.com/authors/emily-organ
- View my other books here: emilyorgan.com

And if you have a moment, I would be very grateful if you would leave a quick review of *Curse of the Poppy* online. Honest reviews of my books help other readers discover them too!

HISTORICAL NOTE

The opium trade has a long and complicated history and I hope that my attempts to summarise it here aren't too clumsy.

Opium was a popular medicinal and recreational drug in China for centuries. Britain first became involved in the late 18th century when its East India Company saw an opportunity to make money. By this time, opium had been criminalised in China but this didn't stop the British who cultivated the drug in their colony, India, and created a complex trade arrangement which saw opium being smuggled into China. The situation escalated into the two Opium Wars in the 1840s and 1850s which concluded with a treaty favourable to the British and other foreign traders.

In the latter half of the 19th century British-controlled India processed opium from the vast poppy fields of Bengal and Malwa and sold the drug to China. This trade was not without its opponents, including the British Prime Minister William Gladstone; critics viewed the trade as an exploitation of opium addicts' misery. The trade continued because the revenue was so lucrative. On August 6th 1884 the Globe newspaper reported that Britain's annual revenue from the opium trade that year would be over £9 million – today this equates to just over £1 billion / $1.3 billion (according to the Bank of England's inflation calculator).

Merchant families grew wealthy from the opium trade including the Baring and Rothschild families in the UK and the Astor and Forbes families in the US. President Franklin D Roosevelt's grandfather, Warren Delano, was another merchant who made his money in the opium trade. Increasing condemnation of the trade led to Britain officially ceasing it in 1917. However, as recently as 1939 it was reported that British-controlled India was still exporting some opium to China 'to treat animals and to cure malaria.' Mahatma Gandhi campaigned against the trade in India and the country won its independence from Britain in 1947. By the 1950s Chairman Mao had eradicated much of the opium trade in China, although legal and illegal opiate use remains a problem there as it does around the rest of the globe.

The Ghazipur opium factory in Uttar Pradesh, India, was established in 1820 by the East India Company and is still functioning today processing opium for alkaloid products in the pharmaceutical industry. Rudyard Kipling visited the factory in 1888 and wrote about it in an essay which was a useful resource for me.

In the 19th century, opium dens could be found in large cities where the Chinese community settled outside China and in locations where there was a population keen to use the drug. In London's Limehouse many frequenters of the opium dens were sailors and travellers passing through the docks close by. Charles Dickens visited an opium den in Limehouse and used it as a location in his final, unfinished novel *The Mystery of Edwin Drood*.

The East India Club in St James's Square was founded in 1849 principally for men who were connected with the East

India Company. It still occupies the same building in St James's Square today, having merged with other clubs over the years. Membership is by nomination and election and women are still not permitted.

The India Office was located in what are now the Foreign Office buildings in Whitehall. Noted for their architecture and spectacular interior, these government buildings were built in the 1860s and still house the Foreign Office today. The buildings are open to the public once a year.

The police station on Commercial Street was once part of Whitechapel H Division. It was this division which investigated four of the five Jack the Ripper murders in 1888 (the other one being in the City of London). The investigating officers were based at Commercial Street police station. The building still stands today and had an extra storey added to it in the early 1900s. A police station no more, it's now residential and is called Burhan Uddin House.

Euston Arch was an enormous sandstone structure which stood in front of Euston station from 1837 until 1962. It was demolished as part of the station's redevelopment, to the upset of many. The broken up pieces of the arch were used to line the bottom of a canal in East London and the gates are in the National Railway Museum in York. A number of pieces were raised from the canal in 2009 and plans are being discussed to have the arch rebuilt as part of an upgrade of Euston station in 2026.

Change Alley, sometimes known as Exchange Alley, is a narrow street in the heart of the City of London. In the 17th century it was home to Jonathan's Coffee House where the prices of stocks and commodities were first published – a forerunner of the stock exchange.

If *Curse of the Poppy* is the first Penny Green book you've read, then you may find the following historical background interesting. It's compiled from the historical notes published in the previous books in the series:

Women journalists in the nineteenth century were not as scarce as people may think. In fact they were numerous enough by 1898 for Arnold Bennett to write *Journalism for Women: A Practical Guide* in which he was keen to raise the standard of women's journalism:-

"The women-journalists as a body have faults... They seem to me to be traceable either to an imperfect development of the sense of order, or to a certain lack of self-control."

Eliza Linton became the first salaried female journalist in Britain when she began writing for *the Morning Chronicle* in 1851. She was a prolific writer and contributor to periodicals for many years including Charles Dickens' magazine *Household Words*. George Eliot – her real name was Mary Anne Evans – is most famous for novels such as *Middlemarch*, however she also became assistant editor of *The Westminster Review* in 1852.

In the United States Margaret Fuller became the *New York Tribune*'s first female editor in 1846. Intrepid journalist Nellie Bly worked in Mexico as a foreign correspondent for the *Pittsburgh Despatch* in the 1880s before writing for *New York World* and feigning insanity to go undercover and investigate reports of brutality at a New York asylum. Later, in 1889-90, she became a household name by setting a world record for travelling around the globe in seventy two days.

The iconic circular Reading Room at the British Museum was in use from 1857 until 1997. During that time it was also used a filming location and has been referenced in many works of fiction. The Reading Room has been closed since 2014 but it's recently been announced that it will reopen and display some of the museum's permanent collections. It could be a while yet until we're able to step inside it but I'm looking forward to it!

The Museum Tavern, where Penny and James enjoy a drink, is a well-preserved Victorian pub opposite the British Museum. Although a pub was first built here in the eighteenth century much of the current pub (including its name) dates back to 1855. Celebrity drinkers here are said to have included Arthur Conan Doyle and Karl Marx.

Publishing began in Fleet Street in the 1500s and by the twentieth century the street was the hub of the British press. However newspapers began moving away in the 1980s to bigger premises. Nowadays just a few publishers remain in Fleet Street but the many pubs and bars once frequented by journalists – including the pub Ye Olde Cheshire Cheese - are still popular with city workers.

Penny Green lives in Milton Street in Cripplegate which was one of the areas worst hit by bombing during the Blitz in the Second World War and few original streets remain. Milton Street was known as Grub Street in the eighteenth century and was famous as a home to impoverished writers at the time. The street had a long association with writers and was home to Anthony Trollope among many others. A small stretch of Milton Street remains but the 1960s Barbican development has been built over the bombed remains.

Plant hunting became an increasingly commercial enterprise as the nineteenth century progressed. Victorians were fascinated by exotic plants and, if they were wealthy enough, they had their own glasshouses built to show them off. Plant hunters were employed by Kew Gardens, companies such as Veitch Nurseries or wealthy individuals to seek out exotic specimens in places such as South America and the Himalayas. These plant hunters took great personal risks to collect their plants and some perished on their travels. The *Travels and Adventures of an Orchid Hunter* by Albert Millican is worth a read. Written in 1891 it documents his journeys in Colombia and demonstrates how plant hunting became little short of pillaging. Some areas he travelled to had already lost their orchids to plant hunters and Millican himself spent several months felling 4,000 trees to collect 10,000 plants. Even after all this plundering many of the orchids didn't survive the trip across the Atlantic to Britain. Plant hunters were not always welcome: Millican had arrows fired at him as he navigated rivers, had his camp attacked one night and was eventually killed during a fight in a Colombian tavern.

My research for The Penny Green series has come from sources too numerous to list in detail, but the following books have been very useful: *A Brief History of Life in Victorian Britain* by Michael Patterson, *London in the Nineteenth Century* by Jerry White, *London in 1880* by Herbert Fry, *London a Travel Guide through Time* by Dr Matthew Green, *Women of the Press in Nineteenth-Century Britain* by Barbara Onslow, *A Very British Murder* by Lucy Worsley, *The Suspicions of Mr Whicher* by Kate Summerscale, *Journalism for Women: A Practical Guide* by Arnold Bennett and *Seventy Years a Showman* by Lord George Sanger, *Dottings of a Dosser* by Howard Goldsmid, *Travels and Adventures of an Orchid Hunter* by Albert Millican, *The Bitter Cry of Outcast London* by Andrew Mearns, *The Complete History of Jack the Ripper* by Philip Sugden, *The Necropolis Railway* by Andrew Martin, *The Diaries of Hannah Cullwick, Victorian Maidservant* edited by Liz Stanley, *Mrs Woolf & the Servants* by Alison Light, *Revelations of a Lady Detective* by William Stephens Hayward, *A is for Arsenic* by Kathryn Harkup, *In an Opium Factory* by Rudyard Kipling, *Drugging a Nation: The Story of China and the Opium Curse* by Samuel Merwin and *Confessions of an Opium Eater* by Thomas de Quincy. The *British Newspaper Archive* is also an invaluable resource.

THE BERMONDSEY POISONER

A Penny Green Mystery Book 6

❦

A culprit is on the run after a fatal poisoning in Bermondsey. It seems like a simple case for Penny Green to report on, until a series of macabre photographs is discovered.

As the poisonings continue, Scotland Yard is convinced they have their suspect. It's not long before they're outwitted and no one is safe. Penny and Inspector James Blakely must avoid the red herrings and track down the manipulative poisoner.

But could there be more than one?

Find out more: emilyorgan.com/bermondsey-poisoner

GET A FREE SHORT MYSTERY

❧

Want more of Penny Green? Sign up to my mailing list and I'll send you my short mystery *Westminster Bridge* - a free thirty minute read!

News reporter Penny Green is committed to her job. But should she impose on a grieving widow?

The brutal murder of a doctor has shocked 1880s London and Fleet Street is clamouring for news. Penny has orders from her editor to get the story all the papers want.

She must decide what comes first. Compassion or duty?

The murder case is not as simple as it seems. And whichever decision Penny makes, it's unlikely to be the right one.

Visit my website for more details:
emilyorgan.com/westminster-bridge

THE CHURCHILL & PEMBERLEY SERIES

Also by Emily Organ. Join senior sleuths Churchill and Pemberley as they tackle cake and crime in an English village.

Growing bored in the autumn of her years, Londoner Annabel Churchill buys a private detective agency in a Dorset village. The purchase brings with it the eccentric Doris Pemberley and the two ladies are soon solving mysteries and chasing down miscreants in sleepy Compton Poppleford.

Plenty of characters are out to scupper their chances, among them grumpy Inspector Mappin. Another challenge is their four-legged friend who means well but has a problem with discipline.

But the biggest challenge is one which threatens to derail every case they work on: will there be enough tea and cake?

Find out more here: emilyorgan.com/the-churchill-pemberley-cozy-mystery-series

Made in the USA
Las Vegas, NV
04 September 2022

54691688R00225